The
Opening Night
Murder

The
Opening Night
Murder

ANNE RUTHERFORD

BERKLEY PRIME CRIME, NEW YORK

THE BERKLEY PUBLISHING GROUP
Published by the Penguin Group
Penguin Group (USA) Inc.
375 Hudson Street, New York, New York 10014, USA
Penguin Group (Canada), 90 Eglinton Avenue East, Suite 700, Toronto, Ontario M4P 2Y3, Canada
(a division of Pearson Penguin Canada Inc.) • Penguin Books Ltd., 80 Strand, London WC2R 0RL,
England • Penguin Ireland, 25 St. Stephen's Green, Dublin 2, Ireland (a division of Penguin
Books Ltd.) • Penguin Group (Australia), 707 Collins Street, Melbourne, Victoria 3008, Australia
(a division of Pearson Australia Group Pty. Ltd.) • Penguin Books India Pvt. Ltd., 11 Community
Centre, Panchsheel Park, New Delhi—110 017, India • Penguin Group (NZ), 67 Apollo Drive,
Rosedale, Auckland 0632, New Zealand (a division of Pearson New Zealand Ltd.) • Penguin Books,
Rosebank Office Park, 181 Jan Smuts Avenue, Parktown North 2193, South Africa • Penguin China,
B7 Jaiming Center, 27 East Third Ring Road North, Chaoyang District, Beijing 100020, China

Penguin Books Ltd., Registered Offices: 80 Strand, London WC2R 0RL, England

This book is an original publication of The Berkley Publishing Group.

ISBN 978-1-62490-047-1

PRINTED IN THE UNITED STATES OF AMERICA

Prologue

The opening night audience crowded into the renovated
Globe Theatre to fill up benches, until even the pit was
packed with milling bodies. The excitement of the reopening,
and the utterly reasonable price of the seats, brought nearly
everyone within walking distance. The roar of voices was nearly
overwhelming; it seemed all of Southwark was in attendance.

The mood in the 'tiring house behind the stage was equally
vibrant. The energy of the cast grew. Actors fidgeted, some
prayed, one talked incessantly until the rest wanted to boot
him out the door. One of the less experienced boys had to run
from the green room to vomit. The cast laughed, though they
all had done the same thing at one time or another in the past.

In her quarters backstage Suzanne Thornton readied herself
to see the play, eager to see her new theatre through the eyes
of its audience. The noise was a roar of thousands trying to be
heard among themselves. As she painted her lips she toyed
with the idea of lurking among the groundlings in the pit to

2 ۞ *Anne Rutherford*

listen in on conversations, but decided she would enjoy the afternoon more if she went upstairs to sit with the musicians in a gallery over the stage. They were a lively crew and would be as fine an entertainment as the play itself. She hurried with her beauty marks, eager to be finished and take her place as a spectator, and her fingers challenged her to keep them from trembling.

Her son, Piers, came to visit for a moment, complained of his father, then left. She made one more check of her coif, then set the mirror on her dressing table and left her quarters.

As the hour of three drew close, Suzanne climbed the steps at the rear of the 'tiring house to watch the performance from the gallery directly above the stage, where the musicians sat. As she found a stool and settled in at the front, Big Willie, Warren, and their flautist friend played an old-fashioned tune that might have been performed in this theatre during Elizabethan times. Suzanne's wistful fancy toyed with the thought that Shakespeare himself might have listened to this very tune from this very gallery half a century ago. She looked around at the theatre The Bard had built, and the idea made her smile. Today was a fine, sunny day, and especially warm even for this time of year. Afternoon light bathed the stage, and there was no fear of a sudden rain from the pale-blue sky overhead.

That day's performance began with a short *commedia* play, involving a cuckolded husband. The mummers had the audience laughing well and quickly, and in a few minutes they left the stage with the entire crowd of nearly four thousand people in a good mood. To Suzanne, this was the wonderful thing about the theatre: to have that many gathered together in one place and everyone having a good time. One could accomplish it in a public house with alcohol, cards, and women, but a pub could host only a fraction of the souls a theatre could.

The play began. Matthew lit up the stage as King Henry V. Such a talent the troupe had in him! The air snapped and sparkled with the energy of all the actors. Henry and his advisors. Henry condemning spies. Henry in France, urging his dear friends unto the breach once more. In her mind's eye Suzanne could see the wall crumble and the actors surge through it, shouting fealty to England and King Henry. She watched the king move among his men incognito, listening to them, hearing how they really felt about him and about their mission in France. Matthew made her believe the story, painting a picture of history so clear she thought she could know how it really had been hundreds of years ago.

The audience was as caught up as she. From the pit they shouted advice to Henry, and in response Matthew invented bawdy asides ad-libitum in spite of the king's directive to keep to Shakespeare's own words. Suzanne hoped nobody in the house tonight was likely to go running to the king, tattling.

Then the battle of Agincourt. The French king and his dukes in desperation. The murder of the boys in the luggage. The horror of that cowardly act, and Matthew's rage was palpable. Suzanne was caught up in the story as if she hadn't seen the play a dozen times before. Even as she gasped along with Henry and his dukes, she thought what a fine time she was having.

A scream lifted from the audience, and she thought how wonderfully involved everyone was. That voice seemed filled with real horror. Then something dropped to the stage and thudded on the boards below. More screaming and confusion moved the audience, some surging forward and others falling back. Suzanne leaned over the banister to look and saw a man lying on the stage, writhing and grasping at a crossbow bolt stuck in his neck. A boy ran forward to yank out the bolt, and a gout of blood poured over the stage. The pool spread quickly, and though two actors tried to stanch the flow with their hands, it was hopeless. The fallen man weakened and stopped struggling, finally going limp in the arms of those who tried to help him. The play had come to a halt.

Suzanne leapt to her feet and ran down the rear stairs to the stage. Round and round the tight spiral, all the way to the stage level of the 'tiring house, then she burst through an up-stage entrance door to the stage. All the actors in the troupe were there, those not in the scene having emerged from the green room to see, gathered around the body while those in the pit attempted to climb onto the stage for a look. Some of the actors tried to hold them back while gawking themselves at the terrifying scene onstage. The audience was abuzz, and some shouted advice to those on the stage. Others wept. Many began to make their way to the exit in a hurry. Suzanne shoved men aside and attempted to take charge, but all she could manage was to enter the circle to see. The dead man lay on her stage in a pool of blood, killed by a crossbow. His ragged clothing was soaking up the blood. The red stain slowly crept along the white fabric, and it ran down the stage boards toward the pit.

She said to the boy standing by with the bloodied crossbow bolt still in his hand, "Go fetch the constable."

Chapter One

May 1660

Suzanne Thornton was in no hurry today. She was never in any hurry, for hurry attracted attention and she'd learned early in life that invisibility was a skill that often came useful. One only ever made a fuss when it was absolutely necessary, and then, rather like drawing a weapon, one always made sure to make enough of a fuss to make it count.

Today her talent for calm came in handy and she could make a leisurely pace through London without annoyance, for today traffic choked the streets everywhere within the city walls. She should have known better than to have ventured out for shopping. The king had returned to England and was arriving in London today. The entire city was in paroxysms of festivity. Everyone who wasn't ecstatic was pretending it for the sake of keeping their heads, their freedom, and their money. Puritans and Presbyterians had gone silent for the moment, and all of London expected things to return to normal. The king was on his throne, God was in His heaven, and all would be right with the world. Perhaps.

In any case, Suzanne was making her way home from the Exchange in a sedan chair, and the two men carrying it kept setting her down to await room to proceed. They were both large, muscular men, but even they didn't care to hold up the chair and Suzanne when traffic was this still.

"Thomas. Samuel." She leaned out to address them as they set the chair down on the street. When she saw they'd slipped from under their yokes again, she realized they weren't getting anywhere. "Circle 'round toward the . . ." Cannon shot roared, followed by trumpets nearby. Excited talk among the surrounding onlookers rose to a pitch and quite drowned out any attempt to speak. The king's procession must be passing close. Suzanne craned her neck to see, but there was nothing yet in sight. "Around toward the river, good fellows, if you please."

"Begging your pardon, mistress, but we're well hemmed in here. There's naught for it until the press clears."

Suzanne made a little noise of disappointment and sat back in her chair. "Very well." Well enough to be sanguine about things she couldn't control, but she hoped this wouldn't take terribly long. William was sure to call on her today, and it never went well with him if she wasn't waiting for him on arrival. Even more she regretted her decision to go to the Exchange today.

William was suspicious by nature, ever ready to leap to an unfounded conclusion if she wasn't where she was supposed to be at all times. His Puritan guilt over his own behavior convinced him that everyone else was equally guilty. After all, if one of God's chosen was weak-willed and susceptible to temptation, then how could anyone else be strong enough to resist? To him, everyone he saw was a sinner, stained with sin and as vile at heart as himself. To Suzanne, it was all too tedious. Keeping company with William was almost sure to cause one to lose faith in people. Sometimes, ironically, it even wore on one's faith in God.

Also, he made it plain he thought her no longer acceptably young and pretty. At her age his already scant patience with her was thinning as fast as his hair, and his prickly temper grew nearly intolerable. Lately he behaved as if her lost youth and fading beauty were an imposition on him for which she must pay. As if her maturity were a diminished value of goods. He'd become terribly critical of her, as if he would shave off bits of her pride as compensation for his loss, as if she were a silver penny and he would have as much out of her as he could get.

Sometimes she wondered whether it might have been worth the effort to find a husband rather than a keeper, considering the little freedom William allowed her and all the effort she put into making him happy and paying her support. He was often quite impossible, and seemed to think she should be grateful for whatever attention he deigned to bestow. Like most men, who always assumed the entire world revolved around themselves and their male parts, he never suspected it was only his money for which she was grateful, and his attention she could take or leave. After all, he was certainly no spring chicken himself, nor Prince Charming, and was an utter bore and not even all that wealthy in the bargain. She thought life would improve immeasurably if he left her alone and simply sent the money by messenger. Her son would soon be of an age and position to be of assistance to her financially, and with any luck she wouldn't have to put up with William and his kind much longer.

She gazed out the window of her chair and made herself relax, for there was nothing she could do about her situation.

She might as well settle into her cushion and watch the parade that, by the noise of trumpets and cheering upstreet, was about to pass by. This might be amusing, at least for the moment.

Idly she wondered what this new king was like and whether any of the rumors were true. She'd heard he was handsome and intelligent, and of an agreeable nature. That his years on the Continent, living by the charity of others, had taught him compassion, which had been lacking in many who had held the throne before him, including his immediate predecessor, the Lord Protector Oliver Cromwell. She remembered well her life under Charles I, when she was a child and people went about their lives and knew what was sin and what was not. She thought this second Charles would have to be better than that Cromwell fellow, just for not being a bloody, stiff-necked Puritan. Life under Cromwell had been joyless even for those with money, who ordinarily did whatever they pleased. And Suzanne had always had little enough of both money and pleasure. Perhaps the new king would be more like his father. All of London cheered the return of the king, and at that moment it seemed every Londoner was on that very street, shouting at full voice.

Excitement rose in the crowds of spectators up the way, and Suzanne leaned out to look again. Fresh cheers went up, hats were thrown skyward, and she could see the approach of men on horseback. Trumpeters at the van heralded the approach of the king. Blaring their enthusiasm with more joy than skill, they could nevertheless be barely heard over the ecstatic crowd. Row after row of horns on horseback played the fanfare continuously, and at sight of the royal party the onlookers burst into even more hysterical demonstration, with waving of handkerchiefs and empty hands, feathered hats and coach whips. Everyone wanted to catch the attention of his majesty, no matter how brief. Even Suzanne, who always struggled not to let her own enthusiasm get the best of her, was moved to rise a little from her seat for a better look. Only half realizing her tension, she gripped the frame of the sedan chair with white-knuckled hands.

Charles could not be mistaken among the mass in the parade, though Suzanne had never seen a painting of him, nor even heard him described. He sat his white steed as only a king could and fairly shone with his own light, wearing a silver cloth doublet and a gold-braided cloak. His flat-topped hat was also heavy with braid and feathers. Suzanne thought him handsome, with an aquiline nose and long, flowing dark hair.

She saw that as he gazed upon his subjects he was looking at individuals. Not with the glazed-over eyes of most men at the center of public attention, who seemed to see only a blur of faces, Charles's glance was specific to each person, and that person knew he or she had been seen. He seemed to have a genuine interest in each onlooker, and each one of them responded with the thrill of having been noticed. Charles seemed equally happy in return. His was the most radiant face Suzanne could remember ever seeing. It lifted her own weathered heart to witness such joy.

Behind the king rode his two brothers, and beyond that, hundreds of Cavaliers and courtiers who had followed him back from the Continent came two by two, their horses prancing with the excitement drawn from the surrounding crowd and the Cavaliers themselves. Once the king was out of sight, Suzanne sat back to idly watch the parade of men in livery and in new suits of silver and gold created for the occasion. Feathered hats and colorful banners and pennants passed, and more feathered hats and colorful banners. Men waved to the crowds, who waved back. Cloth of silver and braid of gold glittered in the sunshine so brightly it soon made her eyes ache.

Then one face among the horsemen caught her gaze and stopped her breath. He was at the near side of the column, close enough she knew it was him. Surely it was him, though two decades had stolen the fairness of youth and she could barely recognize him. Her heart leapt and she laid one hand over her mouth to cover its gape.

Daniel Stockton, Earl of Throckmorton. Yes, it was he! She hadn't seen him since the war, for he'd fled England to the Continent with the King's Cavaliers, where they and the executed king's successor had spent nearly a decade dependent on the goodwill of foreign friends.

Until that moment, she hadn't even considered he might return with Charles. The day he'd left for the Continent he'd been a threadbare young warrior following a king in retreat. Today he rode a fine stallion and wore a doublet of cloth of silver and a cloak of green with gold braid. The white feather in his hat was so long and thick it swished and flicked behind him like the tail of a dancing Spanish stallion as he nodded to the well-wishers nearby. He rode with more grace than even the king, Suzanne thought. Even at thirty-seven years of age he sat his mount like a young Cavalier born to the saddle. Like the mythical centaur, man and horse moved as one. Yes, that was Daniel all right.

For one panicky moment that was unlike her, she wasn't sure whether she wanted him to see her. A terrible urge to duck back inside the sedan chair surged in her, but she hesitated. In that moment of hesitation, he did catch sight of her.

His smile fell. Not just faltered, but fell entirely from his face. Mortified, Suzanne withdrew to her seat, returned her vizard to her face, pressed it there with both hands, and shut her eyes tight. It was Daniel. And he'd seen her, and plainly he was not happy he had.

The welter of emotions that buffeted her made her blink, then she found herself blinking back tears. She drew in her feet beneath the chair seat, and once he'd passed, she put the mask down and rested her hands on her knees. Huddled like that, she felt less noticeable. Less noticeably a fool. Memories washed over her, some pleasant, some that brought grief and made her body clench. Plainly he didn't wish to see her; she wondered whether he wanted to see Piers. Finally she wondered whether after all this time he even remembered he had a son.

Chapter Two

It seemed an eternity while the rest of the procession passed by and the throngs moved like sludge along the narrow London streets. At nearly sunset, long after she'd expected to be home, Thomas and Samuel set her down before the entrance to the town house William kept for her not far from where the bridge met the south bank of the Thames. She paid them according to distance, and a good thing, since she wouldn't have had the cash to pay them for the hours they'd spent delivering her. They gave sour looks to the coins she handed them, but pocketed them without actual comment. She would need their sedan chair again another day soon, and they were always happy for a steady fare and a light load. They picked up the empty chair and moved off into the light traffic in streets cleared of people who had gone home to tell of their exciting day.

Suzanne lifted her skirts above the eternal street muck, and wiped her iron pattens on the filthy scraper by the door as best she could. She wore them to keep her shoes clean, and they did an adequate job of that, but there was no way to keep the much-crusted pattens from tracking dirt and sewage into the house. A wicker mat before the door took a bit more of the muck, then she carried her shopping parcel inside and up the narrow stairs to her apartments on the first floor above the street level.

Still her mind tumbled with thoughts of Daniel, with pleasant memories of their time together and the terrible ones of the war that had separated them. It seemed so long ago, when there was more money, better company . . . altogether more and better of nearly everything. And there had been Daniel before the war. For two years they'd had stolen moments and secret meetings, so much the sweeter for being forbidden. At the time she'd been certain their love was like no other, that when he kissed her they lit up the sky, that when people looked at them they could see they were the truest lovers in creation. She knew when she became pregnant she was the first ever to feel the way she did about her baby.

Then Daniel left. He knew about Piers, but never saw him. The day she'd told him she was pregnant was also the day he'd fled with Charles I. And that was the last she'd seen of him.

Or heard from him. While he was still in England there had been letters, but he hadn't contacted her in any way since leaving for the Continent. She had assumed it was because he no longer wanted to hear from her. After all, he was married. Why would he want a mistress across the channel? Why would any man want a mistress he couldn't sleep with? He was able to forget both her and Piers.

Now, as she entered her house, she held in her mind the

look on his face when he'd recognized her in the crowd. What had he been thinking? Perhaps she would never know. After so many years, he surely would have no interest in her. He'd had little enough interest the night he'd left her.

Her girl Sheila greeted her at the entry upstairs, took her cloak and vizard, then bent to help her off with the pattens.

The maid was an Irish girl, about fifteen years old but spunky and assertive for her years, and she spoke rapidly and nearly unintelligibly under her breath as she worked the straps on Suzanne's footwear. "Himself arrived hours ago, you know, and he's fit to be tied." She set each patten on a piece of oilcloth by the door until they could be cleaned.

"Thank you for the warning, Sheila."

"He's been at me the whole time. I vow if you'd been a moment longer I might have done away with him so as not to have to listen to him anymore."

"I applaud your self-control, Sheila." Suzanne was too distracted to care much about William or his eternal pique. Her mind couldn't let go of Daniel, and she spoke to Sheila without much mind attached to it.

Daniel was older now, of course, nearing forty. Graying some, and a mite worse for wear after these past years of poverty. In the parade he'd worn a new suit provided by Parliament, but even from where she'd sat she'd seen in his face the stresses of those years, written there as if by pen and ink. She could see he'd changed, and now she was curious whether it were for better or worse.

William could wait; she wearied of his shrill, self-centered insistence that her world should not merely turn on him, but consist entirely of him. In the bedchamber she took a moment at her hand mirror to be certain she'd not become too frayed and worn during her afternoon out, then once Sheila had replaced a pin or two, Suzanne drew a deep, refreshing breath and made her entrance to the 'tiring room.

There William awaited her, perched on a chair with a book in his hand. He sat with knees together, elbows clamped to his sides, both feet firmly planted. When she entered he looked up, and he gently folded the book closed and set it on a nearby table. His delicate, oval face was that of a much younger man, for his visage had an immaturity that made him seem eternally a child. His frame was lanky and thin almost to the point of emaciation. Hugging him was like embracing a scarecrow. All bones and angles. And he had the strength of one with little meat on his bones. As a lover he was barely noticeable. To Suzanne, that added to his value as a patron, for there was less of him to annoy her, both of mind and body.

"Good evening, William. I do hope you haven't been waiting long. There was terrible traffic on my return from the Exchange, and nothing moved for hours. I assure you I'm exhausted from my attempts to return in a timely manner." She looked off in the direction Sheila had gone. "By the aroma from the kitchen, I'll wager Sheila will have supper soon. I've missed dinner, and breakfast is a dim memory; personally I'm ravenous. I expect you will stay and have some roast with me." He always did. He viewed her meals as food he'd paid for and he was entitled to. She paused and waited for him to rise and come to kiss her as he always did, like planting a flag on territory. But today he didn't. He rose, but only faced her with his hands clasped at his waist, and spoke in his habitual prim tone, rather like an old lady in church.

"Where have you been?" His balding head stood out in beads of perspiration, in spite of the temperate weather. His rather long neck stuck out the top of his plain white collar, and his Adam's apple took a bob like a fishing float as he swallowed.

"I was at the Exchange, in search of a new tablecloth to replace the one ruined with an entire bottle of wine spilled on it two days ago. On the way back my chair was hemmed in by the crowds greeting the king. Had I gotten out to walk, I would not have returned any sooner than I did." Not that she would have considered walking in any case, but she mentioned it to head off what she knew would be his next question if she didn't.

And so his next question was of something else. "You ruined a tablecloth?" His annoyed tone suggested she should have been less clumsy, but she ignored him. It was habitual.

"To be sure, I'm less distressed over the cloth than I am about the waste of a fine bottle of French wine. The inexpensive cloth is far more easily replaced on the unimpressive stipend you provide."

William's chin came up, his back straightened, and he pulled his elbows in, as if someone had just shoved a rod up his rear end. In theory he was of the Puritan bent, and wound as tightly as a hangman's noose. Often when he was annoyed, he worked himself into such a trembling paroxysm, she thought he might snap and explode all over everything in a shower of tiny parts. He said, "You might have saved yourself the cost of even the cloth; you'll soon need the money."

Her eyes narrowed. His voice carried a darkness of dire warning. Not uncommon for him, but she'd learned to take heed when he became too negative. She dreaded the answer to her next question. "Why do you say that?"

"I must leave England immediately."

Not such a terrible thing, but she could see this wasn't the entire story and probed further. "Whatever for? Have you business on the Continent?" More to the point, why would that affect her income? She patiently waited for him to explain the connection, and her heart thudded in her throat. The knuckles of her tightly clamped hands went to white, although her carefully arranged face revealed nothing. Money was an issue she took most seriously.

Impatience tinged his voice. "Even you can't be so stupid. Even you should know what it means to me that the king has returned."

"I expect it means a great many things to many people. What, specifically, does the king's return have to do with my stipend? Why can't you simply arrange to have it paid while you're away?" For a moment she had a bright, shining hope of an extended time when she would receive his money without enduring his presence, but she knew the world was never that accommodating. She was never that lucky, and now she waited for his explanation as she began to resign herself to the reality she would soon be on her own.

"You know I'm a follower of the Reformed theology."

She nodded. He was a Puritan. And more vocal about it than even the average hardheaded Protestant. Having been raised a moderate Anglican, she often felt herself in a cross fire between the rabid reformers and stubborn traditionalists of every stripe, whether Puritan, Presbyterian, or Catholic, and had little patience with anyone for whom religion was worth going to war. She was no theologian, and even she could see that bloodshed and hatred were not what Christianity was about. But, as always, she held her tongue and only waited for him to proceed.

An edge of increasing impatience came to his voice. "I did business with our Lord Protector, Oliver Cromwell."

She nodded again. He was always on about his connection to Cromwell, tenuous as it was. William sold fabric, and often sold it to the Lord Protector's household. Cromwell himself more than likely would have been hard put to place the name "William Wainwright" unless prompted with the word "cloth."

Impatience rose further, as if she were expected to gasp with realization of his meaning and had failed him. "I can't believe you don't see the truth."

"Please pardon my stupidity, my dear William. Perhaps if you explained to me your meaning." She sat and gestured to the chair he'd just risen from for him to sit again.

He declined the offer, but said in a voice tight with distress, his hands gripping each other even more firmly than before, "I must flee. Surely you realize that. Now that the king has come to London, I must run for my life to the Continent."

Suzanne nearly laughed, but she kept it to herself and mustered a concerned gaze. "Why? Have there been threats?"

He shrugged, as if embarrassed to admit the truth. "None specific. But you know how these things always happen. Unwary men are often caught out, then find themselves carted away to Tyburn without the first notion as to why or how. I might not have warning until the moment the king's men come to get me."

Suzanne would have thought he was joking, except she'd never known him to have any sort of sense of humor. "You believe the king intends to chase down everyone who did business with Cromwell? That would surely empty London."

"Not everyone, but surely some." The assumption being that he was among the elite to cause concern for the monarch. Suzanne had always known William to be a self-important prig, but this boggled even her for its arrogance. She stifled a laugh, but just barely.

"And you think you'll worry him enough to order your arrest? You think you've given sufficient cause?"

William puffed out his chest, offended. "If you knew aught of the world, woman, you would understand that a dissolute monarch won't need cause at all to send good men to the gallows."

Suzanne had no reply to that, for it was true as far as it went. What was less true was that William would ever attract the attention of the crown, for any reason, let alone cause Charles enough concern to send him to the gallows. Or, for that matter, that William was a good man. She gazed at him and hoped her expression was of a kindness she couldn't feel.

Sheila appeared at the open doorway and said softly and with proper respect for William's benefit, "Mistress, supper is ready if either of you would care for it."

Suzanne nodded. "Yes. We'll be in directly."

The girl disappeared.

"Come, William. Let us eat, and discuss this." She rose and held out a conciliatory hand, a little like placating a growling dog.

"No. I must go now. I'll have the clothing I left here." With that he hurried from the room and into the bedchamber. Alarmed, Suzanne followed.

"Oh, be sensible, William. You can't just leave."

He pulled a satchel from under the bed, then went to the armoire and took some shirts and drawers from it to stuff into the bag. "I must. Surely you see I can't stay."

"Then arrange with your money changer—"

"I said, Suzanne, I'm leaving. All my wealth must come

with me." And all his clothing, and one of her shifts as well, as he shoved things indiscriminately into the bag. She wanted to reach over and tug the shift away, but refrained for fear of setting him off irretrievably. She continued her attempt to persuade him to leave money.

"How will your wife live, then?"

"She'll accompany me."

Of course. Suzanne's heart clenched as she saw what lay ahead for her. She truly was being abandoned. The worst of it was that his flight was unnecessary. William's perception of his relationship with Cromwell was more fantasy than fact, and the king would never bother with anyone so insignificant, even were he aware. "Please, William, you're being hasty. There's no need to throw your life away."

He stopped packing, turned, and gazed at her, a grief in his eyes she thought rather theatrical. Having been on the stage when she was younger, she knew something of a performance when she saw it, and now was unsure of what to think. He said, "My life is forfeit. For all intents and purposes, it's over. Fate has betrayed me, and I must face persecution for my faith. I go with heavy heart, but with the knowledge that I am right with God." The tremor in his voice seemed overdone, but she knew he truly was choked up over his fate. He glanced around the room, spotted a small figurine of a spotted dog he'd given to her several years before, and pocketed it.

Suzanne blinked, wondering what God had to do with whether or not the king would be fussy about William's business with Cromwell. To the best of her knowledge, Charles's main argument against the Protectorate was that the usurper caused the death of his father. She realized William must want his martyrdom, and might have suggested he stay and let

Charles have his head to that end, except that William's death wouldn't save her stipend. William wouldn't be worth much to her without his head. "Please don't go, William. You have a duty to me."

"I have a duty to God, to survive and to spread His word wherever I go." She wondered how well he expected to fare in Catholic France. With that, he picked up the bag and went to the outer door. She followed, saying nothing. There he turned, and with another dramatic gaze, chin high, he said, "Farewell, my dear Suzanne. I'll see you in heaven." Then he departed.

Suzanne stood, rooted, staring at the door he'd closed behind him. Sheila came to stand beside her and likewise gaze at the door. Then she said softly, "When he gets to heaven, I wonder how he'll explain to St. Peter his having kept a mistress these past six years."

Suzanne might have laughed, but she was too heartsick for mirth. William had never been lavish with money, for he had little of it compared to others of his rank, which was, of course, the merchant class. She knew she was his only mistress, and he kept her and Piers barely comfortable. Now there would be nothing from him. At thirty-five, she was too old to ever find another man to support her.

"Supper is on the table, mistress. Shall I remove the second setting?"

Suzanne nodded, though she barely heard. Her mind tumbled, in search of some way out of her predicament. While Piers was old enough for employment, he had barely finished his apprenticeship and had not yet found a position, and even then it would be years before he might support her in adequate fashion. She had some money tucked away in a false drawer bottom in the armoire, but that wouldn't last long. And thank

God William hadn't found that while packing. Not only would he have taken it with him, he would have made an ugly, vile scene as he did so.

That evening Suzanne ate her supper in a deep funk of worry.

Chapter Three

Suzanne was not one to dither, ever. Her mind was ever at work, and though it shifted from subject to subject often, her thoughts went a-progress through whatever knotty problem presented itself and usually came out the far end with an answer. The moment her eyes popped open the next morning, her mind began an inventory of her resources and a review of her options. Without any awareness of her surroundings, she sat up in bed and stared into the middle distance as her mind sifted through and sorted the facts of her situation.

She'd always known this day would come, but had only hoped it would not have been this soon, for there was only so much she could set aside from the scant money provided by William. She had some cash on deposit with a goldsmith, but knew it wasn't nearly enough to live on indefinitely, even if she included the coins she'd stashed about the house over the past few years. As much a skinflint as William was, it had been difficult to squirrel away a shilling here and a penny there, but there were coins "lost" at the bottoms of drawers, and small enameled boxes scattered throughout the rooms that held money dropped from pockets or left out where it might be "misplaced" as Sheila tidied up. One such box, a gift from a former client, was half full of guineas and held a number of shillings as well. Suzanne had never added them up but guessed they should come to a substantial amount. Not enough to see her through her old age, though, unless she lived like a pauper, and she'd had quite enough of that in the past.

As she rose from the bed and slipped into her silk dressing gown, the scent of meat left over from last night, being reheated on the stove by Sheila in the kitchen, drifted to the bedchamber. There was an occasional clank and clink of pan and pottery as the maid worked, which brought a thrill of alarm as Sheila entered her calculations. How would she continue to pay a maid? She'd become accustomed to having one, and didn't care to live without her. There had been a time when she'd had no kitchen, and breakfast meant bundling up to venture forth and buy a pot of something cheap and adulterated from a street vendor or stall; now she could hardly bear the thought of facing a cold kitchen alone of a morning.

Numbers tumbled in her head as she worked out how long her money would last. A year or two, perhaps, if she lived frugally, without Sheila. There wasn't much room to cut back from the way she'd lived on William's contribution. His Puritan sensibilities made for a good stability she'd appreciated for the food in her belly and the clothes on her back, but he was not much for luxury. There was little to give up that wouldn't return her to the bad years when her only refuge was a bawd house on Bank Side.

Now, at the age of thirty-five, her youth was fully spent and any enthusiasm for that game quite wrung from her. The beauty she'd enjoyed as a girl had waned so that these days she was generally described with the euphemism of "handsome." Her flesh was firm and her figure trim "for her age." Not only would finding another patron be impossible, even base whoring was no longer an option for her; she would have to find another source of income if she was to live past thirty-six.

She tied the sash of her gown and slipped her feet into a pair of slippers that were ordinary linen but boasted some skilled, intricate embroidery, then she ventured from the bedchamber.

At the dining table she was delighted to find Piers had arrived from Newcastle and was already at breakfast. He looked up from his plate and smiled, rising to greet her with a kiss on the cheek, but she then threw her arms around his neck for a long hug. Her boy was finally back from the north, and she could be happy.

Then they both sat again as Sheila set Suzanne's plate of meat before her. "How delightful to see you so soon, Piers." The window was wide open to a bright spring day, and a breeze on which wafted the odors of manure, sewage, cooking food, and a hint of the Thames just to the north. Voices of street criers below drifted in.

Before seating herself, Suzanne leaned over to blow out the single candle that burned at the middle of the table. The day brought plenty of light through the window, and they didn't need to waste the tallow. Waste was a sin, one of the few things William preached that she thought valid.

"I hurried home," said Piers with a huge grin. "Farthingworth had no more use for me, and so I'm now free to secure gainful employment as I will." He sounded cheerful over the prospect, though his voice held a hint of the knowledge she would not be pleased with the news.

Suzanne tensed. "He had no offer for you?" She'd hoped Piers's apprenticeship would have segued directly into a permanent position, and in fact Farthingworth had alluded to the possibility when the training had been arranged seven years before. It would have meant living in Newcastle, but she would have been pleased to make the sacrifice of leaving London in exchange for a secure life in the care of her son.

"No, I'm afraid." Piers picked at the meat on his plate.

"No references?"

Here Piers perked a bit, he sat up straighter, and the roses of embarrassment on his cheeks faded some. "I've the name of a merchant here in London I'm to contact. And I'd rather be in London in any case, truth be told." He returned his attention to his breakfast, but kept an eye on her reaction.

Susanne's attention sharpened, apprehensive, wondering whether Piers had declined an offer from Farthingworth in order to return home. She opened her mouth to chastise him for it, but thought better of berating her only son over something that couldn't be undone. Instead she said, "Only one merchant?"

Piers nodded. "He's Farthingworth's largest London client. He provides coal for all the great houses. Probably the crown as well, once the king is settled in."

"You'll go to him today, I expect. Before the king's return throws everything in London into confusion. Better to have any position at all than to seek one during the coming upheaval."

"Do you really think it will be all that bad?"

It's already bad, and will worsen. Suzanne replied, "It can't help but be troublesome. Even with Parliament telling the king what to do, there will still be changes made in trade relationships." She remembered how things had shifted during the civil war, so that nothing could be depended on until it was clear Cromwell was in charge and would stay there. "Those whose families stayed loyal to the crown will now have advantage over those too close to Cromwell. If this fellow can't take you on, you must seek an employer with few political ties or, even better, one with ties to the king."

Piers made a wry face, and a dry edge came into his voice. "Yes, that should be as easy as pie." He took a bite of mutton, chewed a couple of times, then moved the meat to his cheek and said around it, "And if I lose my new position during this upheaval?"

"Then you return to the search immediately and take whatever you can get."

"I hear a note of desperation, Mother." He set his knife on his plate and sat back in his chair. "Is there anything wrong?"

Suzanne bit her lip and also sat back to look at her son. Eighteen years old and as handsome as his father. Naïve about the world, but far too sharp where his mother was concerned. She'd never been able to hide anything from Piers, and only wished Daniel had been as attentive. She said, "William has left us."

That brought a snort, and Piers returned to his meal. "Good riddance to bad rubbish."

"Maybe so, except he's taken his money with him. We're on our own again."

Piers paused eating to gaze at his plate, then shrugged and resumed chewing. "We'll manage."

"You mean we won't starve. Yes, that will be a change from some days past. But I would rather do better than that in my old age."

"I'll take care of you, Mother." He glanced over at her. The look on his face broke her heart, he was so earnest and so brave. To her he was a little boy trying to be a man, but his ruddy complexion and bright blue eyes betrayed him for one too young to make good that promise. And worse, for the thousandth time since his birth, he reminded her of his father.

"I know you will. And with any luck I'll find another income that will help buy more than just mutton and bread."

Piers nodded and returned to his meal once more. Suzanne addressed hers and thought hard about what to do.

A knock came on the door, and both of them listened closely as Sheila answered it. But there were no words to hear beyond Sheila's thanks for a delivery and the messenger's muttered thanks for the farthing tip from the dish of small change kept on the stand beside the door. Suzanne looked toward the dining room door, and Sheila came with a folded message in hand.

"Not creditors already, I hope," said Piers.

"There are no creditors, thank God, other than the landlord. William never believed in having things that weren't paid for. Usury is a sin, you know. *Neither a borrower nor a lender be*, he would say, as if Shakespeare wrote the Bible."

"You mean he didn't?"

That made Suzanne smile, and Piers's boyish dimples showed in a grin. She'd so missed him these past years of his apprenticeship. It had been far too long between visits.

She took the message, dismissed Sheila, and her fingers began to tremble, for she recognized the hand on the front. Her name, exactly as Daniel used to write it when she was but a girl younger than Piers. She hadn't seen him or his handwriting in nearly a decade, but she remembered it well.

She broke the seal at the back. Slowly she unfolded the stiff, heavy paper. There was but one sentence on the page. "I must see you today at the stairs."

She folded the paper quickly, hoping Piers wouldn't see it,

but he didn't need to read it and instead saw the look on her face.

"Why so pale, Mother? What's wrong?"

She thought for a long moment, considering a lie, but hated to tell it to Piers. Instead she said, "Piers, your father has returned."

Piers only grunted and picked up a piece of fat to gnaw. "I assumed that. He left with Charles; it stands to reason he would return with him if he were still alive. I can't say as I'm particularly pleased he is."

Suzanne hadn't considered the possibility of Daniel's return until she'd seen him in the procession yesterday. "He wishes to see me today."

"Not me?"

"I imagine his thought is to learn my mind first, then ask about you."

"Perhaps. Perhaps not. Then again, it may be his only wish is to have something more from you."

"Piers!"

He only shrugged and looked away. She wanted to tell him that Daniel loved him, but she couldn't know whether it were true, and in fact she rather doubted it. He'd never met his son, and had never shown any interest in doing so. First the war, then nine years on the Continent. Not one letter from him since leaving England. And now a note from him so soon after his return. It seemed odd. A dim hope rose. "I must go see him."

"You must retain your dignity." Piers's voice was hard and angry, and his young voice cracked with the stress.

"I'm afraid any dignity I ever had was whipped out of me by my father twenty and thirty years ago. And William certainly never had any respect to spare for me, or anyone but himself, for that matter." The familiar clenching tightened in her chest.

"He respects St. Paul, I think. Truth be told, I think he would bugger St. Paul if he had the chance."

Suzanne struggled to suppress a grin, and she drew a deep breath to clear her thinking.

Piers leaned toward her, one elbow on the table, his voice a low growl. "Then allow me to win back some respect for the both of us. Let me go to work and earn our keep. I wish to support you, and never mind the king's man my father."

She laid a hand on his arm and said gently, "You will, son. But just now I need to learn what he wants and hope he wants to lend some support. Even for the interim."

Piers only grunted again, neither approving nor disapproving, but at least he didn't pull his arm away.

Suzanne returned to her breakfast, and her mind turned to work through the problem of what to wear to the old meeting place on Bank Side.

Chapter Four

Suzanne's choice for the day was an elderly dove-gray dress with lace at the sleeves and a bodice that was so old as to be nearly Elizabethan. It was something she'd bought second- or thirdhand during her search for a patron to better herself, testimony to fashion before Cromwell. The costumes she'd worn as a prostitute and an actress had all been cheap, and of course were long gone. Nothing she'd acquired during her tenure with William was any color other than black, and though the fabrics were sometimes silken, all were plain Puritan style, with long sleeves, high necklines, and white collars that on occasion brushed the earlobes. Daniel had just come from the Continent, accustomed to the latest French fashions, so though the gray dress was hopelessly out of style for any country, at least it wasn't unadorned, funereal black. For hair dressing she robbed an old hat of some feathers and pinned them securely over her right ear.

At the door she had Sheila strap on her pattens, drew on her cloak and gloves against the spring breezes, placed the holder of her vizard between her teeth, and stepped out into the neighborhood, headed for Bank Side.

Horse Shoe Alley, where Suzanne's rented town house stood, was a place of bawd houses and pubs, where the streets teemed with the working and criminal classes. It was cheap and out of the way, suitable for the mistress of a Puritan who needed to hide his hypocrisy, but not so filthy as some other areas of London. Suzanne was a longtime resident and knew who her neighbors were, but a stranger shouldn't care to be out and about these streets late at night.

Off down Maid Lane stood the great old Elizabethan structure of the Globe Theatre, closed these past sixteen years. Beyond that towered the even older bear and bull baiting arenas, just as empty as all the theatres during the interregnum, when most forms of entertainment had been outlawed and the majority of theatres had been torn down. The neighborhood was hardly fashionable, even during the Commonwealth when the very idea of fashion was unfashionable and enjoyment of anything was a sin and evil to contemplate. Unforgivable sin apparently, since confession and absolution had been heresy for about a century and a half. Suzanne wasn't Catholic, nor a particularly religious person, but even she was made jumpy by the idea that one could go to hell for wearing the wrong dress or stopping to watch a play. Even worse, to be arrested and incarcerated for it, for that was immediate misery. She longed for the days when those things hadn't even been a question and one had been free to enjoy life.

In any case, though the neighborhood she had lived in for the past two decades was rather dodgy, the house she lived in was sturdy, proof to the weather, not too terribly overrun with rats, and it boasted a kitchen roomy enough to please Sheila as well as southern-facing windows to let in whatever light could be had from the street. Today the sun was out, but still spring-thin and almost watery as it moved toward summer. The gentle warmth on her shoulders helped her think the meeting with Daniel could be a pleasant one. The neighborhood had a glow about it today, which could only mean good fortune. She didn't need to consult her astrologer to know the stars were aligned well today. She could almost smell the hope drifting in the air.

At the north end of the alley a narrow passage let out onto the Bank Side, which ran along the Thames between the Skin Market and the Bank End Stairs. Whenever the wind came from the west, the tannery stench of the Skin Market overpowered even the sewage-filled Thames with a reek that only the most seasoned residents could ignore. Fortunately today was not such a day, and only the ordinary smells of street food, horses, garbage, and dank river were evident during Suzanne's walk from Horse Shoe Alley.

Children played in the street, ones belonging to families in the house next to hers named Andrews and Williams. They kicked around an inflated pig's bladder in an enthusiastic though unskilled game of football involving goals known only to the players. Most of the children were barefoot, though a couple wore ill-fitting shoes and one boasted a rag tied around one foot, which had probably been injured, though no limp was evident as she tore this way and that after the ball. They dodged the occasional horse rider and the even more rare carriage, and their laughing and hollering echoed from the surrounding buildings.

Other, more industrious children hawked wares of prepared foods, the odor of edibles mingling with the stench of filthy muck underfoot. Johnny Kirk and his sister Annie offered their usual pasties and sheep's feet, but Suzanne declined today, having just eaten breakfast. The smells should have been unpleasant, but Suzanne had lived here so long it all now smelled of home to her.

On Bank Side at the far end of the passage, Big Willie Waterman stood in his usual spot with his fiddle, dancing up a storm and playing the same lively tunes he'd been scratching at for the ten years she'd known him. Just as a large man might have been called "Tiny," Big Willie was so named because he was very small and gaunt, even smaller than Suzanne, who weighed very little. Suzanne greeted him and dropped a farthing into his hat.

"New stitches, I see," she said. His remarkably white shirt had no discernible holes and sported all its ties, though few of them were actually tied. His breeches were old, but she could see they were fresher and less frayed than those he'd worn last she'd seen him.

"Found 'em just this morning. Finders, keepers, say I, milady." His grin was mostly toothless, but sincere, and his tune became just a little more lively for the cash. To him any woman who dropped money for him was "milady" and all the men "milord," no matter how humble the actual circumstance. Children sometimes liked to toss him farthings just to hear him say "Thankee, little lord."

"Found them on a clothesline, did you?"

Willie's grin widened, and his eyebrows went up in feigned innocence. "I never steal, milady. Never! They was a-lying on the ground when I picked 'em up, they was! I swear it! And I'll tell you for a fact, I was forever a-shaking that line. I thought they'd never fall. But I swear I never touched 'em on the line!"

Suzanne laughed and turned eastward toward the bridge.

Bank End Stairs had always been the meeting place for her and Daniel, as far back as when she had still lived in her father's house. Back in the days before the war, when the world held bright color and hope. In the days before she'd learned how the world really worked. Today she went to meet Daniel once again, at the very spot where she'd seen him last more than half a lifetime ago, now to learn whether he'd changed as much as she had.

At the top of the stairs, standing on the stone embankment, she gazed across the river at the jumble of old buildings and cobbled streets teeming with people. The spire of St. Paul's Cathedral rose above the nearest structures, a tall, thin spire pointing the way to heaven. To the east the bridge squatted on the river, looking more like a spit of land than a bridge, so built up as it was with houses and offices. Crossing that bridge was little different from walking down any other street.

From where she stood she couldn't tell whether there were any new heads on the spikes at this end, but she assumed there would be a sufficiency before long, once the king caught up with those who had murdered his father. Oh yes, there were always executions whenever somebody new took the reins of power, and London would surely have public and bloody executions and rotting bits of nobility on display before the first day of summer. None of them would be William, to his disappointment, but for a brief moment she held a fantasy he could be among the dead. Then she shook off the evil thought and sought a more pleasant theme for her musing.

It shifted from the king to the war, then to Daniel and the last time she'd seen him in this very spot, so that when his voice came to her it was nearly as if it had originated in her imagination. It gave her a start.

"I'm surprised you came after all," he said.

Her heart leapt, and she had to restrain herself from spinning on her heel to greet him with a big, stupid grin. Her own excitement shocked her, for she'd convinced herself long ago his hold on her heart had failed. She'd thought the thing in her that made her pulse race at the sound of this man's—or any man's—voice was long dead, and there should have been no girlish smile nor excited greeting in a voice an entire octave too high. But today her body betrayed her and she forced herself to wait a beat, then turn slowly. Graceful. Self-possessed. Dignified, in spite of what she'd told Piers earlier. She held the edge of her vizard in one gloved hand so she could speak without the button between her teeth. "Daniel."

"I'm happy you came. We've much to say."

The sun was at his back, and she stepped aside so she could see him without his face in shadow. He turned with her, a tiny smile at the corners of his mouth as he realized what she was doing. He reached out and gently removed her vizard from her face to gaze at her. With one flick of the wrist he flung it, spinning, over the bank, where it floated down to the river like an autumn leaf. There it danced and bobbed on the glittering surface of the Thames, making its way toward the sea. She watched it go and thought of the shilling it would cost to replace the thing. Then she regarded Daniel thoughtfully.

He'd changed more than she'd ever imagined he could. After so long, he seemed even older than he should. Too thin, too gray, too . . . weary. His long limbs and lanky body took an insouciant stance, hipshot, casual, in the eternal boyish pretense of superiority that had once impressed her as actual superiority. But now she saw it for the immature bluff it was, a posture cultivated by those on the defensive, and understood that the intervening years had not been kind to him.

Nevertheless he wore a cheerful countenance that lifted her heart. Plainly he was happy to see her, and his smile appeared genuine. She wondered whether she should also be glad to see him, and she remembered the events leading up to the meeting on that terrible night eighteen years ago, when she was but seventeen and her life changed so horribly.

SUZANNE stood before her father in the 'tiring room of his house, her heart thudding in her chest so hard it seemed her stays must bulge in time with it and her lace collar lift with each beat. Her fingers knotted together behind her at her waist, bloodless and slippery with perspiration. A suitor stood near the archway, who had that look of hope which sickened her for its weakness.

Why her father wanted her to marry someone so needy and spineless was a dark mystery to her. One that put a crease in her brow such as her father could never quite beat out of her. This one was a coal merchant named Stephen Farthingworth, not terribly much older than herself, whose father mined and transported coal from Newcastle. His entire family for two generations had mined and sold coal to the London nobility and had become quite wealthy from it. Not overwhelmingly rich, but well off enough, considering their background involved nobody of significant rank even at a distance and their money did not come from land. Father was quite taken with him, and Suzanne knew where that must lead. She also knew she could never marry Farthingworth. Ever. Nor anyone else, for that. The baby within her had quickened, and she knew it was far too late to pass it off as his.

She was to meet Daniel at the bank at sunset, and she

twitched to be let go so she could sneak away. Poor Mr. Farthingworth would have to find a girl more desperate than she to marry.

When her attention came back around, Father was saying, "Mr. Farthingworth has made an offer, and we should be well pleased with it." It was unseemly groveling. Shameful, and it made Suzanne cringe. If only he'd held her worth a little better, she might have had a better offer than this. But Father had always made it clear she was a burden to him and he resented having to pay a dowry at all. Plainly he didn't care if her future were secure; he wanted only to be rid of her and her sisters, so her brothers wouldn't be burdened by them when they would one day inherit what there was. The paltry money he'd set aside for her wasn't enough to attract a man of character, never mind one of rank. She knew she was pretty enough, but even great beauty would be no help if the dowry was inadequate. Farthingworth was the best she could ask for, and he wasn't enough. She could never love him. She didn't intend to marry him.

Poor Farthingworth stood straighter at Thornton's words. Father wasn't nearly as wealthy as Farthingworth's father, but was well respected in London and held minor office, so Suzanne knew Farthingworth was getting some social advantage to make up for the tiny dowry. In addition, Suzanne had a realistic assessment of her looks. She was the prettiest of her sisters, and at her age understood the attentions of men and what that meant to her future. Particularly her future with Daniel Stockton, who would one day be the Earl of Throckmorton and, more important, who loved her as Farthingworth did not.

Stephen Farthingworth had only met her once before, knew her not well at all, and certainly hadn't made his offer of marriage out of love. Nor out of regard of any kind. He was a pleasant enough fellow in polite company, but certainly was not the most intelligent creature she'd ever met and seemed a little more interested in the whores on Bank Side than in Suzanne during his visits to London. Though on this visit at least, while requesting her hand, he didn't stink of French perfume.

"You're to know, Suzanne, that I've accepted his offer on your behalf." He might have at least made a pretense of inviting her opinion of this offer. Most girls at least had veto power; Suzanne was offered nothing.

Father continued, "He's accepted a very reasonable dowry." Ever the miser her father. He fancied himself a loving and responsible parent, but she knew in this family her brothers were the important ones. He might even be happy to learn the truth about her and Daniel, for it would save him the dowry entirely. As Daniel's mistress, she would be the responsibility of the future earl and Father needn't be bothered with her anymore. There would be both love and security, and she'd had little of either in her life before Daniel. It seemed to her the best thing for everyone involved.

She drew a deep breath, steeled herself, and said, "Father, I'm afraid I can't accept Mr. Farthingworth's eminently generous offer, and you cannot accept for me."

"Why not?" Father's voice carried the edge it always did when he sensed she was about to embarrass him. And he was right. This time the news would be devastating.

Another deep breath, and she plunged into her confession. "Father, I could hardly give myself in marriage to a man when I'm already with child by another. Particularly, given that my dowry is so 'reasonable,' I expect Mr. Farthingworth will want to withdraw his offer." The last she said in a voice rather thick with sarcasm, and she lowered her gaze to the floor for it. Bluntness was her worst fault, and she wished she could be more tactful because her straightforward nature was never helpful and always made Father harsher toward her when her impatience with dull people showed through.

One glance at him, and by the look on his face she saw she'd severely overestimated his willingness to accept the situation. She wished she could reel in the words she'd just spoken. His eyes went wide, and his jaw dropped. The silence in the room lengthened, and tension grew until she thought the very air would snap to pieces. She glanced at Mr. Farthingworth, who stared a hole in the wood floor, his lips pressed hard together. Father said in a trembling voice, "What did you say?"

"I said I'm pregnant, Father. By the time I could be married to Farthingworth here, it would be apparent to all that you had sold him devalued property. He would be embarrassed, you would be scandalized, and I would be trapped in a marriage to a man I don't love." She addressed Farthingworth, "I'm so sorry, but it's true. And neither do you love me, so I think we're both better off not being married to each other, don't you agree?"

Farthingworth opened his mouth to reply, but nothing came out. She returned her attention to her father and said, "Don't you think, Father? Isn't it better to marry someone you love than to make a purely financial arrangement without regard to feelings or personality? Particularly since my dowry is so very . . . *reasonable?*"

She waited in silence for a reply. Saying more would not be helpful, so she knitted her fingers together to the point of pain to keep her mouth from uttering another word. Nobody spoke.

Finally Farthingworth cleared his throat and drew in his chin. He looked at Suzanne, and she saw some pain in his eyes. No anger, but real pain. Even more she regretted having blurted in front of him, for she had never wished to be unkind. He said, "Thank you for your honesty, Miss Thornton. So rare in a woman, and I should have liked that in a wife." Suzanne opened her mouth to reply, but he spoke over her. "Well . . . I expect there is much to be said here that doesn't involve me. I'll take my leave now. A pleasant evening to you both, and I hope all turns out well." With that, he bowed to Father. "I'll find the door myself, thank you." And he departed with alacrity uncharacteristic of him.

Father waited until he was certain Farthingworth was out of earshot, then he reached out and smacked Suzanne on the cheek. She staggered sideways, but from long experience was able to make a quick recovery. Her cheek burned red and it took a moment for her vision to clear as she resumed her stance before her father. Her hands remained at the small of her back, and she faced him in defiant silence. Her thoughts were on Daniel, and she hoped he would wait for her at the stairs. When this beating was over, she would hurry to him. If he came, all would be right with the world and he would help her to know what to do.

Father raised his cane and proceeded to beat her. He pulled none of his strokes. He never did. She protected her baby with her arms and presented the parts of her she knew could withstand the punishment with only bruises. It seemed to go on forever, and soon there seemed never to have been a time when she wasn't being beaten with Father's cane.

When it finally stopped, it was as if she'd begun a whole new life filled with pain that would never end. She lay huddled on the floor, her arms swollen and possibly broken, blood running from her lacerated scalp and down her neck. Her nose was intact, but one side of her upper lip had risen to the size of an egg. Her father ordered her to her bedchamber, there to await supper, and he left her on the 'tiring room floor. On his way out he ordered the downstairs maid to leave her alone. Suzanne was to make her way upstairs and clean up by herself.

Slowly she struggled to her feet and climbed the stairs to the room she shared with her sisters. There she wet a towel in the washbowl and dabbed at her face. Her hair was hopeless, matted with blood. Taking it down and trying to comb it out would take all night, and there wasn't enough time for that, so she tied it up with a kerchief. The cloth soaked through immediately, but there was nothing for it. Time was of the essence, and being caught just now might bring another, worse beating. This bleeding would stop when it would. The swollen lip would go down, the cuts would heal, the bruises would fade. They always had. And these would be the last of them, she swore.

None of the family were present at the moment, so she was unhindered as she packed a small satchel with clothes. Then she drew on her cloak and pulled the hood over her head as far as it would go to hide the kerchief. Quietly she made her way down the stairs and out to the street. She didn't know what she would say if she were apprehended, but luck was with her to the extent that nobody saw her and she strode purposefully to the corner as if on an important errand. And in a way she was.

It was a fair walk across the bridge to Bank Side, and full dark when she arrived at the stairs. Only the full moon and a torch near the bank's edge lit the area. Daniel was waiting for her, sitting on the top step of the stairs to the river. When he saw her, he leapt to his feet and hurried to her. "Suzanne!"

She burst into tears and let him fold her into his arms.

"What happened?" One finger touched her swollen upper lip.

She pressed her face against his cloak, and it muffled her voice. "Father accepted a proposal from a man named Farthingworth. I told them about the baby."

Daniel grunted. "So you've packed up and left, I see."

She looked up into his shadowy face. "I had no choice. He

might kill me next time; this time I believe he tried." One arm wouldn't take the weight of her bag, and the other was also in terrible pain.

"You know I can't take you in."

She nodded. Daniel was married, and had been for a year, to a girl not quite sixteen. She was the daughter of a duke, so Suzanne knew it was not a love match. He loved Suzanne; it was so certain she never thought to question it. He was wealthy, and so would establish her and her child in a house somewhere. She would be his mistress, and she could live the rest of her life knowing she was the one he really cared for. Far better than to be the wife of someone who didn't love her.

"In fact," he continued, "I won't even be in London much longer."

That was unexpected. She stepped back, and he had to catch her arm to keep her from accidentally stepping over the edge of the cobbles into the river. A cry of pain escaped her as the jolt shot up to her shoulder. Now in his eyes she saw he meant to tell her good-bye. She sank to her knees next to her bag, gasping and searching for something to say. Finally she choked out, "Why?"

He knelt beside her. "The king needs me. He's already off to York, and I need to catch up with them immediately. I only came tonight to tell you farewell."

She sat on her heels. Her head swam with the revelation and the realization of what she'd just done to herself. And even then she deluded herself about the enormity of it, for it was too horrible to grasp.

Had she known fully what the following years would bring for herself and her child, she might have fainted. Or thrown herself into the river. Even at that moment she didn't realize that tonight was the last she would see of Daniel for eighteen years. In that time there were only three letters from him while he fought with the King's Cavaliers, then fled with young Charles II. He never saw Piers, and had no contact with either of them while on the Continent. From that moment forward, Suzanne was entirely on her own in the world.

Chapter Five

"How have you been, Suzanne? Are you well?" Daniel's voice held the too-casual tone of someone who had just met her on the street after an absence of only days.

"I'm a whore, Daniel, but you always knew that." As much as she struggled to keep the bitterness from her voice, there was no hiding it entirely.

Hearing it, his reply was nearly as tart. "Well, then I expect you've had a far greater income than I've had these past few years. Loyalty to the crown is well and good, but it does tie one to the fortunes of another, for good or for bad, and I can hardly say the past eighteen years have been particularly good."

Without pause except for breath, he changed the subject with a wide, friendly grin and his finest charm. "Shall we retire to a public room for some refreshment? Is the Goat and Boar still in business or has London forsaken it, as it has every other earthly pleasure?"

"The public room survives. Men will have their indulgences no matter what they profess to the world. In fact it thrived beneath the notice of Cromwell and with the patronage of many in Parliament." She looked toward the pub, for it was just up the bank from where they stood. "Old Dent has died and his son has taken over, but it's the same old place."

"Then by all means, let us claim the table in the back and have a chat. Like old times." Suzanne remembered the old times as less chatting than other pastimes.

She hated to spend this bright, lovely day in a dark, stuffy pub, but she was terribly curious what had moved Daniel to ask to see her today. She clung to a hope that was thin as a wisp of fog, and wanted to grasp it closer in to see if it might turn out to be more substantial. She took his offered arm under her hand and strolled with him to the Goat and Boar up the street.

The pub lay tucked into an alleyway so small it had no name, and it had no sign besides. The attitude of the proprietor—and anyone else in the neighborhood—had always been that anyone who didn't already know where the Goat and Boar was didn't need to be there and therefore wasn't welcome. Though its upper floor could be seen from the river, it had no window on that side. No view. Nobody could see out, and nobody could see in, and most of its patrons liked it that way.

However, today the place was less stuffy than usual, for Young Dent had thrown open its two tiny windows at the back and propped open the door onto the alley. The cooking fire at the far end of the room near the staircase had a haunch merrily roasting and dripping grease every so often, making the flame leap and lick for more. Only two other patrons sat at a table, and that left the rest of the room to Suzanne and Daniel. They chose the table at the back next to the little windows to catch whatever breeze might come from the south. One of the other patrons was a former client of Suzanne's who frequented the pub, whose name was Alfred. Most men in this neighborhood had been clients during the years before William, and though none were clients these days, they were all quite friendly. Suzanne was like an old hunting dog that had outlived its usefulness but was too well liked to shoot.

Alfred nodded to Daniel and smiled. "Ah! I see you found her, my lord!"

"Right where you said she'd be," Daniel replied as he guided Suzanne toward the empty table at the back.

Suzanne didn't question how Daniel knew Alfred. Sometimes it seemed as if everyone knew everyone else in London, or at least all the men did. She was no longer surprised to learn that clients knew each other.

Suzanne gestured to Old Dent's son for an ale. He was a young man and had grown up in this pub, and so knew everyone and everyone knew him. There was very little about the city of London he didn't know.

Daniel enquired after some Scottish whisky, but at Young Dent's blank look quickly changed his mind and asked for an ale as Suzanne had. They settled into chairs, and Suzanne said to Daniel, "It's good to see you survived the war."

"Yes, a good thing. I tend to agree. Though I did come close to dying once, with a ball through my arm that brought fever." He touched the outside of his left arm as if feeling for the scar."

"We had no idea whether we'd ever see you again."

"We?"

"Piers and I." Could he have forgotten Piers?

"Ah. I must say it's also good to see you've prospered."

The last thing she wanted was to explain to Daniel how William had abandoned her. Humiliating enough that she was talking to Daniel at all after he'd abandoned her and Piers; she didn't care to whine and appear a weak ninny. But neither did she want Daniel to think his treatment of her hadn't been callous and hurtful. She said, "After you left, I had no choice but to sell what I had. I became a tart."

"While you were pregnant?"

"There's a market for everything, Daniel. Surely you understand that. I had my clientele." He said nothing in reply, and she continued. "After Piers was born, I worked for Maddie near the tannery and he stayed with me." She nodded in the direction of where Maddie's house had stood on the Bank Side before it was torn down. Daniel nodded, and she realized he'd probably known Maddie and her girls as well as any other man did with money to pay for whores. And many without money as well.

"Did she treat you well?"

She took a sip of her ale and considered her reply. It had been years since she'd let herself remember her time in the brothel, and she'd never thought much about Maddie herself, even back then. It had always been the clientele she'd hated, and the knowledge the men she'd serviced thought her no better than an animal. Again, she didn't want to whine about her fate to Daniel, so she told him, "As well as could be expected. We didn't starve. Piers grew up with a dozen aunties who all cared for him, and there were other children for company. But we had to find a way out of that place so he wouldn't grow up to be a cutpurse. Or worse."

"I'm sorry. I wish I could have helped."

She shrugged, irritated to hear lip service, and so long after the fact. "Well, if wishes were horses, then beggars would ride, wouldn't they?"

"Seriously—"

"A letter now and again would have been help enough." The anger blossomed in her breast, and though she struggled to swallow it she only choked on it as if it were a too-large bit of bread she'd bitten off by mistake. She coughed to clear it, and continued. "It would have helped for Piers to believe his father had some regard for him." It would have helped her own peace of mind to believe he loved her and she hadn't been a complete fool when she'd thrown her life away on him. Her cheeks warmed, and she sat back in her chair with her arms crossed over her chest to calm down.

Daniel lowered his head just enough to appear chastised. He knew he was wrong, and she knew this was as close to an apology as she would ever get. He said, "You let him hate me."

"He has the same regard for you as you did for him. I had no reason to change his mind, particularly when the truth was so very undeniable. You deserve that he hates you."

Daniel picked at a chip in his cup and there was silence. Finally Suzanne's anger abated and she sat forward again, picked up her drink, and said, "In reply to your question, I joined a theatre troupe for a while, just for the sake of getting Piers away from the criminal element at Maddie's."

Daniel's eyebrows raised in surprise. "Out of the frying pan, I'd say."

"The actors weren't so very bad. We'd set up a performance in a street or alley, run the play for a penny a head, then tear down and move on the instant it was done. Another alleyway, another performance, and we rarely had to go far from London. Unlike with Maddie's patrons, there were few fights among the actors and almost never any blood. They stole from the audience, but nobody boasted about it much. The fellow who ran things became something of a father to Piers, or uncle, as he was to all of us. He called me 'niece,' and I rather liked him. He taught Piers some things about business. Kept us all safe. The troupe became like a home, and more hospitable toward us women now that we're sometimes accepted on the stage without a terrible amount of fuss."

Daniel sat back in his chair and crossed his arms over his chest. "I wasn't aware Cromwell allowed actors at all, never mind female ones."

Suzanne made a face and waved away the thought as if it were a bad smell. "Of course he didn't. We were ever on the run, just like any criminal, and that made for some very exciting times."

SUZANNE'S son was nine years old when she joined the troupe that moved in and around London and the surrounding towns. The war was nearly over, and dark Puritanism had been the law of the land long enough that some had become accustomed to life under Cromwell. Most, though, found ways to circumvent the new laws. Or they ignored them completely. Men who dressed in Puritan black, who professed morality and purity of thought and body, nevertheless took mistresses they hid much as children would hide forbidden sweets. Musicians and tumblers performed in closes and alleys. To some it was a form of polite protest, but for people like Suzanne it was simple survival and an inability to be anything other than what God had made them.

Suzanne, wanting a better life for Piers than that offered in a bawd house, ran off from Maddie's brothel on Bank Side with a man everyone called "Horatio." He told it around he called himself that because "Horatio is a friend of Hamlet," and for him the world revolved around William Shakespeare. Nobody knew his real name, and some wondered whether he remembered it himself. He had certainly not forgotten life before Cromwell, and had dedicated his life to living the way he always had, with the joy of the theatre as practiced by Shakespeare.

Suzanne first met Horatio as a client. He'd frequented Maddie's for some months, and she'd seen him sitting in the public room on the ground floor once or twice. He was a large man, and his wig was nearly always slightly askew, which happened often with men who were entirely bald and had nothing to keep a wig from skidding. His voice was as large and impressive as his form, and whenever Horatio spoke, the entire room stopped to listen. Even when he whispered it was with a force and authority that commanded attention. He always sat quietly and patiently, waiting for his favorite girl, Betsy. She was an older whore, nearly thirty. He liked to talk, and she had a talent for listening.

"Strange one, that Horatio," Betsy would say at supper with the other girls. "Always wantin' to talk." She shredded her meat and let it fall to the plate as she chewed. Then she picked up a shred to fold it into her mouth in between sentences as she talked.

Suzanne nodded. "Right. I've several who never do anything but talk. Mostly they complain about their wives or their mothers. Sometimes about the Lord Protector, but those are rare."

"But never so much talk as to be treasonous, and don't you never say anything suchlike in return," said Maddie.

"Yes, Maddie," Suzanne allowed. "Wouldn't want the Roundheads battering the door to round up us rabble-rousing tarts."

A general snicker rounded the table, and even Maddie had to chuckle.

Betsy said, "Well, this one does his business all right, doesn't dawdle none and never takes but a minute or so, and before and after he's talking on and on about his acting troupe. And that Shakespeare fellow from a hundred years ago."

Another girl asked, "Who's that, then?"

Betsy shrugged. "Some old play writer. Back when Elizabeth was busy bein' all virginal and such."

Everyone snickered again at that. Betsy continued, "I seen one of his plays once. Before they shut down the Globe."

"Was it good?" asked Suzanne.

"It made me laugh. It wasn't boring. I like a good play, and I wish they'd kept the theatres open. Crying shame they've been closed."

"A good play is worth a penny, I suppose."

Betsy leaned her head back, dropped a long sliver of beef into her mouth, and chewed thoughtfully on it. She said, "Yeah, that Horatio is an odd sort."

So when Betsy died of a cough that winter and Horatio was orphaned as a client, on his next visit Suzanne stepped forward to offer her services in Betsy's place. She liked the idea of having a regular client who didn't take long with his business and liked to talk instead. As soon as he walked into the public room downstairs she went to him and offered her condolences at the loss of Betsy.

His unhappiness at Betsy's death was plain on his face as she led him up the stairs. She would have to do something to take his mind off Betsy, or spend the entire afternoon urging him to finish his business, so she encouraged him to talk about himself. All men loved to talk about themselves, and most were accustomed to being allowed to do so frequently.

"What's your name?" She shut the door behind them and began to undress. All she wore was a frayed silk robe, so stripping was accomplished in but a second. She draped the robe over a chair, draped herself over the blanket on her bed, and spread her knees. All the girls did their business atop the blanket, for it helped keep vermin from the mattresses. Coyness was not Suzanne's style, and her customers appreciated that with her there was no fuss and no folderol.

"I'm called Horatio, for I am a friend of Hamlet. I'm an actor, you know. My troupe . . ."

That was all it took, and he was off and running. In his big, booming voice, probably heard as far as downstairs, he told her all about the troupe he directed, and his history as an interpreter of Shakespeare's work. As he dropped his breeches and climbed onto her, he continued on about his talented performers and how they all understood The Bard, Shakespeare. Once finished with his business, he buttoned himself and sat on the edge of the bed to explain some of the finer points of Shakespeare's work.

Oddly, as Suzanne rose from the bed, cleaned herself at the washstand, and drew her robe back on, she found herself listening to him. Not the way she did with clients, but as if he were her friend and she cared about what he was saying. The way Betsy probably never had. Any other client might have gone on for hours and she would never hear a word. But this theatre talk interested her. It sounded like fun, and though she'd never heard of a woman acting on a stage, she thought she might like to do it if she could talk someone into letting her try.

When he wound down some and she could get a word in, she said, "Have you ever had a girl actor?"

Horatio clapped his mouth shut, thinking for a moment.

Then he said, thoughtfully, "Of course we have not. But now that you mention it, I can't think of why we shouldn't, other than that no woman has ever asked me before. I'm not certain whether any woman would want to be on the stage."

"I think perhaps you should have them onstage."

"Of course, only a whorish sort would be interested."

"That would be me, I expect."

He looked at her now, as if seeing her for the first time. "You?"

She sat on the bed next to him and leaned toward him, insistent. "Of course me. I think I'd be perfect for your Shakespeare plays, don't you?" She had no idea whether she would even be adequate, but there was no harm in encouraging him in this train of thought.

He now peered hard at her, and she let him do so without interruption. He was the one paying for the time, so it was certainly no skin off her nose if he spent it thinking. Finally he said, "Yes. I think possibly yes. A Juliet whose voice won't crack. A Viola one can suspect is female. A Lady Macbeth played as an ambitious woman rather than a weak man." As he warmed to the idea, his voice rose to a trumpet sound. "Yes. You might do very well."

"Then when can we leave?"

"Leave?" That startled him.

"I can pack my bags in a trice. My son and I—"

"Son?" Even more surprised, he laid a hand over his heart.

"Piers. He's nine years old and a hard worker. He'll be no trouble at all."

Horatio's mouth worked, but nothing came out.

Suzanne rose from the bed, threw off the robe once more, and began to dress in street clothes as she continued, speaking rapidly in order to not be interrupted and told no. "You said it yourself. Juliet. Viola. Lady Macbeth. You need me."

He shut his mouth and appeared to warm to the idea. "Have you acted before?"

"Every day of my life, I vow."

That made him smile, a wide, crooked-lipped grin, showing a row of very small teeth. "Very well, then." He stood and straightened his clothes, checking to be sure his breeches were securely tied. "Come to the Goat and Boar. I'll wait for you there."

"I'm coming now." She drew a valise from under the bed and began throwing clothing into it. Everything belonging to herself and Piers that would fit went in, and anything that didn't she left where it was. When the valise was full, she found a duffel bag in the armoire and filled it as well. She pulled closed the tie, then shut the lid of the valise and tied it with a scarf. As she did so, she called out to her son. "Piers!" She put her head out and called down the stairs. "Piers! Come here!"

The boy popped from the kitchen and ran up the stairs. "What's going on, Mother?"

"Come. We're leaving."

"Leaving? You mean forever?"

"Yes. I've got your clothes in this duffel. We're never coming back."

"All right, Mother."

Horatio took in the tableau of mother and son ready to travel. He leaned down and said to Piers, "You don't seem very upset to be leaving your home."

Piers gave him a slightly puzzled look. "I'm leaving the house, not my mother." He said it as a matter of fact that should have been obvious to Horatio, who must be terribly dense or just not paying attention to not know it.

Horatio thought about that a moment, then said, "Good boy. You understand what is important; someone has taught you well." He glanced at Suzanne, who replied with a bland, knowing smile. He again addressed Piers. "You'll do well when you're a man."

Suzanne said to Horatio, "Lead the way. Where you go, we follow."

Luckily, Maddie wasn't in at the moment, or there might have been violence. As it was, two girls currently unoccupied and sitting in the downstairs parlor raised a fuss in her stead.

"You'll be sorry if you leave. Maddie will raise hell when she finds out!"

"She'll come after you!"

Suzanne had never much liked her fellow tarts. She ignored them, handed the duffel off to Horatio when they reached the bottom of the stairs, and drew Piers away from the area before either of them could think twice about what was happening. She knew they had to get out of that brothel, Piers was nine and there was no time to lose, and this was an opportunity that wouldn't present itself again. As she, Horatio, and Piers emerged onto Bank Side, the river air smelled like freedom.

Over the next two years she and Piers made Horatio's troupe their new family. Suzanne thought it a monumental improvement over the brothel. Playing on the stage was ever so much more interesting than banging one man after another all night long. And from Horatio she learned a great deal about William Shakespeare, who became nearly the idol to her as he was to Horatio.

"Shakespeare was the greatest storyteller who ever lived,"

he declared to anyone who would listen, and then he would enumerate the reasons he thought it, no matter who his audience or how many times it had been said. He knew every word of Shakespeare's plays by heart, even the roles he could never have possibly played, and quoted them so often that some days it seemed he never spoke any sentence that was his own.

Before meeting Horatio, Suzanne had barely known who Shakespeare was, but Horatio taught her more about The Bard than was known by most Londoners. As the troupe's first female performer, she memorized the roles of Juliet and Viola readily enough. Horatio declared he'd always thought it odd and confusing to have a young man playing a woman pretending to be a young man, and so welcomed the new thinking toward women onstage. Shakespeare himself would have been appalled, but on this one point Horatio disagreed with the world's greatest storyteller.

The troupe made a tidy living by setting up a portable stage in alleyways to stop traffic and collect money in exchange for an afternoon of spontaneous entertainment. *Henry V, Richard III, All's Well That Ends Well, Romeo and Juliet* . . . though they also knew Marlowe and Congreve, Horatio's troupe performed Shakespeare's plays far more frequently than those of any other playwright, and it was his good luck that the old plays were popular with folks in the street. Whenever word got out the troupe was setting up their stage, the ordinary people flocked to see them. And sometimes the not-so-ordinary people as well. In a fine spirit of participation, many in the audience brought rotten fruit and vegetables to throw if the performance was unsatisfactory, and Suzanne counted it a good day if they finished a performance without being pelted. Often the audience was offended to find the first woman any of them had ever seen onstage, so she felt especially accomplished if a performance held the attention of the crowd well enough to make them forget the soft, oozing rubbish in their pockets.

Suzanne thoroughly enjoyed being onstage before a crowd. Pretending to be someone else made her own painful existence more bearable. For four hours or so each day she could be a young girl in love or the daughter of a king. She could writhe in the throes of a pretend death and know she would rise again. She could lose herself in the madness of a woman whose father had been murdered by her lover. All of it was better than what had been doled out to her by her Maker, and she was happy to live those other lives every day just before sunset.

Then once the bows were taken, the sun was down, and the audience had gone home, the troupe would dismantle the stage, load it onto a wagon, and move to other parts, always one step ahead of the soldiers of the Protectorate. They had down to a science the process of breaking down the stage and loading the wagon, and could accomplish the task in half an hour. Then they were off to a spot at the London outskirts, a different camp every night. The troupe would make a cook fire, receive the day's pay, and cook and eat whatever provisions might be available that day. They'd discuss where to set up in the morning and what play they would perform. Sometimes they stayed more than a day in a given location if the crowd was enthusiastic, and on those occasions there was time for rehearsal. They would use that time to invent new bits that might be too complex to toss into the mix willy-nilly.

But generally practice was unnecessary, for most of the players knew their roles from long experience and being a quick study was a large part of success as an actor. Usually new bits came from improvised moments during a performance. Anything that worked stayed in and became part of the blocking. Those who weren't inventive enough, or couldn't keep up with those who were, never stayed long in the business.

Suzanne was fortunate in her ability to memorize quickly and accurately, and whenever a line slipped her mind she was nimble enough to invent something similar to Shakespeare's text, so her fellow players had no trouble picking up the thread and carrying on. At which point her memory would refresh and she would be back on the correct path. Those two years were the happiest of her life.

Then one day when Piers was eleven and waiting offstage to hand some properties to actors awaiting their cues to enter, Suzanne was onstage in *Twelfth Night* and her character was in the midst of flirting with another woman, who was played by a boy not much older than Piers. The corner of her eye caught a glint of steel far off down the alleyway. Ever alert for trouble, and understanding the consequences of arrest, she broke character, gave a hard look, and saw the shining glint of a helmet making its way toward the stage.

One enormous breath, and she shouted, *"Roundheads!"* And without any more ado, she leapt from the stage, grabbed Piers's arm, and hauled him, running, away from the soldiers. There was hollering behind her, of soldiers, actors, and audience. Horatio's voice rose above the others, urging the actors to run, then cut short with a cry of pain. The soldiers had grabbed Horatio.

Suzanne never saw or heard what happened to the rest of her fellow thespians, for all she knew or cared about was to keep Piers out of the hands of the authorities, and any other loyalty came second to that. All their clothing and money she left behind in the trunk she and Piers kept in the wagon. Everything she'd accumulated with the troupe over the last two years, gone. She and Piers ran as far as they could, then when Piers could run no farther, she ducked into a doorway to gasp for breath. She held her son to her side, tight so that he wouldn't move and couldn't be flushed from hiding in a panic. She whispered for him to be quiet, an unnecessary caution, for he was as silent and alert as a rabbit.

She listened for approaching soldiers, unsure which direction she would bolt if she heard them. When the actors and audience had been dispersed and the noises in the distance were reduced to normal street sounds of horses and vendors, she continued to wait until she was certain no soldiers lurked in search of stragglers.

Finally she guided Piers away from the street and they walked as far as they could, until the boy began to complain of exhaustion. She found an alley that offered some protection from view, and they sat against a brick wall for the scant warmth it offered from fires inside.

Piers kept quiet, though his eyes were wide with terror. Suzanne fought tears as she realized they were on their own once more, with no money and only the clothes on their backs. Suzanne happened to be wearing the man's clothing for her role as Viola. With Horatio in custody of the authorities, there was no troupe. They would have to return to Maddie's, at least for now. There was nothing for it but that.

But she couldn't take Piers there again. At eleven years old, he was ripe for a career robbing people. He was no longer a toddler to be passed from auntie to auntie, and Suzanne wouldn't have him taught what those women would teach him now. Something had to be done for him, for she wouldn't have him a thief or beggar. His father was an earl; it would be wrong for Piers to live this way any longer. She said in a low, secret voice, "Piers, how would it be if you went away for a while?"

His voice quaked with terror and shock. "Are they going to arrest me, Mama?"

"No! No, son. They won't arrest you, not so long as I'm here. But what if you went away where they couldn't arrest you?"

He didn't reply right away, and when he did his voice was small. "I couldn't leave, Mama."

"I mean, to work. Learn a trade."

"I don't want to leave. I can't leave you. Not ever."

"I could find you an apprenticeship somewhere. How would you like that? It would mean a warm place to sleep every night and enough food to keep your belly from complaining."

Piers was silent, thinking about that. Though he ate every day, it was rarely enough. The idea of having more to eat was surely appealing. But he said, "I'd miss you too much."

"But you could write to me."

"I don't write so well, Mama."

"Then you'll learn. Practice makes perfect. You'll learn to write, and cipher, and then you could find employment and never be hungry again."

A great, rolling snuffle in the darkness told her he was crying. "I want to stay with you."

"You want me to be proud of you?"

"I think so. But why can't I stay here? We should find the others and go where the soldiers can't find us. Then we could continue to be in plays and stay with the folks in the troupe."

"They can't teach you to be a fine man; they can only teach you to pick pockets and cheat people. You should have a real master who will teach you how to make a decent, respectable

living, so you won't have to run away from soldiers or steal for
your supper. It will take a few years, but when you're old
enough you'll be a fine man, with a job and a place in the
world."

"But what will become of you, Mama?"

"I'll be all right. I'm always all right, so no worries about
your mother. Do you understand?"

Piers made a reluctant mumble of assent. She knew he
would do as he was told, but also knew she would have to keep
pressing him in the right direction if he were to succeed at an
apprenticeship.

As soon as they were rested, she nudged her son to his feet
and they began walking south, to the other side of the river
and Bank Side, where the next day she imposed on Maddie's
goodwill for the night. She found Maddie stiff with anger, still
unhappy at having been left by one of her girls. She crossed
her arms over her ample chest and didn't reply to Suzanne's
request for a temporary bed. The other girls in the room
gawked in silence to see what would happen next, each of
them fascinated and amused by the proceeding. Suzanne knew
how silly she must look in her breeches and doublet, but kept
her chin up as if she'd chosen the outfit from a closetful of fine
gowns.

She said, "Horatio is still your customer. He comes here when
he's a need. I haven't stolen that." Horatio had a policy of never
sleeping with the women attached to the troupe, so he had
always had a need that brought him to Maddie's. Suzanne join-
ing the troupe hadn't changed that, and Horatio had visited
Maddie's as often as he ever did. "He's not touched me once
since I left, and you know you see him twice a month, just like
before."

The frown on Maddie's face smoothed out, and she gestured for Suzanne and Piers to go upstairs. "Your old room happens to be empty today. One night only, and then you're on your own again." Suzanne was glad for this one night.

Then the next morning she begged her former employer for pen, ink, and paper to write to her former suitor and ask if Farthingworth would take her son. She wept as she wrote, knowing that if this letter accomplished her goal it would be years before she saw Piers again, but she pressed on because it was the only thing that would ensure his survival.

The following weeks she and Piers spent on the streets. Suzanne engaged in as much commerce as she could cadge around the periphery of Maddie's house, servicing her customers on a pile of rags tucked into an alley. Privacy there depended mostly on luck, and so her revenue was little and spotty, but in breeches and doublet she was able to sell herself as either girl or boy.

Piers occupied himself however he might in a given day, loitering with the fiddle player on Bank Side, clearing tables at the Goat and Boar for tips, or hawking prepared food for a merchant on Maid Lane. Whenever he came to her with money, she prayed he hadn't gotten it by stealing, but she never asked, and accepted that he'd worked for it. At night they slept on that pile of rags, rolled in a blanket together for warmth.

After three weeks had passed, each day before venturing onto Bank Side to sell herself she checked in with Maddie to learn if there was a reply to her letter north. Piers began to speak hopefully of rejection when they'd had two weeks of disappointment.

But finally one afternoon Maddie handed her a letter enclosed in a real envelope sealed with green wax. The thing was terribly fancy, and it made her nostalgic for her father's house and the niceties of her childhood. Quickly she shook her head clear of the memory, broke the seal, and pulled out the pages. She read:

My friend, Suzanne;

She couldn't imagine how Stephen could still consider her his friend, particularly since he never had before, but took the salutation as promising.

I am in receipt of your letter regarding your son, Piers. Frankly, I find myself taken aback that you even remember me. I had the impression you thought me beneath notice. The night you confessed your condition was surely a difficult moment for all of us, and I expect it was a terrible strain on your family. I'm sorry your situation didn't turn out as you'd hoped. It appears there was disappointment for everyone in it.

I married not long after you left your father's house. My wife is a fine and gentle woman, pious and responsible. She is the essence of what St. Paul would call a good wife. I am most pleased with her, so my own disappointment is, in the end, not crushing. For me the situation turned out better than I could ever have hoped. I did admire your forthrightness in confessing your sin and your reluctance to foist a child on me that was not mine. I believe that sort of honesty to be rare in a woman, for even my own dear wife is prone to disingenuous behavior whenever there is difficulty. I cannot help but respect honesty in you, and as I said that night, I would have liked it in a wife. But that was not to be.

You have asked me to take on your son as an apprentice. Though my wife, as pious as she is, would not be sanguine about accepting the illegitimate son of a former fiancée, regardless of the boy's actual parentage, I feel I can be charitable toward you and your child. So long as my wife never learns of our previous arrangement, I am open to the idea of having Piers as an apprentice in my offices for the customary seven years.

Find enclosed a letter of credit sufficient for transportation to Newcastle and a suit of appropriate clothes, as I suspect your straitened circumstances would make obtaining them difficult. Send Piers to me at the earliest opportunity, and be assured he will learn a trade and live as safely as my own children during his tenure here.

I wish you the best of luck in making your life in the future what you would have it be.

Suzanne watched Daniel's face when she spoke of his son's childhood, but there was no flicker of guilt, or even of acknowledgment. He only looked at her as he listened, with a slight smile on his lips and a distant look in his eye. She couldn't be entirely certain he even heard what she was saying. Her chest tightened, but she continued. "I was terribly lucky to succeed in obtaining an apprenticeship for him."

That finally brought a glimmer from Daniel, but of surprise. "But you obtained one. Certainly if Farthingworth hadn't come through, you might have wheedled it out of a patron."

Suzanne's eyes narrowed at the intended slight, but pretended to ignore it. "I wasn't yet so experienced in such things, had not yet had what might be termed a 'patron,' and wouldn't have known how to convince such a man to put himself out for my son by another man. At the time I believed I had no choice but to make the arrangement as if I were Piers's father myself, and the only man I had ever known who was in a position to give Piers what I wanted him to have was Stephen Farthingworth. He was my first and only thought."

Deeper surprise showed on Daniel's face. "Rather bold of you. What made you think he would be of help?"

"He was the only man I knew who might be charitable enough to help. When he was my suitor, he'd seemed a reasonable sort, and though I didn't care to marry him, I nevertheless saw him as kind. Extraordinarily kind, enough to seem weak, and that was why I disliked the idea of marrying him. Besides, desperation makes one do odd, otherwise unthinkable things. I wrote to him in Newcastle and asked if he might be agreeable to taking on my intelligent, obedient, hardworking son. The worst that could happen was that he might say no, and I was used to that by then."

"Did you explain that said son had been raised in a whorehouse and was currently living on the street?"

She straightened in her chair and raised her chin. "I couldn't have him thinking Piers might have been raised to be a thief or thug. I told him we were in extreme need. I said we were temporarily reduced to taking a room at Maddie's, which was true on the day I wrote the letter. I'm certain Mr. Farthingworth must have known enough of my circumstances, given he was there the night I left home."

Daniel only grunted and drew on his drink. "You've changed since I last saw you. The Suzanne I once knew would have announced the situation loud and clear, and devil take the hindmost."

"I had to change, otherwise I would die. And certainly so would my son." There was a long pause, then she said, "Your son."

He looked over at her, then away. The lines in his face seemed to deepen, but he said nothing.

Finally she asked, "Why did you invite me here today?"

"I wanted to see you again." He said it with a warm smile, as if she should be pleased he'd favored her with his attention.

"Why?" Attention was well and good, but money would be better, if some were in the offing.

"Why did I want to see you again? I've always wanted it. Since I left for York with Charles, and especially during the time we were on the Continent. I've missed you."

The sentiment touched her, and she felt the old feeling rise, but she tamped it down as useless to her. "I've certainly missed you, as well. I could hardly breathe for eighteen years of having no support and no father for Piers."

"I couldn't help that."

"Your helplessness didn't change our need." She took a deep draught of her ale and said, "Is your wife still living?"

He nodded.

Suzanne's heart sank, and only then did she realize she'd harbored a tiny hope he would be a widower ready to marry her. She tucked that dead wish away, never to entertain it again. "Children?"

He shook his head. "None came before I left London, and I haven't been back since. So . . . no children." Then he said, "You ask to know whether I would support you and Piers."

"You owe us. You owe him."

"I've no money. Since the death of her father, my wife has lived comfortably these years with her brother, and it's only by force of law she's returned to me." Suzanne mentally cursed the law that chained Daniel to that woman. "While following the elder Charles during the war, then his son in exile, I've had no income other than what could be begged from those on the Continent who hate Puritans. The very clothes we wore on our entrance to London were provided by Parliament so we wouldn't appear to the commons as beggars unfit to rule."

Suzanne then noticed the outfit he wore today was the same as he'd worn yesterday, but with the gold braid removed from the green cloak. He seemed to be telling the truth, and had more than likely sold the braid for cash.

"So you say no, you cannot support us."

"That is so. As I said, there is no money even to support myself."

"I cannot go back to the brothel. Even if it were still there, my days of selling myself are over. Certainly I would starve on what I could get for my aging body. Anymore, I can no longer attract even a Puritan rotted with lust and hypocrisy, one too ashamed of himself to be seen with me in public."

Daniel grinned, and suddenly reminded her of the youth he had once been. "Nonsense. You're still quite attractive."

Suzanne surprised herself by blushing, though she noted the word "still" had the same mitigating power as "handsome."

"What of Piers? He should be old enough to provide an adequate living."

"Adequate is different things to different people. And besides, Piers hasn't yet found employment, so there's no question that the living he currently provides is inadequate by any standard."

Daniel considered for a moment, then said, "I'll make some enquiries, though there will be a great number of more worthy men seeking positions, and finding a place for a young man with no connections and little experience will be difficult."

"He's you for a connection."

"Not so much as one might think. Nobody knows I have a son."

Were she still able to blush with shame, she would have. "They don't? Nobody?" His wife might have been kept in the dark, but it shocked Suzanne that Daniel had never told anyone at all.

"I would prefer it didn't get out, and therefore possibly back to my wife. My position with Anne, and her brother who is now duke, is precarious enough, I'm afraid. He spent the past decade garnering power in Parliament, and that hasn't changed since the restoration of the monarchy. And he hates me in the bargain, even without knowing about Piers."

"You won't be dependent on the brother for long. Surely the king will restore your lands to you."

"If he can."

"He's the king."

"And he has just slightly less power than Parliament and astonishingly less money. There are hundreds of loyal royalists climbing all over each other, seeking restoration of their lands taken from them by Cromwell. And equal hundreds of Parliamentarians who have been in possession of those lands for nearly two decades. I'm just one of many petitioners, most of whom are of better rank than myself, and it remains to be seen whether I will have my own income soon or whether I will remain dependent on my brother-in-law."

"But you sacrificed everything for loyalty to Charles and his father."

"It's true. Charles is a kind and reasonable king, and he appreciates those who are loyal to him. I may come out well. As I said, it remains to be seen."

Suzanne sighed and sipped on her ale. A gloomy frown darkened her face.

"Don't look so defeated, Suzanne. You've always appeared so sad all the time, even when you were young, and you're so much prettier when you smile."

"Those who complain about my sadness would do well to give me something to smile about." She offered her tankard with the comment as a toast, then drank and tried not to feel disappointed that Daniel's only interest in her anymore was curiosity.

Chapter Six

When they parted, Suzanne watched Daniel walk away from the Goat and Boar until he disappeared into the traffic on Bank Side, then she stood alone for a moment and looked around, trying to decide what to do next. She wasn't in the mood to return home right away and didn't care to go back inside the public house for another ale, so she went for a walk. Her vizard was gone, having been tossed irretrievably into the Thames, and she felt exposed in public without it but not so much that she wanted to return home for another. There was nothing for it but to press on without the mask. She strolled off down the alley toward Maid Lane, took some random turns that weren't really so random, and accidentally-on-purpose found herself once again in front of the Globe Theatre, the very venue the great bard Shakespeare had built decades before.

She loved this place. It had stood empty since Cromwell had outlawed theatre performances, but she'd attended several plays here as a young girl. Now it was boarded up, poorly, with only two boards crossed over the door frame. She shoved the tall, heavy door, which swung inward, heedless of the boards on the outside. Then she stepped over the lower one and ducked under the higher.

Loose dirt gritted under her pattens, which tottered on the littered floor, and she held her skirts up to keep from dragging them through the dust and cobwebs. The building had not worn well during recent years, for most of it was open to the weather above even without the gaps in the roof over the galleries. Birds nesting in the rafters sang and flitted from perch to perch, annoyed at her intrusion, and a small animal made a shuffling noise under some debris nearby in an attempt to flee the invading human. Probably a mouse, perhaps a cat chasing a mouse.

The chairs that had once filled the upper levels were all gone except for some broken ones that lay scattered across the lower level. The pit had a mud puddle, left from a rainstorm the week before. Some birds bathed in it, aflutter with feathers and water drops and chirping away at each other in the spring sunshine. The stage, which protruded into the pit from the far side of the circled galleries, appeared intact, though Suzanne thought the rotted wood must be a danger to any actor treading it. The entire place smelled of rot. Twenty years of neglect had taken its toll.

She loved this place. Ever since her two years with Horatio's acting troupe she'd been fascinated with it, drawn to it as if it knew her and knew she belonged to it. She'd imagined what it might be like to act on a real stage, to play to the galleries, to an audience of thousands. She imagined how magnificent it would be to have the proper amount of room to really perform what Shakespeare had intended, in the theatre he'd built.

Shakespeare himself had worked here. He'd trod those very boards near the end of his life. In rehearsal he'd observed his actors from this very pit, and in performance had waited in the 'tiring area for the pleasing sound of applause or the annoying chatter and catcalls that signaled a bored audience.

Now Suzanne looked over the array of galleries, arranged in a circle and towering three stories high. The heavens covering the upstage area still betrayed a hint of blue and white cloud, though the paint was quite faded, dirty, and molded in spots. Moss grew on the roof, and great, rounded ridges of gray fungus were devouring some of the rain gutters along the heavens.

An enormous sigh took her. She wished to have been born in a different time, when theatre had been not merely allowed, but nurtured. When Shakespeare was still alive and working his magic on the stage. If wishes were horses . . .

One more sigh, and she ducked back out to continue on her walk. Far enough away from the Globe Theatre, she consoled herself with knowing that even had she lived during Shakespeare's time, she would never have been allowed onstage.

DANIEL didn't contact Suzanne again, for a chat or anything else. During the days a wistful daydream distracted her, of what it might be like to have a tumble with him once more, for he was the only one she'd ever really wanted in that way. She reminisced of the days when lying with a man was something other than a chore, and with him it had been a soaring joy. But his silence told her he didn't remember her in the same way she did him, that the curiosity he'd shown on his return to England had been nothing more, and mild at that. Her daydream stayed a fantasy. Proof enough that her days as a kept mistress were over, she supposed, and it was probably just as well.

Piers contacted the coal merchant friend of Farthingworth, but waited and heard nothing. Suzanne wasn't sure whether it was better to not hear and hope, or to hear and have a rejection. To not hear at all could mean Piers was being ignored, and that was the worst. The days passed into summer, and still no word. Gradually hope faded.

Now that William was gone and forgotten, Suzanne was free to frequent the Goat and Boar as she pleased, just as she had when living in the brothel. On one hand it was a return to bad times, when she had never known if she would eat that day or whether she might be arrested for one thing or another. On the other hand, it was a return to the world and friends she'd seen infrequently in recent years. Being a mistress hidden away by a guilt-ridden hypocrite, in an England that at the time had been in paroxysms of pretending mistresses didn't exist, had been a lonely existence. Nowadays it was a pleasure to socialize with people she understood. A circle of old friends convened there of an evening once the sun was down and street traffic had waned. She was pleased to spend her time listening to their woes in order to ignore her own. She would nurse a cup of ale to laugh or gripe as the moment demanded, and her fears went away for a time.

One night she was sharing a jug of wine with some of them when she looked up to see Daniel at the door. He looked across the room, searching, and when his eyes caught hers, he smiled. His doublet of fine brocade and well-cut breeches suggested he was doing well, and that piqued her curiosity. Suzanne wondered whether his father's lands had been restored to him, and her heart lifted in hope they had. He settled into his habitual insouciant hipshot stance, and her heart skipped as warm, throbbing memories rushed in. She sat up, suddenly self-conscious. She checked her hair to be sure it had not fallen out of its pins, and tucked back a hank that had.

He claimed a small table near the door and tilted his head to suggest she join him. It didn't take more than that to convince her to do so. Without a word to her companions she left her cup and the jug, and went to sit with Daniel. Nobody said anything, for nobody would blame her for wanting to spend time with the earl rather than their motley bunch. They understood the economics of people in their station.

"Hello. How have you been?" Daniel's mood was especially warm tonight, and Suzanne had already consumed enough wine to be especially happy to see him. A bright spot opened up in her, and hope filled it. Daniel gestured for service, and Young Dent hopped to it.

"We've been well enough, I suppose." She knew better than to complain about her life to someone who plainly was looking for a good time. Daniel surely had not come to the Goat and Boar to listen to her problems. "Piers has been looking for work, but there's no hurry." True enough, in the sense that they wouldn't go hungry this year if he didn't find it right away. Next year would be another matter entirely.

Daniel's smile faded some. "Yes. Piers." Young Dent waited to hear his order, and Daniel requested a bottle of French wine and two clean glasses. He would pay more for them, but it was worth it to not have someone else's ale or milk in his expensive wine. Dent nodded and disappeared to the back. "What about yourself? How is Suzanne Thornton today?"

She had to think about that, but in the end replied what she thought he wanted to hear. "I'm well, thank you."

"Are you certain?" He lowered his chin and peered closely at her, doubting she was well.

She laughed, and hoped it was a convincing laugh. "Of course I am."

"You don't sound terribly sincere."

She gave him a well-practiced coy smile. "A woman must maintain a certain amount of mystery, don't you think?"

Daniel shook his head. "I can certainly do without it. I rather enjoy a woman who comes straight out to say what she means. I've grown to dislike the game of hide-and-seek most women play. What I always liked about you was that one always knew where one stood. I wonder why you've changed."

"Many men have told me that, you know. You all love to know where you stand, and you insist you prefer honesty. But over the years I've found that men only want to hear the truth when it happens to be what they wish to hear. One must conclude that a man's wish to know where he stands is more a desire to know early on whether he is going to get what he wants, in order to not waste time or money in pursuing it. I've never known any man to prefer unvarnished truth of any kind."

Daniel appeared to not know what to say to that, then finally said, "Well . . . I suppose you've just made your point."

Suzanne sighed and graced him with a rueful smile.

The wine came, and when Daniel poured it, she took a deep draught. It warmed her and numbed all her sore spots. She didn't want to think about where she stood with Daniel, because for tonight at least it felt like old times. She took another long drink, then smiled at him.

They engaged in small talk for a while, then moved to

weightier subjects. He complained that his father's lands had been given by Cromwell to someone Charles wished to keep as an ally, and so the king would not be able to restore those lands. It was a huge disappointment and something of a slap in the face for the king to prefer a Roundhead over one who had always been loyal to him and his father. But that was the way of politics, and Daniel understood his place in the current regime just as the king understood his own precarious perch in the scheme of things.

On the other hand, there was good news in that Daniel had been provided with other lands outside of London, and a patent involving the manufacture and sale of certain types of metal bits and harness pieces for horses, oxen, and donkeys. There were other patents in the offing, and these things promised a living more or less appropriate for his station. Before long he would be wealthy enough to no longer depend on his brother-in-law to keep up appearances.

She avoided speaking of her own financial situation. One truth she'd learned men never liked to face was that women required upkeep. As a prostitute she'd always been insistent about being paid, and as a mistress she never held back in asking for money, but she never mentioned money to anyone who was not a client. Every time Daniel asked a question about her, she deflected with an answer that focused on Piers.

"How have you kept yourself entertained of late?" he asked.

She glanced around the room. "I come here. Or I stay at home and read. Piers has recently bought for me a number of the classics, and I enjoy them immensely."

"In the original Greek?"

Her cheeks warmed. He knew better, and was teasing. He should know she hated that, and her spotty education was a terribly sore subject. It annoyed her even more that he didn't seem to know or care she was embarrassed. "No. My father felt education for girls was a waste of money. Mother taught me and my sisters to read, but languages other than English were beyond her." Then, to steer off the subject she said, "Piers is terribly attentive, you know. I don't know how I got along without him for those seven years he was in Newcastle. We can spend the evening in conversation and never know where the time has gone. Or he reads to me while I simply sit back and listen. I especially enjoy that. He's the most entertaining delivery when he reads. All that time spent on the stage when he was small, I suppose."

"Are you happy and safe?"

"As much as anyone can be without an income, as I'm sure you're aware." She hurried to cover the slip into money talk. "But Piers will alleviate that soon, I'm certain. He's hard at work finding a position, and before long will be supporting us both adequately. I have complete faith." She didn't like the look of doubt in his eyes, and went on. "Piers did well in his apprenticeship, I'm told." She was told no such thing, but Daniel didn't need to know that. As far as she knew, Piers had done well and there was no complaint from Farthingworth. "He's smart as a whip, and terribly strong. Farthingworth taught him swordsmanship, you should know, to have him as a sparring partner, and Piers tells me he became a formidable opponent." That much was true. Piers liked to tell her about the times he'd bested Farthingworth in a contest, and she was proud of him for it. Gentlemen carried swords, and it pleased her that Piers had learned swordsmanship and manners from his master.

They talked on, the evening became quite late, and Suzanne hardly noticed how the time was passing. The bottle of wine emptied, and another was brought and likewise emptied. The drink warmed Suzanne so the world fell into a fuzziness that comforted. Daniel's presence had always taken the hurt from the day, and when he took her hand in his all pain fell away. There was no thought that he should have done anything but that. He held her hand, and she let him. Then he kissed her palm.

The sensation took her back to the time when she was a young girl and had never been kissed by anyone else. Back when the only man she would consider kissing was this son of an earl. He had been so handsome! So intelligent, so strong. She had thought herself in love, and when she was young, perhaps thinking it made it so. Now, two decades later, a kiss on her palm made her feel young again.

"Would you care for a drive in the moonlight? The weather is warm and the moon is full."

"I would like that." The seventeen-year-old still residing deep within her danced with joy at the prospect, though the adult she had become held deep reservations. The wine, in dulling the pain of her life, had also robbed her of her maturity. A wide, happy smile lit her face and she could hardly wait to get out of the Goat and Boar.

Daniel held her hand as he guided her to the carriage that awaited him on Bank Side. It was true the night was clear and warm, and moonlight reflected from the Thames and outlined the silhouette of the bridge that stood to the east. He helped her into the carriage and she settled in. The upholstered seat was deep and soft, covered in fine leather that gave way in all the right spots. As the driver urged the team off down the street, Daniel laid an arm across her shoulders and drew her near. She leaned against him, happy to be there once more.

Conversation waned as they moved away from Southwark and south to the countryside. The highway became narrow, and the view was endless fields glowing silver in the moon-light. It was quite late, and they saw no traffic. No animals in the fields, no farmers at work. All was silent except for the thuds of horses' hooves and the creak and rattle of leather, wood, and iron as the carriage moved onward. Every so often Daniel would murmur something about the beauty of the night landscape, and she could only agree. His fingertips brushed the lace at her neckline, higher than was fashionable this year, but low enough that her bosom tingled with pleasure. Daniel was the only man ever to have made her feel that, and it was a pleasant surprise to learn she still could.

When he kissed her, the touch of his lips lifted her heart, then set it free to soar. She returned it with all the passion and joy left in her. She laid a hand aside his face to keep him there, and he stayed.

Soon he encouraged her to lie back on the seat so he could lift her skirts. His hand went beneath to release her drawers under hoops and petticoats, and for the first time in twenty years she felt excitement. Her knees splayed on their own, and there was no thought but to open herself to him. She reached for the tie of his breeches and loosened them. It set up a fire in him she could feel on his skin, and he moaned into her mouth. Suddenly urgent, where before he'd been casual, he shoved down his breeches and drawers just far enough for service, arranged her and her skirts on the carriage seat, and entered her.

She still loved him, she was sure of it then. He was the only man she had ever loved, though she'd been with thousands. He shoved himself into her with a passion nobody else ever had. She knew he loved her as well, as he had never loved his wife. That thought made her want to laugh, for the victory was sweet.

He finished quickly, and Suzanne took that as a sign he'd not been with anyone for a while and was not sleeping with his wife. It was a small victory, but sweet nonetheless. He restored his breeches, helped her arrange her clothes, then he checked his wig to make sure it was straight. They righted themselves in the seat, and the carriage rolled onward as if nothing special had happened inside it. The silvery country-side passed, as beautiful as before, but Suzanne thought she would never look at a night landscape again without remembering tonight. She and Daniel rode in comfortable silence.

Suzanne never noticed the carriage turning around toward London, but soon they were back among the close buildings and narrow streets of Southwark. When she realized they were going north instead of south, it was as if the entire world suddenly spun beneath her, dizzying her. It nearly made her laugh.

Daniel delivered her to Horse Shoe Alley, silent and still in the predawn darkness. There, standing on the cobbles next to the carriage, he kissed her good night. Or nearly good morning, based on the lightening sky. He took her hand and pressed a gold guinea into it. "Thank you," he said. Then he gave her one last peck on the cheek and stepped back up into his carriage. A word to his driver, and he was off, leaving Suzanne standing in the street.

She looked at the coin in her hand. At first she didn't want to realize what had just happened, for the happiness of having been restored to Daniel's affections was still full in her heart. For it to evaporate so quickly would be too painful, would leave too big an emptiness to bear. But as she stared at the gold piece, shining bright in the full moonlight, she knew the love she'd thought was hers hadn't existed at all. She'd been paid for sex, and furthermore she'd sold herself cheap. A real mistress would have been able to negotiate a yearly stipend, and a wife would have been entitled to the complete support of all her husband's wealth. One guinea, while a fortune to a street whore, was evidence he did not love her even enough to pay her more than once.

The emptiness, where glowing happiness had been only moments before, darkened and hardened quickly. The edges of it dried and curled so that her chest felt tight and she couldn't breathe. Tears tried to come, but she wouldn't let them. She grasped the coin hard in her hand until the edge of it hurt her palm. Then, slowly and with deliberate care, she slipped it into the pocket beneath her skirts. She turned and made her way into her house and up the stairs to her bedroom. There she washed herself well in the washbowl, dressed in her nicest nightgown, and slipped under the covers. She lay there, thinking about how good a thing it was that she now knew exactly where she stood with Daniel. She could now harden her heart to him and never wonder whether he might care for her. Nobody had ever loved her except Piers. Not her father, not her brothers and sisters, not Daniel, and certainly not any of the men she called clients. She now told herself what a good thing it was to know the truth. To rid herself of hope and never let disappointment cut her again, and never again waste her time pursuing something Daniel would dangle before her but never give her. She closed her eyes against the dawn, to make the world go away in sleep.

Fall came, then winter. As the days grew shorter, so did the money. By spring they would have to let Sheila go and move to a less expensive house. Each day when Suzanne awoke to hear the rattle of rain on the windows or feel the sharp chill of snow in the air, she dreaded the future. Soon rising in the morning took enormous effort and a steel will.

One evening in mid-January a crowd of five or six gathered at the Goat and Boar, around the large table near the stairs, and perhaps another three or four stood nearby, listening to the boisterous conversation. Suzanne sat with her back to the wall, the only woman at that table; a couple of young whores were chatting up three well-dressed men at the other table, ignoring the less-moneyed locals at the front. Big Willie Waterman was carrying on in a loud, braying voice to another street musician whose name Suzanne didn't know, but she thought he played a flute. "I heard there's a new theatre a-gonna be built." He nodded as he spoke, with an air of inside knowledge, though he'd surely had the news by eavesdropping in the street. His perch was the back of a heavy wooden chair, his feet in the seat and his elbows on his knees, a tankard clutched in both hands and his chin nearly dipping into his ale as he hunched toward his listeners gathered about the table.

"Where?" said the other, whose round face and cheeks like apples made him appear fat, though he was not.

"Dunno," Willie replied. "Somewhere across the river, I thinks." He made a broad, sweeping gesture with his tankard to indicate the general direction of the river and potential theatre.

Suzanne's attention sharpened, and she listened closely. The other musician wanted to know how Willie knew this.

"I heard it from a drummer I sometimes let play with me on the corner. You know Arthur." He made another gesture to indicate the direction of his corner, though everyone present well knew where it was and who Arthur was. "He were angling to be hired to drum for it, he says to me. I laughed, I did." Big Willie let go a chuckle as if to demonstrate how he'd laughed. "That one playing for the king? Not bloody likely. But in any case, I hears the theatre is a-gonna be a big and fancy one.

A right palace, they says. One might call it a sort of fare-thee-well to Cromwell, if you will. A bit of a nose-thumbing, I thinks. Take that, you old fire blanket!" He raised his tankard to cheers and laughter, then took a draught and emitted a belch that caught the attention of the patrons at the other end of the room.

Suzanne asked, "What sort of theatre will it be?"

Willie turned to focus on her as if he'd just then realized she was present. At his bright grin she thought it might be possible he only just then knew a woman was listening. "I hear they're bringing in all the new plays from France. Ones with backdrops and such."

Backdrops?

"What are those?" *Backdrops?* "Do you mean paintings on the back wall of the stage?" Suzanne found it hard to imagine. Every stage she'd seen, including the temporary ones Horatio had used in alleys, were slightly sloped affairs with two large curtained entries at the back wall and no attempt at decoration.

"Oh certs, 'tis paintings, it is. And set pieces."

"But how can the audience imagine the scene if there's a painting behind it?"

"I ain't certain myself, but I think the painting is of where the scene is supposed to take place."

Suzanne squinted, trying to picture it. "But how, then, do they do a new scene that's supposed to be a different location?"

Willie shrugged. "I can't tell ye. But I hear 'tis all the rage, it is. Set pieces and backdrops, to make the scene real-looking."

Suzanne took a sip of her drink, then said thoughtfully, "Well, it strikes me as awfully silly. And awfully cumbersome as well. Good actors should be able to create their own scene, with words and voice and posture. You should be able to picture the place by how the actors act and not have to have a painting behind him to tell you where they're supposed to be." She tried to imagine what Horatio would say about such a thing as backdrops, and had to smile. Yes, the friend of Hamlet would have a great deal to say, and none of it very nice.

She asked Big Willie, "What do people say of these things? Do they like the French theatre? What sorts of plays are they?"

Willie screwed his face into a thinking pose, then said, "Dunno what sorts of plays they is, but you know them nobles and all will like anything the king likes. He lived there long enough, I suppose he's as much French as anything."

"No, he's English," said the round-faced musician.

Another standing nearby with an ear to the conversation said, "Nae, he's a Stuart and Scottish, and dinnae allow anyone to tell ye different."

"His grandfather was a Scot, and not such a good one for all that."

"In any whatever," said Big Willie in a loud, overriding voice, "he appears to like to see a play now and again, wishes to let the followers of Cromwell know it, and now he and his brother is both o' them putting money into bringing back stage plays. For the nobility, at any rate."

One of the listeners at the table said, "I wish they'd bring back the bearbaiting. I like a good brawl."

"Oh, they will," said another. "Sure as anything, they'll have the bear arena opened soon, I'll just wager on't. There's good old English entertainment, says I."

"I wonder whether they'll let us ordinary folk see them new French plays," said the Scottish fellow.

"Can't see why not," replied Willie. "They always let us in before."

"But I hear there's nae pit. Nae pit, nae groundlings, and ye ken they must charge a dear price to sit in a chair."

"There'll be a pit. Sure there'll be a pit."

"I hear the stage will be all up under the heavens."

There was a brief pause as the listeners absorbed that, then Willie snorted. "Nonsense. You can't have a play without a downstage." A general murmur of agreement burbled about the table. Willie continued, "They'll have to let us in. Without groundlings, nobody will watch the play. They'll all be watching each other."

That brought a laugh, for they all knew it was true. *Groundlings.* The hoi polloi. The unwashed masses who loved to spend their money on entertainment as much as did the nobles. They had less of it, but also there were more of them. They were willing to pay to stand where the rich folk wouldn't care to sit.

A thought sparked in Suzanne's head that actually made her blink. It surprised her, for the idea was outrageous and impossible, and she couldn't yet see any of its defining characteristics. All she could see was the Globe Theatre. Nothing else, but the Globe as she'd seen it months before, rain-soaked and overrun with vermin. But still a theatre. One as they had been before the war. It made her heart race as she began to imagine how the return of sanctioned theatre could change everything. Not just the entertainment options of the rich, but it could change everything and everyone. For her, at any rate.

She said to the cluster of men, "So, what plays would you fellows care to see?"

"I want to see the bears and bulls."

"Aye, ye said that already, Warren."

"Seriously, tell me, all of you." She leaned forward in her

excitement and held her drink in both hands. "What plays do you like best?"

"I likes the ones where everyone dies," said Willie.

"*Hamlet*," Suzanne nodded. "The Scottish play as well."

"Oh aye, the Scottish play. But I also likes the ones as make me laugh. The one about the forest faerie in particular."

"*A Midsummer Night's Dream.*"

"Aye, that one."

They all seemed to know the Shakespeare plays, but nobody knew any of what had been brought from the Continent.

She asked, "Would you pay to see those plays again?"

There was a general roar of approval at the table, and Willie added, "Sure enough, Suze. I always loved to see them stories. Hard, though, to find them during the past twenty years. I misses them, I does."

"Anything you would see other than Shakespeare?"

"I suppose were I the king I would be pleased to be entertained by whatever means was at hand, but I do so miss the ones I know best. Maybe Marlowe a bit, but old Willie Shakespeare wrote all the ones I truly like." The others murmured in agreement.

The idea that had popped into Suzanne's head took root, and she could almost feel it grab hold behind her eyes. She sipped her ale and continued to question the fellows. Her heart pounded and breaths came hard, though she struggled to control herself and not let on how excited she was.

The next morning, at home, she spoke to Piers when he rose for breakfast. She hadn't slept much that night, and in the small, quiet hours of the morning had risen to sit up next to a candle, thinking. When that candle had guttered, she continued to sit in the dark until dawn, when Sheila rose to poke the fire in the kitchen. The sun was well up when Piers came for the breakfast Sheila had prepared. He walked through the 'tiring room on his way to the table without noticing her presence. When she spoke, he startled.

"Your hair is a disgrace," she said.

He stopped to peer at her in her dark corner. "Oh. Mother." He ran a hand through his hair and checked his collar to be certain the cravat he wore was straight, graceful, and proper. Even in his unemployed state she wouldn't allow him to neglect his appearance. It was a constant struggle, but she knew if she let him give in to the heartache of his situation he might never regain himself. If this kept on and their finances sank enough, he might think it advisable to turn to illegal means of support. With no job and no cash, desperation would certainly force him to more nefarious means, and for a man that meant crime of some sort, and that usually involved violence for those who were not wealthy or sly. Piers had been raised among actors, but had never been a good liar. He had never been raised to be a criminal; he could not succeed at it.

"Good morning," he said, remembering his manners.

"Good morning indeed. We must talk."

Suzanne rose from her chair and went to the table in the next room, but ignored the meat put before her. Piers followed her, a little hesitant at her manner. She read curiosity all over his face.

He tucked into his food as soon as it was set on the table, and Suzanne watched him eat for a moment. She began in a casual voice, as if she hadn't been waiting all night to ask him this.

"Piers, do you remember when you were ten or so and we worked for Horatio?"

Piers stopped chewing for a moment, thinking, then smiled. "Yes, I do. Good times, those."

That rather surprised her. "Good times, you say?"

"Indeed. You were happy then. I don't think I've ever seen you happy except for then."

Suzanne was mildly surprised to learn Piers had a thought for her happiness; she'd always been so focused on his well-being. Then she smiled at the memory of those days and knew he was right. She had been pleased with the life the troupe had offered. There had been far more money since then, but never the joy of a fine performance, lively audience, or the camaraderie of fellow troupers. Not even the playacting when she pretended to be enthralled with tedious William. She said, "And you liked the work?"

He nodded. "Oh yes. The apprenticeship was good for the learning of business, and I hope to put that knowledge to work for me soon, but playacting is like a game. There's a great deal of fun to be had, knowing that an audience is enjoying themselves. And when you've moved them to throw money, it's so much the better."

Suzanne had to laugh, remembering the times coins were tossed at her feet. Usually copper, but even copper could be a pleasure when you knew the giver was giving freely, in appreciation of a skilled and inspired performance. She said, "What might you think about doing that sort of thing always?"

At first he chuckled, but she said nothing and he realized she was serious. "You mean, to make money?"

"Why not?"

"Will the king allow it?" They both knew any business venture was subject to approval by the crown, and the only people who acted with any freedom were the nobility. Their only chance of obtaining that approval was to have the support of a peer, or else demonstrate they were in a position to provide something that couldn't be had from anyone else.

She shrugged. "I hear he and the Duke of York are very much involved with theatre as one way of setting themselves apart from Cromwell's rule. Perhaps they would like to encourage theatre among the rabble as well."

Piers made a face. "The rabble might not be so willing to pay for admission."

"They were eager enough to hand over their coppers when we were playing in alleys."

"A pittance."

"I don't recall starving for lack of ready cash."

"Where will you stage your plays? Cromwell was a tyrant to make the king appear careless, but even Charles won't care to have unsanctioned plays popping up in the streets. He'll want to control the stories if he's any sort of ruler at all. If you're to have a theatre in which to perform, rather than a temporary stage on the street, you'll need to pay for it. If your audience is groundlings only, you might be hard put to ask for more money. There is a reason not all the audience is in the pit."

Suzanne went silent. She hadn't thought of that, and now she turned over in her mind what to do about it. Money. They would need money to even begin such a venture. A loan from a usurer would be impossible, for she was a woman and her son untried and unconnected. She would need to go to someone she knew, with spare cash and connections, and the only man she might touch for this was Daniel. Slowly, thinking hard, she said, "I'll talk to your father."

"No, you will not."

She looked over at Piers, who wore a red scowl. He was such a puppy, growling and squealing and pretending to be the one in control. "Why not?"

"He hasn't even asked to meet me. He has snubbed you

these past months, and wasn't terribly curious about how well you were doing when he did ask. He doesn't deserve to hear from us."

Suzanne smiled and laid a hand over Piers's. He was such a dear, thinking that a visit from her was to be coveted rather than avoided. "On the contrary, my son. He richly deserves a visit from someone asking for money. And that someone knows exactly where his most tender places can be found. I will go to him not with a feather, nor even a bludgeon. But I will carry a needle, long and sharp. I will stick him where he is most sensitive, and he will be ever so pleased to help us."

Piers thought about that for a moment, then a sly smile crept across his face. He said, "I only wish I could be a cat on your shoulder, Mother."

That made Suzanne laugh aloud.

Chapter Seven

S uzanne wasted no time. No point in sending a letter; that would be too easily ignored. She would need to go to him in person. One enquiry on the street let her know he was currently at court, which was good in that he was in London but bad in that it meant she would need to gain entrance to Whitehall. Not such an easy thing unless one looked the part. Fortunately for Suzanne she was well versed in looking and acting as if she were not herself, and now she readied herself to play a role once again.

Since William's departure she'd had one new dress made, to be seen in public and not look like the discarded mistress of a Puritan hypocrite. Now she donned it as a knight going to battle. French couture had always been more revealing than English, because of the warmer weather in the south. These days, though, the bare bosoms brought over by the king and his court startled even Suzanne, who had never been afraid of revealing clothing. At her age the breasts had deflated and the bones had become just a little too prominent. It behooved her to not show too much flesh that might be lined, sunken, and discolored.

Today she wore a loosely gathered golden-brown silk over a bleached white linen shift trimmed in delicate lace. The front she clasped with a brooch that was finely wrought silver and appeared rich though it boasted no jewels. Her shoulders and chest were all bare, revealing her fine collarbones, but her bodice pressed her breasts up and together enough to cover her rather knobby breastbone. A padding of handkerchief to the outside of each helped them to appear more substantive than they were. Her long neck was still smooth, without the horizontal lines so common in women her age, and rose gracefully from ladylike shoulders. She dreaded the vulture neck she knew awaited her in extreme old age as it did every woman, and vaguely hoped she might not live that long.

She viewed herself in the handheld glass and lifted her chin to be sure she wasn't creating unnecessary wrinkles. She already had more than enough, and didn't need more. Then she let Sheila help her into pattens and cloak, and ventured into the street.

She contemplated hiring Thomas and Samuel if their chair were about, but thought better of that and walked to the Bank Side to secure a carriage. It would be expensive, but creeping up to the palace gate in a sedan chair would take ever so long, would impress nobody, and would make it that much more difficult to gain entrance. She wished there were a carriage she could borrow that wouldn't appear hired, but she was of limited means and needed to make do with what was available to her.

Bold and blithe had always been the way for her. To the best of her knowledge no woman ever got what she wanted by waiting with her hands in her lap for someone to notice she needed it, and she'd learned long ago that if she acted as if she assumed she would have her way, then she often had her way. Nothing bad ever happened for it. Nobody ever died from being told no and sent away. To be sure, she hated being told no, so it was no small thing to her. But she succeeded often enough to make it worth the risk. She approached the palace gate with her heart in her throat and a gracious though bored smile on her face.

Bored, because the worst thing one could do among the fancy folk was to appear overly impressed by them. One must, of course, have proper manners and correct deference according to rank, but going all boggle-eyed and panicky in the presence of a duke or earl pegged one as not just a commoner, but one without the slightest connections or grace. This was her first visit here, and it took a mighty effort not to look around at the street and the traffic through the gate as she descended from her carriage. She must appear to know where she was going even though she had not the faintest idea which way to head. Without so much as a pause to collect her skirts and gain her bearings, she dove straight into character and strode toward the gate as if she knew she was on course. Like a ship at full sail, she breezed past others who were stopped and questioned by guards in armor and carrying pikes.

"Hold!" she heard, but she kept going. Her aim was a small door beyond the gate. Once she was inside the complex arrangement of towers, apartments, and galleries, she could make herself "lost" and end up nearly anywhere she pleased. Then it would be a simple matter to find Daniel, for the king's personal guard protected the king and never his lesser courtiers. She had no need to test their mettle.

"Hold!" A guard ran to intercept her and placed himself

and his pike between her and her goal. A small groan of frustration escaped her, and she stamped her foot in a theatrical pique.

"Let me through, guard." Her tone conveyed that she condescended to speak to him. His instinctive reaction would be to wonder whether he'd misjudged her rank and would be in trouble for stopping her. Though any palace guard worth his pay would fight that instinct, it would still throw him off balance for a moment and that would give her a slight edge she could exploit.

"Who are you, and what business do you have?"

Then, to keep him further off balance, she graced him with a wide smile, for she had been taught at an early age the art of pleasing men, and it had been her vocation for two decades. She was very good at it. "My name is Suzanne, brave soldier, and I can't imagine you need to ask what my business is." She gave her bosom a slight shake and hoped the guard wouldn't notice she was nearly old enough to be his mother.

She needn't have worried. He never saw her face because his gaze never left the cleavage between her breasts. She drew an enormous sigh in the softest voice she could manage, and her bosom swelled and fell directly beneath his face. For a moment she thought he might fall into it and his nose would be stuck there, and wouldn't that be a jolly thing?

Nevertheless he had the presence of mind to say, "Where's your escort? You must have an escort." The poor fellow's speech was slurred, as if he'd been drinking, and though he struggled to look at her face he never quite managed it.

She giggled, pretending it was of no consequence that she was out and about alone and breezing into Whitehall Palace without a man to vouch for her. "Oh, you know how he is; he's fallen down drunk at the public house. He drank a barrelful,

I vow. Too drunk to walk, and too big for me to carry. I knew the king would be in a perfect snit were I to tarry there, so I hired myself a carriage—out of my own pocket, I will add—and here I am, and I can only hope his majesty will make up for my loss. So I really must be on my way, or the king will have someone's head. Or, I should say, someone else's head, since he's got so many perched on the bridge already." Then with a bright grin of good cheer she waved the guard good-bye and proceeded on her way.

The guard hadn't the nerve to stop her again, probably assuming the king's bodyguard would be able to identify a fraud, and once she was through the door she was on her own. Out another door, across a courtyard, and through yet a third door, and she'd surely lost anyone who might have followed her. She paused in an alcove a moment to discard her filthy pattens, gather herself, and button and straighten her cloak.

Now to find Daniel.

Whitehall Palace was an amazing confusion of buildings surrounding several odd-shaped courtyards, sparsely populated for the cold weather. Some were wooden and some stone, some dating back to the time of Henry VIII.

People passing by paid her little attention. Servants in livery ignored her, intent on whatever mission had them hurrying through the palace. Those who obviously were not servants also ignored her, and she could guess why. Though the dress she wore was her very finest clothing, compared to the rich velvet, brocade, soft leather, fine embroidery, and accents of gold, silver, and jewels, her finest dress seemed a rag. Women wearing the latest fashions from Paris strolled past, so involved with themselves and each other they never spared Suzanne a glance. Men might catch their eye on her bosom, but never her face, and that was the end of it. She wasn't deemed worthy of flirting. When she realized it, at first she was a little embarrassed, but then she reminded herself that she wanted to be invisible here. She could go where she wished and not be apprehended, so long as nobody noticed her. She looked around to see which direction to make her search for Daniel.

To her left was a jumble of lesser structures and to her right stood an archway that appeared to lead to a large courtyard before a majestic, imposing building that towered over the smaller ones. Her guess was that she would find the king there, but Charles was not her objective. A passing boy in livery caught her attention, and she reached out to grab his jacket and detain him. He was in such a hurry, she nearly pulled him off his feet.

"Boy!" He was perhaps ten or twelve years old, and nearly wriggled from his skin to be out of her grasp and on his way. She dug her fingers into the fabric of his jacket, and her hand followed him whichever direction he took.

"What is it, milady?" He finally stood still, though he leaned away from her to be gone if her grasp should fail for even a second.

"I seek the Earl of Throckmorton. Can you tell me where I might find him?"

"In his apartments, I expect. Or else in the presence chamber with the others at court." He glanced up at the sun, which had nearly reached its zenith, then added, "This time of day, I'd look to the apartments. The king will still be abed this early, and probably so will a great number of his courtiers who join him in his amusements of an evening."

Suzanne hadn't thought of that, but then considered that it might be a good thing to approach Daniel in his bedchamber. Assuming he was alone, though she knew she couldn't count on that. "And where would one find the earl's apartments?"

The boy pointed with his chin toward a stone building in the direction of the river. "That one there, milady. Enter from the north, and 'tis the first door you come to on the right. Knock loud and long, as 'tis my experience his grace likes his privacy and orders his valet to ignore the door."

Suzanne wondered why Daniel liked his privacy so well, but didn't dwell on the question just then. She thanked the page, handed him a threepence, and let him go. Whereupon he thrust the money into a purse inside his belt and scampered away as fast as his feet would carry him.

She glanced around to see who might be watching her, and when she saw everyone in sight was absorbed in his own business and cared not a fig for her, she picked up her skirts and headed straight for the building indicated by the page.

North entrance, first door on the right. It was a rather dank, old place, being so near the river and likely built when the palace was new. The door was small by current standards, badly worn in spots, medieval-looking, and bound in old iron. She raised her hand to knock.

The door swung open beneath her knuckles before she touched it, and she found herself face-to-face with Daniel. The sight of him melted her resolve in an instant, and her courage quite deserted her. She quickly retrieved her hand, wishing she could run away and forget she'd ever thought about knocking on his door. They stared at each other for a moment, neither sure what to say or who should speak first. Then Daniel did.

"Suzanne."

Now it was her turn to speak, and he'd given so little on which to base an opening. Her lips parted but she found her voice nothing but a squeak, then she cleared her throat and tried again. "Daniel." There. Now the ball was in his court.

"What are you doing here?" His tone gave her to understand he meant *How on God's earth did you get into the palace?*

She ignored his true meaning and answered the question as asked. "I have a business proposition for you."

"I've already a mistress, thank you."

Anger flushed her cheeks, but she held her temper. This meeting was far too important to ruin it with a fit of pride. She said evenly, "How lovely for you. But I expect you'll want to send her back to her husband for the nonce, since we need to speak of business and you'd rather hear what I have to say without any . . . distraction."

He thought about that for a brief moment, then said, "I happen to be alone . . . *for the nonce* . . . and was on my way to dinner, though it be de facto breakfast. However, I can order food brought in for us. Come in and we'll sit." He stepped back and gestured graciously that she should enter. She stepped inside.

His quarters appeared to consist of several rooms in a succession ever deeper into the old tower. The outer room contained a table and several chairs against one wall, plus another two more comfortable chairs with upholstered seats near the hearth. A boy wearing Daniel's dark blue livery had just finished stoking the fire and now turned to his master to be given further orders or dismissed. He appeared perhaps seven or eight years old and had the translucent, ruddy-cheeked complexion of high rank, good food, and indoor occupation. More than likely he was a distant cousin of Daniel's on his mother's side, where Suzanne knew were a couple of dukes and a Scottish marquis. Daniel requested dinner be brought for himself and Suzanne, and the boy bowed before making his exit.

There was movement in the next room, and through the door Suzanne saw a valet going about his business, tidying up. She sensed that though Daniel was alone at the moment, she'd missed the mistress by bare minutes. In any case, she reminded herself she was no longer attached to Daniel in that way, had no desire for a repeat of that night in his carriage, and pressed ahead with her business proposal.

"Daniel, I've a venture in mind I'm sure will interest you." She allowed him to help her out of her cloak, then settled into one of the upholstered chairs, liking the softness of it. The fire was just comfortable, not too high and not dying embers. "So ask me what my idea is." She said it as if she were bursting to tell him some excellent news, and in a way she was. The idea had taken hold as if it had a hand at the back of her neck and was shaking her, and more than anything she wanted to grab it in return and bring it under control.

Daniel thought a moment, an indulgent smile on his face, then he draped her cloak over a chair, removed his own cloak and laid it on top of hers, then took the seat opposite hers before the fire. "Very well. I'm curious. Tell me your brilliant idea."

"Well!" Suzanne leaned forward with all her energy, her hands in her lap and her chest thrust toward Daniel. It was a posture that generally made men agreeable, and she was pulling out all the stops. "You've surely heard that the king and his brother the duke are very much interested in the theatre and are encouraging its return to English culture."

Daniel nodded. "I've seen a number of plays staged here in the palace, and some of them are quite entertaining. Some of those are even English." The last was said with a wry smile and a tilt of his head.

"And you are aware I acted with a troupe during the interregnum."

Again he nodded. "You've mentioned it."

"Are you also aware that there are several theatres about town that stand empty and only lack some repairs and an acting troupe to make them useful?" She paused for emphasis, then leaned forward ever so slightly and added, "And profitable."

Daniel smiled. "Let me guess; you've a lover you would have gain that profit."

She sat straighter in her chair and looked down her nose at him. "No, I mean to have it myself."

A bark of a laugh escaped Daniel before he caught himself and realized she was serious. "You're serious."

"I am."

He laid his elbows on his chair arms and clasped his fingers over his belly. "You couldn't possibly imagine you might be one to manage such a venture yourself. Besides being a woman, you're a common whore." He said it as matter-of-factly as if he were referring to the color of her hair, and she knew him well enough to understand that he meant it as harmlessly. It was a fact, and no getting around it.

"Yes, a common whore who is the mother of your only son. Surely that deserves some consideration"—here she allowed her voice to go a bit low and ominous—"particularly since you wish your relationship to him kept quiet." She paused ever so briefly to allow her implication to sink in, and when there wasn't a flicker of alarm from Daniel, she then pressed on in a newly bright and chipper voice. "Besides, I don't expect to manage the theatre myself; Piers is my guardian now and he will be charged with those things more easily accomplished by those possessing male parts."

"You want me to loan him money so he can hand it over to you. Then he will take responsibility for your use of it, yes?"

She shrugged. "In essence. Had I a husband it would be the same. He will lease the building and hire out the work to restore it. I will manage the troupe itself and guide the business to its success. Piers will handle the money, take legal responsibility, and thereby give the appearance of control over the venture."

"And what will you do if I decline your business proposition?"

"More than likely I will spin out the next year or so in my present state, then become a burden on my son, who so far has been unsuccessful at finding gainful employment and runs a risk of being seduced by the criminal element, for which life he is so unsuited as to find himself dead or incarcerated within a very short time, and then I will be left to my own devices as a whore and at my age must starve in that profession. So, without your help, within two or three years you will find me dead in the gutter somewhere, I imagine. My life will end in poverty, for lack of assistance from the man whose son I bore for love rather than money. A story that, should it come to light—and I can assure you the chance is great—would shock and dismay your wife." The threat was entirely bluff, but Daniel didn't necessarily know that, and whatever alarm he received from it was most deserved after his behavior at their last meeting.

Daniel thought it over for a moment. Suzanne thought she might have seen a small blush of shame on his cheeks, or perhaps ire, or it could have just been a red light from the fire. But he said, "How much money do you require, and why do you think I have any in any case?"

That made her chuckle, and bounce a little in her seat. "Oh come, Daniel. It's been nearly a year since you returned with the king. Surely your business interests have paid something.

When we last spoke, you said you had lands and a patent, with the promise of more."

His head bowed slightly in agreement. "I confess I'm better off than I was this time last year."

"Then you must see the advantage in becoming a patron of the theatre, something the king supports and encourages."

"There you are again, looking for another patron."

"Indeed I am, and this time my proposal is entirely legal, and moral as well. Let us all collapse from the shock of it! The king wishes for the theatre to thrive, and he and his brother are providing entertainment to those with money. I and my friends can bring similar pastimes to the commons in the setting they prefer. Dramatic art will flourish once more because of it. England will be known for its fine theatre enjoyed by all; we shall surpass even the smug, arrogant, self-satisfied French. I know it in my heart."

"I like your enthusiasm, but again I ask: How much cash will this venture require?"

Only then did Suzanne realize her error in not learning the answer to that question before coming here. She'd not thought any further than just to know whether Daniel would be willing to talk to her at all; she hadn't considered what to tell him if he proved willing to listen. Without hesitation, she invented a number and it leapt from her mouth.

"Five hundred and fifty pounds."

Daniel blinked, and Suzanne's heart sank. She must have asked for too much. "Or thereabouts," she added. Still he was quiet, but he didn't say no and only sat for a moment, considering.

Yes, considering. Suzanne's heart lifted. He was considering giving her more than five hundred pounds. Father would have choked and turned purple at being asked for so much money.

He certainly would never have had that much available. But Daniel was in an entirely different class. He thought of himself as barely solvent, but only because he compared himself to the king. He surely had the resources to help her. Her head then went light. Dizzy, that she might have that much from Daniel.

But then he said, "I don't know whether I can spare it all at once."

Quickly she replied, "Half to start. To lease the theatre and make repairs on it. The poor thing has been neglected horribly these last two decades. I think I can bring together the actors and pay them later. Within a year or two the venture might even be self-supporting."

"And Piers will accomplish the business tasks?"

"Other men will speak more comfortably to him than to me. Were I to attempt to do it myself I would spend all my time proving I cannot be taken advantage of. Piers would only have to prove himself once; I would be challenged every minute of every hour of every day, ad infinitum. The job will simply be easier for him than for me."

"Of course, everything will be in his name. He uses one, then?"

"Of course. Anyone who asks is told his mother is a widow. Most don't bother to ask." Few asked because they already knew her history and assumed Piers was the son of an anonymous client at Maddie's brothel, and she wondered whether that might be the reason he'd not found a position. It briefly crossed her mind that Daniel might be undermining Piers, but she set the thought aside. Daniel might have no interest in his son, but surely couldn't wish him harm.

"And what name would that be?"

Suzanne blinked, surprised. She hadn't realized she'd never

told Daniel the name their son went by. "Surely I mentioned it in my letters."

Daniel only shook his head and waited for a reply to his question.

Suzanne nearly stammered, unhappy the issue had come up at this most unfortunate moment. "Naturally he uses Thornton; you've never shown any indication you might acknowledge him. He calls himself Piers Thornton after me, though the name is meaningless. You certainly wouldn't want him to call himself Stockton, lest your wife hear rumors."

"Of course." Daniel was examining his thumbnail and appeared to have drifted off the discussion. This reaction puzzled her; everything she knew of him made her think he wouldn't care, but now he seemed to. Now she didn't know what to think.

"He could hardly have presumed to call himself Stockton. As you said, you wish to keep him secret and therefore cannot acknowledge him. By law he is not your son, and so the name he uses has no bearing because it is false. By your statement you wish his paternity to remain unknown, so it's far better he call himself Thornton."

Daniel considered that and grunted in grudging agreement. "Well, in any case, Piers must handle the money, no matter what he calls himself. Three hundred pounds to start. That's all I have for him, so he must secure the theatre building and make it useable with that much."

In a sudden burst of energy, he sat up in his chair and grabbed the arms of it. "And, come! There is another thing we must address. Someone else to convince as you have me." He rose from his seat, took her hand, and drew her with him. "We will need the goodwill of the king."

Suzanne's heart leapt up and choked her. *The king!* She

hesitated and hung back. "Why? What will you tell him? Why must we go to him?"

"You wouldn't wish me to be in conflict with the king, would you? How would it be if I were to sponsor a theatre when he and the duke are both doing that very same thing? Surely you realize he must have control over what plays are performed. He cannot have actors acting willy-nilly about the city, without sanction from his majesty and control of the crown."

"And you wish to speak to him now? This very moment?"

"Now is all we have. There is no such thing as later. And if he declines permission, then that will be that and there will be no further need of discussion of this venture." He settled her terribly ordinary cloak about her shoulders, then donned his own, and his broad-brimmed hat from which flowed an enormous red plume. "Come, let us catch him early in his day, before the crush of courtiers, while he is still in a pleasant mood."

Now Suzanne saw his plan. He would take her to the king and let Charles tell her no, so he wouldn't have to say it himself. As he guided her from his rooms she blinked back disappointment. But as anger rose to take its place she swallowed that also because she realized what Daniel said was true. There was no theatre without the king, no business without his approval, and so they must petition him. The sooner the better. She nodded and allowed Daniel to draw her along with him to the presence chamber so the king could tell her to go home.

Daniel walked much faster than Suzanne and pulled her along at a slight trot across the courtyard, through some rooms and out to another courtyard. They crossed it at the same pace while palace denizens and workers stared at their hurried passage. They entered another stone building and breezed past the guard with no more than a nod of recognition to the earl. Up some stairs and to the opposite end of a great gallery lined with windows, through another door, and they were finally halted by a row of more guards with pikes just before the entrance to what appeared to be the royal presence chamber.

One of the guards came forward to hear Daniel's business with the king, then disappeared deeper into the palace. Perhaps a minute later he returned with news that the king would hear him, and Daniel drew Suzanne onward.

Just inside the chamber loitered a cluster of nobles in private conversation that didn't seem to involve their sovereign. Dressed in the height of French fashion, they wore the long wigs in vogue because the king never let himself be seen without one. Everyone knew his hair was thinning badly, and he never left his privy chamber without a prodigious head cover with great masses of dark curls that draped over his shoulders, down his back, and over his chest halfway to his waist. His court, filled with older men whose hair was gray and thinning, were happy to emulate him, so enormous wigs could be seen nearly everywhere in London these days. Even Daniel, whose hair was thick and not yet entirely gray, wore an elaborate wig befitting his rank.

She recognized each man as a former client from the early days of the Commonwealth, when everyone had been much younger. Names escaped her. She had never kept track of names because even if she was given one it was usually false. She remembered faces according to their preferences, physical oddities, and limitations both physical and emotional.

She remembered the tall one with a bright red wig required her to moo like a cow when he was in his throes. He paid her extra because her animal noises were so enthusiastic and "realistic." She dared not contemplate what that might mean.

The one who appeared in control of the conversation at hand, whose brocade jacket glittered in the sunlight streaming through the window, had never taken much of her time but paid well regardless. She thought him a true gentleman and remembered him warmly.

The third was a vague memory of those days, though she was certain she'd seen his face before. The three glanced at her as she passed, and she could see not one of them recognized her.

Good.

Voices of children came from ahead, and as Daniel and Suzanne entered a well-lit chamber with large, wide-open windows, she realized the king was entertaining some of his children by mistresses he'd kept in France. Neither of those women seemed present at the moment, but several courtiers watched as two boys of eleven or twelve played at sword fighting with wooden swords, chasing each other about the room with great noise of shouting and laughter. Their governesses observed from the side, laughing and applauding as if they were the boys' mothers, and Charles laughed with his sons as he lounged on a great wooden chair raised on a dais. He tossed advice to whichever boy was losing at the moment, and egged them both on with an enthusiasm Suzanne had never seen in a father toward his sons. Particularly her own father had never enjoyed any of his children this well, not even her brothers. A warmth crept into her heart, and she was gladdened to see a ruler who appreciated his family.

Daniel drew her onward by the arm, past the cluster of courtiers who appeared not to notice their passing, but Suzanne could sense their attention on her like the heat of a large fire. This close to the king, they now noticed her ordinary costume and lack of fine jewelry. She was a commoner, and there was no hiding it.

She then realized she was hanging back, which surprised her because it was unlike her. Very little frightened her, so she shouldn't be intimidated by even Charles. There was nothing magical or immortal about him. What made this encounter different from meeting anyone else was that this was the king. What made the king different was that he wielded a great deal of power and could take things away as readily as he could give them. Suzanne was accustomed to being in the presence of men who had more power than she, because most men were more powerful than most women, particularly herself. Though she currently lived in more or less comfortable circumstance, just then she had nothing much that could be taken from her beyond her freedom and her life. Since she had no reason to believe she would be thrown into the Tower of London and beheaded even if she misspoke today, she had nothing to fear from the king. At the moment, to her, he was little more than a richly dressed man who was in a position to make her dream come true, which would surely be good. Either he would or he wouldn't, and neither case was life-or-death. All fear fell from her and she began to imagine the king would give her what she wanted.

She picked up her pace as she and Daniel were announced. The king turned a genial smile on them, and Daniel immediately halted his approach for a deep bow. Suzanne followed suit with the deepest curtsey she could manage without any practice. She faltered in her balance, but counted herself fortunate not to trip to the floor like a collapsed tent. A breeze lifted curtains at the window, and she welcomed it for taking the sudden sweat that beaded on her brow. She regained her balance and stood as straight as she could once she stopped teetering.

"Greetings to my loyal Throckmorton! How fare you today?"

"Well, your majesty. And I hope the day has treated yourself well."

"What brings you to me this fine morning?" Morning had passed at least an hour ago, but Suzanne felt her heart lift that the king seemed in a good mood.

Daniel replied, "Please forgive the unscheduled visit, your grace. I have an urgent and private petition that should require but a moment of your valuable time."

Charles had been caught somewhat in disarray with his coat thrown across a chair and the neck of his shirt quite open, but he didn't seem to mind much. He waved off the apology as if it were nothing to barge in on the monarch during a personal moment with his children, closest advisors, and immediate servants. "Dear Daniel, what is the matter at hand?" The breeze lifted a curl in his tall, heavy brown wig, and he brushed it back. It lifted out of place once more, and he tucked it back in so it would stay. It appeared a bit odd, stuck in like that, but it apparently didn't annoy the king anymore and nobody was likely to tell him he looked odd.

"I wish to petition your majesty for a patent to stage performances of plays within the city."

"Plays? Theatre?" It was a fairly unusual request, and his majesty might have thought it too minor for consideration. But the mention of theatre brought a light of curiosity to his eye.

"Yes, your majesty."

Charles's smile dimmed, and he had the beady look of a crow eyeing a fresh carcass. "You're aware, Daniel, there are already troupes sanctioned by myself and my brother. The first theatre is under construction and there are plans for a second. We've no need for a third."

"Yes, your majesty, the nobility are well served by the king's and the duke's fine players. There is no theatre that is to be preferred over the royal troupes, for they bring the best from Paris and make it their own. However, there are many in London who could benefit from a theatre more suited to commons. Less sophisticated folk, who might not understand the new plays. A friend . . . that is, the son of this woman here, whom I've known for many years, wishes to address this need among the commons. That they might also enjoy performances of sanctioned plays."

The puzzlement deepened, and the king straightened his seat in the chair to lean forward as if to hear better. "Why can they not pay their penny and stand with the groundlings in our theatre once the duke's troupe has their public venue? Or else be happy with the commedia dell'arte, which is more to their liking and understanding in any case? What interest could the masses have in serious theatre?"

Suzanne knew she had to reply to that, for Daniel wouldn't answer well. "Your majesty, if I may . . ." The king thought for a moment, then nodded that she might speak. "Your majesty, perhaps it's not well known that the commons have a thirst for the older plays. Ones well established in the culture of England and the monarchy. Shakespeare. Marlowe. But especially Shakespeare, whose work has surely been performed somewhere every day for more than a hundred years, even during the dark days of the Commonwealth. A troupe offering those plays to the masses, and the lower theatre as well, would be a service to the city and therefore an advantage to the crown."

"But my brother's new theatre would offer the serious plays. The common people could see them there."

"Yes, your majesty, in another part of the city, and in a much fresher setting. Which will be very good indeed. I hear the new theatre will have many innovations such as backdrops and set pieces, and an arch to frame the scenes like a painting. But the common folk don't share a taste for innovation. They rather prefer the traditional. The familiar. They find comfort in it, and the Lord knows that there is little enough comfort in the lives of commoners. Our venue would not be like the new theatre, but would present plays as they've been staged for the past century, in the traditional manner."

"And where would this theatre be?"

"Southwark, your majesty. It's the Globe Theatre my son wishes to restore."

Surprise put a curl to Charles's lips. "That old place? You can't be serious."

"I'm afraid I am, your majesty." Suzanne lowered her gaze and bent her knee as if about to curtsey in apology for contradicting the king. "'Tis a poor building and in bad repair, but 'tis good enough for the audience my son would serve." She nodded toward Daniel. "Throckmorton here has pledged money to make repairs enough for the theatre to be presentable to the commons. Again, not suitable for fashionable company as yours will be, but pleasing to the low folk."

The king addressed Daniel with a twinkle of humor in his eye. "You wish to make yourself a patron of the theatre like myself?"

Daniel bowed quickly. "Never like yourself, your majesty. I only wish to bring the renegade entertainments of street performers under the purview of the crown, as should be any public amusement."

Charles chuckled. "And gather in some cash in the bargain."

"Perhaps, your grace, but even were it a losing venture there would still be the benefit to the crown and to the overall culture of London. To elevate the sensibilities of the commons is to elevate us all in the greater scheme of things."

Charles gazed at them both for a long moment, thinking. He said to one of the bewigged nobles near the door, "What think you, Richard?"

The one who liked cows considered his answer for a moment, then spoke from where he stood. "This theoretical troupe wants to perform Shakespeare and Marlowe? Are we certain they will do justice to serious plays?"

The man with the vaguely familiar face said in reply, though he hadn't been addressed, "Well, one can hardly damage Shakespeare. So long as the words are spoken clearly, the play is excellent drama."

The first said, "I've heard of people changing the words of plays. In fact I've seen enough damage done to Shakespeare that I could hardly recognize the play and it was so much gibberish." To the king he said, "That is a consideration, your majesty. What will this new troupe do to these well-loved plays, many of which are about your ancestors, I would remind your grace."

Charles said, "Indeed."

Desperation leapt on Suzanne. She hurried to say, "I agree, your majesty. The things some actors do to the words should be deemed criminal. And they do it without sanction, every day. Somewhere in this city each day a play is performed in an alley or close, without permission from the crown. Actors do what they please, say what they like, take the audience's money, then pack up and move to another street to do it again the next day. How good would it be to have a venue meant especially for those who live on the south side of the river and perhaps cannot travel to stand in the pits of your excellent new theatres? What advantage would there be to have a sanctioned theatre troupe answerable to my lord Throckmorton and therefore to your majesty, serving the poorer folk and giving them what they like and what you need them to have? Traditional theatre, whether serious or comedy, as it was before the Commonwealth?"

Charles nodded, warming to the idea.

The first noble said, "But your grace . . . serious theatre for the commons? Can they possibly appreciate it?"

"They've always enjoyed standing in the pit in the presence of Shakespeare or Marlowe," said Charles. "By my estimation they appreciate the old plays as much as anyone."

Suzanne saw an avenue and went down it to press her case. "Yes, the old plays. They prefer the old ones, and their sensibilities cannot compass the newer, bolder plays. They won't understand the ideas of backdrops and set pieces. They like what they're accustomed to. Too much change and they'll be happier to attend plays presented in alleys than to travel across the river."

"You may be right," said Charles, still nodding slowly. "However, I balk at the idea of letting the Globe Theatre and an untried troupe have their way with serious plays that carry weight in the mind. Too much leash could lead to . . . satire."

Suzanne wondered why the king didn't feel that way about the commedia dell'arte, which was easily made political satire by extempore performance, but let her question go and asked another. "Perhaps a patent that will specify only the plays of Shakespeare?" Suzanne watched Charles's face, and when the king's expression didn't change, she added, "And perhaps additionally specify that nothing be changed from the original scripts?"

Charles raised his eyebrows, apparently liking the idea. "Yes, that might be to the advantage of the crown. A theatre for the commons, sanctioned and controlled so that it might be another voice of the monarchy. The more subtle for not bearing the name of myself or my brother, but under the patronage of a loyal courtier." He gestured to Daniel. "One who has been loyal for a great long time."

"An excellent idea, your majesty," Daniel said.

"Yes," said the king. "I like the idea. There will be a patent allowing the theatre in Southwark to use Shakespeare and the lower forms only, under the patronage and responsibility of the Earl of Throckmorton."

Suzanne couldn't keep a grin from her face. Her dream was going to happen.

Chapter Eight

Now that financing and performance permission had been secured, the next step was to secure actors to perform those plays. Though her life with William hadn't kept her entirely sequestered from the world, she had been fairly sheltered by him. And her life in the care of her father certainly hadn't prepared her for the task of convincing people to work for her. It had been over seven years since she'd seen any of the old troupe. In fact, the last time she'd seen Horatio was that ugly day when he'd been arrested. In seven years a man could become very lost or even more dead, and she'd never had any knowledge of what had become of him. London was a large place, dotted with backwater neighborhoods where one could disappear accidentally or on purpose and never be found by the authorities.

But a few enquiries among the musicians along the Bank Side gave her to know Horatio was still alive and plying various trades here and there, none of them involving theatre.

Rumor had it he was currently residing somewhere in the vicinity of Newgate, a section of town even Suzanne found menacing for its locals prone to violence. But in spite of the risk, she wasted no time in hiring the chair of Thomas and Samuel to venture across the river in search of him.

Newgate was an area of London into which spilled former occupants of the notorious prison, some of whom were still under sentence and had bought their way out. Much like the Bank Side, which had its own prison and sinful amusements, the streets were filled with vendors of all kinds: food, magic potions, astrology readings, gambling, stolen goods, and sex. Lots and lots of sex, of all kinds, willing and unwilling, human or beast, adult, child, or deformed, paid by the hour, by the day, or by the month. These streets made Bank Side appear positively God-fearing.

Suzanne rode through the streets in the chair of Thomas and Samuel, who also served as bodyguards if for no other reason than that they wished her to survive to pay them for their work in carrying her. In her search she bade them pause whenever she saw someone who appeared likely to have information of the neighborhood in general or Horatio in particular.

Of course none of them knew where he was, because they didn't know who she was. Some said they had never heard of Horatio, and one or two may have told the truth. As the day wore on, the search took on the patina of a wild-goose chase. Those who had information sent her hither, where someone else would turn her around and direct her yon. None of it ever panned out, and she entertained the thought they were stationing themselves in her path as a game, to make her dizzy.

Late in the day she enquired of a street musician playing a squeeze box, who turned out to be a little more forthcoming than the vendors and beggars she'd accosted earlier. When she spotted him and ordered Thomas and Samuel to stop, she leaned out of the chair and greeted the musician with a pleasant smile as she asked for the whereabouts of her old friend Horatio. She'd heard through a current acquaintance that he occupied a vacant building in the vicinity, but "vacant" didn't exactly narrow the search. She hoped for more specific information.

The squeeze box player kept playing, a sort of vamp that laid a cover of sound over his words. He glanced around to be sure nobody could hear, though everyone in sight was eavesdropping as best they could. Suzanne slipped a silver penny into the tin cup he wore around his neck on a length of twine, and he told her an address in a close several streets over where Horatio might be found. It might have been a lie, but she politely thanked the man and directed her carriers to take her there in case it wasn't.

The place was of Tudor construction, so old and neglected it appeared as deserted as the Globe and in far greater need of repair. Against the protests of Thomas, Suzanne left the chair and asked her carriers to wait. She assured them if she needed them she would scream. Then she crossed the close and stepped through a ragged hole in the wall that had once been a window. Inside the dank, rotting place she found debris everywhere on the ground floor and a ceiling beam with one end lodged in the floor above and the other resting on the floor. She looked up at the hole in the ceiling, through to the room above, and somewhere on the first floor was a flicker of hearth or candlelight reflected from the brick walls. This appeared promising. She peered into the darkness around her and found a spiral stairs that might be sturdy enough to take her upward.

She lifted her skirts and picked her way across the treacherous floor to it.

Quietly as she could manage, she went up the steps, each one so worn at the center, the stone appeared to sag. The light from above flickered and danced, and her eyes adjusted to the dimness. At the top she paused to get her bearings and determine the source of the light.

A hearth and chimney stood in what was now the center of the room but may once have been a division between rooms where the wall had been knocked down, leaving crumbling brick blackened by centuries of cooking and heating. The hole in the floor she'd seen from below was just beyond it, and the wooden flooring on this side seemed sturdy enough. The stone fireplace slumped like a hunchback, and some of the smoke from its coals threaded its way into the room and up, following a slight draft out through a gap near an outer wall. The coals weren't bright enough to have made the flickering light, but a candle set on a rickety table to the side made the room jump with shadows. It all smelled of decay, scantily laced with the odor of burnt meat and stale beer.

A bed stood to the side, aslant to everything else, its curtains thick with dust though the bedclothes were relatively clean and recently used. Hung from hooks about the bed and from the beams above were a confusion of clothing and other odds and ends, which Suzanne recognized as costumes and properties for the stage. Frayed brocade and velvet in faded colors that had once been rich and bright hung aside yellows and grays meant to represent cloth of silver and gold. Everywhere hung wooden practice swords and daggers adorned with chunks of stained glass to represent jewels. Old feathers and decrepit furs shed bits here and there that floated in the air each time they were disturbed. A fairly new reed mat lay between the bed and the hearth, and on it stood a table and chair. On the table were a platter containing the remains of a roast poultry of some sort, a half-empty bottle of wine, a plate of food and wooden spoon, and a large pewter tankard.

Horatio sat in the chair next to the table, his dagger in his fist, peering across the room at the shadows where she stood. "Who goeth there?" He squinted as if he couldn't see very well.

"Horatio, 'tis I, Suzanne Thornton."

He squinted harder. "Suzanne? Gay Suzanne?" He laid his dagger on the table. "Little Suzanne? My lovely Suzanne?"

"Yes, my friend. How have you been these years past?"

Horatio rose from the chair. He was a few years older now, but without a wig he'd always had a smooth head free of hair, and to her he looked the same as he ever had. His large frame, broad at shoulder and thick about the middle but narrow at the waist and dwindling to spindly legs, towered over the table, and he hunched over to peer at Suzanne. "How now, my niece? How farest thee these past many years?" His voice was hesitant, as if he weren't entirely certain he wasn't hallucinating her.

"I've done well, Horatio."

"And thy son? Has Piers grown well?"

That he remembered Piers at all touched her. "He has, truly. He's a fine young man and about to launch into a venture I'm certain would interest you."

"Come!" Horatio fairly shouted, his actor's voice booming and echoing in the large and mostly empty space. He threw his arms wide and stepped aside to indicate she should sit in his only chair. "Come! Sit! Tell me of thine adventures out in the world!" Horatio had an odd habit of dropping in and out of archaic Elizabethan language, depending on his mood. Sometimes he quoted his favorite plays, other times he just peppered his speech with "thee" and "thou" because it amused him to mock the stuffy Puritans. He was a staunch Catholic and wore a crucifix under his shirt at all times, and didn't think highly of Protestantism in general.

He waited for Suzanne to step over some debris on the floor and take the offered chair, then he picked up his half-eaten plate, and after a couple of turns to see where to put it, he set it on the hearth. "Would you care for some meat? As you see, I've still half a hen untouched. And some wine. Would you care for some wine?"

She sat with her hands folded demurely on her lap. Horatio, in spite of his vocation and circumstance, and in spite of having known her as a prostitute, was something of a prude and appreciated a woman who was not overly casual in her demeanor. The insistence that all women function as either Madonna or whore seemed bred into all men, and she knew when and which to evoke. "Yes, Horatio. I'd love some."

The big man took another pewter tankard from a box containing several of them along with a number of wooden cups and wooden candlesticks that had been painted gray to appear pewter. All stage properties. Horatio blew into the tankard to clean it of dust, wiped it with his shirt, then poured some wine from the bottle on the table.

"So, Horatio, I'm curious how you escaped the Roundheads when last I saw you."

He laughed and handed her the tankard. She took a sip, but though the wine was palatable, she didn't care to throw it back too quickly. She liked to keep a clear head when out in the town, even with someone she trusted as she trusted Horatio. He said, a laugh in his voice as he recalled that day, "I was caught, dear Suzanne. The soldiers caught me and bound me in chains, but I never was incarcerated."

"No prison for you?"

He shook his head. "'Twas simple enough. I merely paid a fine on the spot, and was released on the promise that I would never, ever break the law again."

"Which, of course, you'd broken the law by paying the bribe."

Horatio shrugged. "One does what is necessary to get by. I had the means, and they had the key to my shackles. It was an equitable exchange, much as it went against the ideals of the Lord Protector, who was a usurper in any case and his ideals should never have carried the weight of law." He took a deep drink of his own tankard, and added, "I daresay Cromwell never knew of the bribe and was therefore never distressed by it."

She nodded. In general, those who made the laws never seemed to be the least aware of those expected to abide by them, and neither did the lawmakers ever seem to abide by those laws themselves. One might think Parliament was nothing more than a recreational pastime for rich men with nothing more interesting to do than argue with each other. "And what have you done with yourself since then? Did you reassemble your troupe?"

"I'm afraid I could not. I tried to find the scattered actors, and found a very few. Some had been arrested, some left town or, as thou didst, simply disappeared. Our stage was confiscated, and so was every costume and property, along with the wagon and horses. I hadn't the money to keep myself walking the streets every day, and even less to replace all we'd lost. I was forced to find other means of support."

"Honest work?"

"Some of it."

"Bravo, Horatio. That, at least, is something."

"I'm telling you, it was not easy. I carried a sedan chair for a time, but had little luck being paid at the end of the day by the owner of the chair. So I began keeping back a portion of my fares, until my employer noticed the shortage and sent me on my way. He shouldn't have taken exception. I only held back what was due me, making up for what I knew from experience would not be paid to me."

"And what then after the sedan chairs?"

"I sold meat pies. Of a morning I bought a boxful of them from the vendor just down there on the corner." He gestured with his tankard in the general direction of a shop Suzanne had seen on her way there. "But at the end of the day I always had at least half my pies left over. I ate them, of course, but that brought me little cash. I finally deduced that people prefer to buy their food from children and old women, and that a large, loud man such as myself is not considered a suitable source of meat pies." He shrugged. "So I needed to find something else for cash. Odd jobs, errands, digging holes or filling them in . . . I worked at whatever I could find that would pay me."

She looked around. "You still have many costumes and properties."

"These I've acquired recently. I hope to return to the stage."

"They must have cost a penny or two."

"The cost is unimportant. I need them, for what would I do, then, if I had an opportunity to play once more on the stage? I haven't in so very long, but it would be too, too sorrowful to know I could not have a troupe again. That hope has kept me alive since the day I was arrested."

"Well," she said, smiling, "I've come on business I think will please you."

He sat on the edge of the bed with his hands folded between his knees and attended her like a little boy awaiting instruction. "Do tell, then. What brings you to my humble establishment?" A rat ran across the room, then paused to sniff the plate on the hearth, but when Horatio stamped his foot at it, the creature scurried away to the shadows again.

"I wonder, Horatio, whether you can still perform."

"Of course I can." He made a broad, theatrical gesture. "*All the world's a stage*, you know."

"*And all the men and women merely players*, which is as close as Shakespeare ever came to allowing women on the stage, I expect."

That made Horatio chuckle. "You certainly proved yourself in that. No young boy could ever match you for veracity as a young maid."

"One would hope that I, being genuinely female, would have the advantage in that."

Another chuckle. "Devoutly to be wished."

"In any case, my good and true friend, I bring you an offer to not only act, but to do it in the Globe in Southwark."

Horatio's jaw dropped quite open. "The Globe? I'd thought it had been torn down."

"No, it stands even yet. If ever its destruction was ordered, the thing hasn't been done. And won't in the foreseeable future. I passed it coming here, in fact, and see that it is structurally sound in spite of nearly twenty years of neglect."

The smile on Horatio's face was wide though not particularly toothy. "*The Globe!* I acted there once, you know." Suzanne knew, for it was a story he told to anyone who would sit still for it. "'Twas as a lad, and I played Juliet's nurse for being so large." He gestured at his enormous frame, as if Suzanne might not have already noticed his size.

"I expect you were an excellent nurse."

"I was an excellent nurse!" Horatio boomed. He wasn't hearing her, for he had drifted off into his own memories. "How the audience howled with laughter for my antics!"

"'Tis a pity you were born so late, and never met the great bard."

Horatio sighed and gazed at the floor for the pity of it. "Indeed. I would so loved to have known him. To have seen him on the stage or in rehearsal, directing the players." He touched his right-hand fingertips together in the Continental manner to indicate just how sublime it would have been. "To have had his tutelage would have been the finest thing I could ever have dreamed of."

It was true that Horatio valued his craft more than he did the money he made from it. Suzanne prodded him a little more toward accepting her plan. "So, you would act on that stage once more?"

"Of course I would. No actor worth his skin would decline such an opportunity."

"And would you act there for me?"

Puzzlement crossed his face. "For thee? What have thee to do with the Globe?"

She drew a deep breath and plunged into her explanation. "Well, Piers has leased it and today has begun hiring workers to make repairs on it. Within the season it will be returned to its former glory and will be ready for a troupe to occupy it."

Horatio's expression reverted to one of gobsmacked astonishment. "You? You control the Globe? My little Suzanne?"

She nodded. "As much as anyone other than the king controls anything."

"And you wish for me to act on that stage?" He spoke with awe, as if he could hardly believe his luck.

"Not just perform. I wish for you to lead the troupe that will act on that stage. You are the finest man I know to do it. You know The Bard better than any man living, and I've seen you guide actors in their work. You can teach young actors, who have little experience and no tradition these past two decades, what it is to perform a role so that the audience believes and understands."

Horatio rose from the mattress and fell to his knees before her. He took up her hand and pressed his lips to it. He looked up into her face, his eyes filled with such joy she might have just told him she was St. Peter about to give him entry to heaven. "Bless you, my young friend! Bless you and your descendants unto seven generations!" He was orating now and gesturing to the heavens. "I shall accept with great happiness! Thank you!" He kissed her hand once more, then hugged her so hard she squeaked.

Then he leaned back to gaze at her. There was a long silence, in which neither of them quite knew what to say next. Finally, Horatio stood and said quite conversationally now that his theatrical fit was over, "How did you obtain permission from the king to perform serious drama?"

"The same way I acquired the money. Piers's father. And I confess there are some limitations to the patent."

Horatio crossed his arms, waiting for the bad news.

She continued with a blithe air, as if it were no matter, "Though we are allowed to play Shakespeare, and of course the commedia dell'arte, mummeries, and such, we will not be allowed to perform any of the new plays, or plays of any playwright other than Shakespeare."

"No Marlowe?"

"Nobody. Only Shakespeare."

He thought that over for a moment, then drew a deep,

thoughtful breath and declared in his clean, projecting baritone as if it were word from on high, "As Shakespeare was a finely honed dagger, Marlowe was a bludgeon, crude and unwieldy. All others were at least as clumsy, and ever beat the audience over the head with a story so that in the end they lay senseless." He gestured and raised his chin as if speaking to the third gallery. "Shakespeare's dialogue was poetry that came trippingly from the tongue. His words held flavor to be enjoyed well by an actor, and a sweetness for the listener's ear." He returned his focus to Suzanne and waved dismissal. "'Tis no loss to be disallowed Marlowe and his kind."

"And we cannot stray from the original text. We must perform the plays as written by Shakespeare."

Horatio narrowed his eyes at her. "Not even the prologues?"

She shook her head. "Especially the prologues. And we'll be kept to that. Any deviation from our patent will cause us to fall into bad odor with the king. His own troupe might be free to step out of bounds with satire, but we'll be held to a tighter standard. Charles will have no humor for those of us outside the royal troupes."

Horatio shrugged and waved away the issue. "No matter. 'Tis no burden to be true to Shakespeare's own words, for it would be an impossible task to improve upon them. What else?"

"We cannot perform any play within a week of when it is performed by the king's or the duke's players."

That made Horatio pale. "A week? How far in advance will we know what we can play?"

"I'm not sure yet. At least a week, maybe two. We have an advantage in that they use backdrops and set pieces, which will require construction. We'll be far more versatile and ready to change because our only staging burden will be costumes and properties. So long as we have a repertoire ready, we can adjust to accommodate the king and not conflict with the royal players."

"There are two royal troupes. They could monopolize as many as six plays a week."

"Yes. We'll need to be on our toes."

Horatio sighed, then threw up his arms. "No matter! It can be done, and we will do it well. Throngs will attend our plays, and we will be known all over England for our artful performances! France will hear of us, and weep for their inferiority!" He clapped his hands and rubbed them together in anticipation. "When do we begin?"

Suzanne, with Horatio committed to the venture and contributing to the artistic decisions, decided they would open with the history *Henry V.* Though the histories weren't the most popular of Shakespeare's works, beginning with one was a gesture of compliance with the patent and an effort to not steal thunder from the royal troupes. Every word would be as Charles would have it, and the play was less likely to upstage the royal companies than would a more popular comedy or tragedy.

It had more than forty roles to fill, and gathering talent for The New Globe Players was an enormous job, requiring several weeks to find enough experienced and talented actors to form the kernel of a troupe. Though droves of men and women from all over London came to audition, very few pleased Horatio. He sought actors from the old troupe, but could find only four who were still alive and at large. Seven others he would have liked to bring into the fold were reported to be incarcerated in Newgate, and the rest were dead or had disappeared long ago.

So by audition, one by one more players were accepted into The New Globe Players, and soon the hearth in the 'tiring room was surrounded of an evening by actors taking up residence in the Globe. Many lived there and slept on pallets on the floor, and were happy to have a place to sleep other than the street.

Suzanne vacated the house she lived in and moved her residence to the Globe, again to save money. Inside the 'tiring house structure to the rear of the stage were three stories of various rooms for readying the actors and for storage of costumes and properties. At one end of the 'tiring house, at the bottom of the stairwell that traversed all three stories, were tucked some nondescript rooms private enough that Piers had the restoration crew close them off, leaving a single entrance door near the stairwell.

There were five rooms, and they formed entirely adequate living quarters with windows to the east, which let in the morning light. One window in Sheila's kitchen, high over the pallet she slept on, looked out on the cellarage below the stage. If Suzanne stood in that room, she could hear rehearsals on the stage as clearly as someone waiting under a trapdoor to make an entrance. It proved handy for the sake of keeping track of happenings on the stage without the disrupting presence of herself or Piers. Suzanne found the rooms cozy enough for comfort and roomy enough for her belongings, and the interior access gave Suzanne a sense of safety she'd never known before in her life. In fact, it felt odd to know that she was in control of her fate, no longer at the mercy of a man who may or may not have her best interests at heart. Also, there was the relief from paying the rent on that dreary house where William had placed her. Her outlook brightened every day that she awoke in the theatre to the sound of workmen restoring it. Soon she associated the sound of hammering and the smell of sawdust with hope and freedom.

In that spirit of coming into her own, she sometimes wore men's clothing, partly for comfort but also for the sake of blending in with the men and boys who surrounded her. She relished being able to climb stairs or step over obstacles of lumber and tools without having to grab her skirts and have them snag on the debris regardless. In breeches she could even climb ladders without fear of tangling her feet in her under-skirts. Nobody minded her costume, and without skirts and a woman's neckline she did not distract the workmen from their work. She was no longer on the market as a potential wife or mistress, so nobody cared whether she looked like one.

While workers hammered away at construction, Horatio auditioned actors. Aside from the forty roles in *Henry V*, he also needed to consider plays they would perform in the future. Versatility was key. Though some actors could be cast in multiple roles, and Suzanne encouraged it, too much of that generally brought laughter from the audience when a single face appeared too obviously too often. The most treasured actor was one who could change his voice and demeanor to disappear into several roles in one play without eliciting snick-ers or hoots from the pit.

Horatio needed acrobats and clowns in addition to charac-ters, for part of their repertoire would be the medieval *com-media* and mummeries, which were very broad physical performance and tumbling, involving slap sticks, comedic costume, and face paint. When an already formed troupe of old-style mummers came to them and asked to play, Horatio chortled and raised his voice in praise at his excellent luck. Immediately he began planning out what they would perform throughout the opening week.

Some of the would-be performers were women, having heard the king was now allowing genuine females to perform onstage. All were of the very lowest classes, which annoyed Horatio, who understood that such folk were not competent to portray most of the characters Shakespeare wrote. An actress raised on the street who had never met a gentlewoman could hardly be expected to mimic the behavior of Lady Macbeth, Desdemona, Ophelia, or Juliet Capulet. So Horatio was forced to reject the most eager, starving applicants and seek those who might have connections and not need him so much.

A true gentlewoman, of course, would never do such a thing as perform in public; these days even some women of the lesser classes had acquired sensibilities delicate enough to wear vizards that hid their faces whenever outside their homes. None of the girls who auditioned were above the age of twenty-five; even the most base whores and thieves were only there because they thought acting must be better than prostitution and robbery. A sea of humanity flowed to the Globe, but the pool from which Horatio drew was quite small.

All the hopefuls, male and female, gathered at noon outside the theatre doors and waited for summons to enter. Some were patient and silent, respectful of this rare opportunity. Some were not at all, drinking and gossiping as they lounged about the doors. Some missed their audition for being too drunk by the time they were called, and these were left lying in the street where they had collapsed.

Suzanne enjoyed listening to the auditions from high in one of the galleries. Often she sat on a folding chair and leaned her chin on her arms resting on the banister in front. One afternoon while observing Horatio in his talent search, she noticed a young girl loitering in the pit, waiting among the boys and men who had just been called from outside. When she saw Horatio gesture the girl to the stage, Suzanne settled into her seat for some amusement.

Horatio stood in the pit at the edge of the stage, surrounded
by ends of sawn beams, boards, and bent nails, and waited for
the girl to respond, but she was chatting with one of the workers and not paying attention. Finally he called out, "You!
Child!"

The worker hurried off, lest he be chastised for slacking
from his job. The girl came to attention, her hands behind her
back, a picture of innocence that spoke volumes of guilt.

Horatio once again gestured for her to ascend to the stage.
She picked up her skirts, hurried up the steps, and picked her
way across the rickety boards to a relatively sturdy spot, then
turned to face Horatio with a wide grin and her skirts still in
her fists, exposing her ankles for all to see. The boys in the pit
saw all they could as they ducked their heads to peer up her
skirts at her bare calves. She appeared oblivious, though
Suzanne knew she probably was not. "I'm Liza, yer honor." Her
accent was crude and northern, and barely understandable
even to Suzanne.

He said, far more serious than she, "Very well, then, Liza.
Have you read the play?"

"Ah cannae read, yer woorship."

"My name is Horatio, girl. Address me by that, if you
please."

Some of her smile faded, but she carried on gamely. "Aye,
then. Soorry ta 'ffend ye." The girl's tone was impertinent,
which made Suzanne sigh. This one already wasn't going to
be accepted, she could tell.

But Horatio continued, slipping into his annoyed taste-of-sar-
casm quasi-Puritan speech, complete with rolling R's, "Well. If
thee cannot *rrread*, then how will thee learn thy lines?"

"Ah 'spect I'll have ta ask ye to read 'em ta me."

He emitted a bark of a laugh. "Not bloody likely, I'd say. Doest thou have someone else who might read them to thee?"

"Oh aye, I've a client who would be ever so pleased to help."

"A client?"

"Aye. He's right regular, comes every fortnight sure as anything. He'll do nearly whatever I ask. He can read me the lines, and I'll remember 'em, sure enough."

Suzanne groaned to herself. Horatio gazed blandly at the girl for a long moment. The girl sensed that things weren't going well, so she held her skirts tighter and higher, and said, "Read me some o' what ye got. A long passage. Ye'll see I can remember."

Horatio hesitated, but the girl urged him on with a nod. So he recited to her a random passage from memory. "From *Henry V*, we have a speech by the Bishop of Canterbury speaking to King Henry, which readeth thusly: *Then hear me, gracious sovereign, and you peers, that owe yourselves, your lives and services to this imperial throne. There is no bar to make against your highness's claim to France but this, which they produce from Pharamond. 'In terrain Salicam mulieres ne succedant:' 'No woman shall succeed in Salique land:' Which Salique land the French unjustly glose to be the realm of France, and Pharamond the founder of this law and female bar.* Now say that back to me, girl."

She dropped her skirts and crossed her arms. "That innae long. Ah c'n say that back standin' on me heed."

"Then by all means, do so. I am *rrrapt* with anticipation."

The girl threw back her head and obliged. Every word and syllable, even the Latin, exactly as Horatio had pronounced it.

When she finished, there was dead silence in the theatre, for even the workmen listening were stunned. All sawing and hammering had stopped. Even Suzanne was wide-eyed with wonder at the feat, but at the same time wondered whether the girl understood any of the words she'd spoken.

Horatio opened his mouth to speak, but the girl said in a rush, "What I cannae ken, ye see, is hae come, since this bishop feller must be a-talkin' to King Henry about France and all, I mean, he's a-tellin' Henry why the French willnae give him his inheeritance, how come he says all these things auld Henry must a'ready ken, being king and all, and being the one as didnae get his inheritance in the first place he must ken why. So, what I mean is, who ever goes around a-tellin' folks things they a'ready ken?"

Horatio recovered from his shock and replied, "Well, girl, you see, Canterbury knows that Henry already knows these things. He's saying them because he's trying to talk Henry into invading France. So he's not informing, he's *reminding*. Also, he's pointing out that the French king and his cohorts are liars and hypocrites, and have unjustly stolen land that should belong to England."

"Ah."

"Besides, if he didn't say these things, the audience would be in the dark about the history, and history is what the play is about."

Again the girl said, "Ah."

"What's your name, girl?"

"Liza, as I said earlier."

"Yes, you did. You know the play."

She shook her head. "As I said, yer grace, ah cannae read. Nae a word, if it please ye." She dropped a quick, bouncy curtsey for good measure.

"You have remarkable comprehension of the scene from just one speech."

She nodded. "Ah'm good wi' folks, yer honor, sir. I ken things that often leave others a-scratching their heeds."

Horatio absorbed that for a moment, then said, "If you would go have a seat over there in the gallery, I'll talk to you again soon."

The girl grinned, lifted her skirts again, and obliged, happily flouncing off the stage in a flurry of skirts and barely contained bosom.

Horatio, the boys in the pit, all the workmen, and Suzanne watched her plop down on a pile of lumber, and for a long moment there was silence. Then Horatio turned his attention to the waiting hopefuls standing in the pit, selected one for the next audition, and the workers went back to their hammering and sawing.

Chapter Nine

D aniel stayed away from the theatre during this time, and
that annoyed Suzanne. It had stood to reason he should
come to the theatre, and part of her had assumed it would be
often. That he didn't was a surprise and disappointment.

Then it annoyed her that she was annoyed, because she
hadn't thought she'd wanted to see him. Yet another part of
her knew it was foolish to think he would loiter about the
theatre for the sake of financial interest. Surely that hadn't
been her reason for going to him for money. She told herself
this more than once, all the while glancing out over the stage,
past the pit, and to the large entrance doors in hopes of seeing
Daniel's carriage in the street. Surely her only reason for
involving him was that he was the only man she knew with
real money he might be willing to give her. Naturally he had
been the one to ask. Wanting to see him had nothing to do
with any of it. Did it?

Particularly after the way he'd treated her that night last summer.

But when all was said and done, it still annoyed her that he didn't come. All those years he'd been away with Charles, she'd never thought of his wife as a rival for his attention, because he had been in France, not with Anne. His wife never entered into the picture, and Suzanne could imagine him pining for his mistress. After all, who could ever long for a wife selected by one's parents? Suzanne thought it impossible to love a spouse one had not chosen, and so assumed that if Daniel's heart yearned it must yearn for herself. Surely it must.

But now that he was living with Anne in the new house he'd had built in Pall Mall, Suzanne began to wonder why she heard from him so rarely, and then only when there was business regarding the theatre and only by messenger. She was the liaison between him and Piers, and so passed messages back and forth. For some reason she couldn't fathom, Daniel was reluctant to deal directly with Piers, and so she took care of some business details that might have been handled by her son. It suited her, for she was not shy about telling people what to do and what she wanted to happen, but soon she wished Daniel would address her about something other than business. Eventually she wondered why he didn't, and then found herself annoyed.

One day in spring, when the weather had warmed nicely, on a whim she hired Samuel and Thomas to carry her across the river and around toward Whitehall. She had no thought of what she would do once she got there, but like so many things in her life it was an impulse she couldn't resist. She went to the palace just for a look, as if to see whether any of it had changed since her last visit, or whether there was anyone about she might want to espy. Such as Anne. It annoyed her that Anne might be there, where she herself was not welcome, and in a moment of honesty she admitted to herself she was going there to spy on Daniel.

The trip was not a short one, and it was past noon when she was set down in the street across from the palace entrance. Traffic through the gate was lively today. Carriages made their hoof-clopping way in and out, while pedestrians wended between them, some occasionally hurrying or sidling to avoid being run over. The guards kept a sharp lookout, but Suzanne knew they couldn't eye everyone who came through, especially the passengers in vehicles. As Suzanne had come to realize during her last visit, the king depended on guards closer in than the gate, and his personal bodyguard, to protect his person. The closer one came to the king, the more likely one was to have a pike thrust into one's face.

As she watched, the entire guard came alert as one and busied themselves clearing the entrance. Suddenly nobody was allowed in or out of the gate, and those approaching it found themselves barred by pikes held parallel to the ground, like a human fence. Suzanne came alert herself, sat up in the sedan chair, and peered at the palace gate to see who was coming out. For several minutes nothing happened. Everyone near the gate leaned in as far as they were allowed and stared into the palace. There was nothing for Suzanne to see, though it was apparent something was expected by those near the gate.

Finally some people began to emerge at a stroll. Those standing near the entrance gawked.

At the front was the king, tall, leggy, and aglitter with silk and jewels. He was too far off for Suzanne to see details, but every so often the sun would glint from a bit of his costume. A small entourage accompanied him, nearly as rich and fashionable, shining in the sun and bouncing with feathers. Two women and several men walked within speaking distance of him. A small cluster of men came behind at a slight distance, not entirely on their own, but neither were they part of the king's immediate circle. Each company was more or less surrounded by a sprinkling of guards armed with swords and pikes, and near the king walked two wielding arquebuses. The guns, held at ready, glinted in the sun as if they were part of the king's jewelry.

Charles and his courtiers headed for St. James's Park, directly across from the palace. The park had recently been opened to the public, and everyone knew the king enjoyed a stroll through it now and then. Today Suzanne could see that when the king went on an outing, nearly half the palace tagged along. So did some of the gawkers at the gate follow at a distance. Charles seemed to be enjoying himself, chatting with the woman at his elbow, a wide smile visible even from where Suzanne sat.

Then she caught sight of Daniel, strolling amid some friends in the cluster that followed the king. He laughed at something and touched a hand to his hat as a breeze came up and made the wide brim flap and feathers wave.

To Thomas and Samuel, Suzanne said in a hurry, "Here, have your pay now, you're dismissed." She slipped from the sedan chair and handed Thomas enough coins to cover the one-way trip. "If you find another fare before I return, I'll make my way home some other way." Perhaps she might talk Daniel into taking her home in his carriage.

The men didn't appear happy she was leaving them, but Thomas bowed to her without comment. Samuel acknowledged her with a nod. They would probably still be there if she returned, for folks in this part of the city wanting to cross to Southwark were few, and those who did had carriages. The men would stay long to have her fare for that trip.

They slipped from her mind as she drew her cloak around her and hurried to reach Daniel before he entered the park. He was absorbed in a joke being told by one of his companions, and didn't see her approach.

"Gracious good afternoon, my lord," said Suzanne.

All three men turned to see who was addressing them. A guard with a pike stepped in to bar her, but Daniel held out a hand for the man to stand down, that she was with him. His friends relaxed when they saw she was a stranger, a commoner, and nothing to concern either of them. Daniel gave her a small, conditional smile. "Good afternoon, Mistress Thornton. How are you today?"

His formal tone was like a pinprick to her heart, but she reminded herself that they were not in Southwark today. Regardless of who she was to him in private, or had been in the past, out in the sunshine and fresh breezes she was nothing more than a reformed whore and the mother of a business associate. Notwithstanding the new freedoms offered by the king, in its own way the moral climate of the restored monarchy was as hypocritical as that under Oliver Cromwell.

She replied, "I'm quite well, thank you, my lord. I wonder if I might walk with you a distance today. It's such a fine afternoon, one can hardly resist a stroll in the park." She turned her face to the sky, and it was very nice to feel the warmth of the sun on it.

"I think I might enjoy that, Mistress Thornton." He addressed his companions. "If you both will excuse us, gentlemen."

The two nodded their acquiescence, and Daniel and

Suzanne fell away and to the side of those accompanying the king, while following the same general path.

Daniel's mouth was a hard line when he turned back to Suzanne, but his words were mild and he offered her his arm. She laid a hand on it, lightly. He said, "You really ought not to come here, Suzanne."

"I embarrass you?"

"Not today, but what if Anne were here? She does sometimes come to the palace, if not to see me specifically, then to visit with her brother."

"She can see her brother anytime. She doesn't need to come to the palace."

"She likes to socialize with others of her rank. At home are only servants, and no family or friends to keep her company. No children. I can hardly blame her for wanting to spend time here of an afternoon. Very often, she does."

"But she doesn't happen to be here today. Aren't you the fortunate one."

Daniel gave her another thin-lipped look, then said, "What might I do for you today? Is there anything wrong at the theatre that couldn't have been brought to my attention by messenger?"

His tone stung once more, but she pretended it didn't, and kept her own voice light. "I was wondering when you would come to the theatre and see what your money has bought you."

He grunted and gazed out across the park lawn as if enjoying the view, though she could sense he was enjoying nothing about this stroll. "I'll be along soon enough. Meanwhile, I trust you to make certain nothing goes awry. You've always been skilled at getting what you want; you don't need me to meddle in your affairs."

Suzanne didn't quite know how to take that. She was quite certain she rarely got what she wanted, and wondered why Daniel thought otherwise. Further, she wondered why he sounded as if he thought success a character flaw. Succeeding in getting what one wanted was a skill she valued, and envied in those who were more wealthy and charismatic than she. Why should one ever want to be the sort who failed to get what one wanted? How was that more virtuous than success? She sighed and decided she was eager to see the park and was quite enjoying the walk, and never mind what Daniel thought about anything.

She allowed an excited smile to lift the corners of her mouth, and she began looking around, trying to see everything at once, like a squirrel in search of danger. The place was beautiful; she'd never seen such orderly nature. Smooth, mowed grass, perfectly trimmed trees and shrubs in shapes nature never imagined. Even the birds seemed to behave as if they'd been born to the nobility and taught manners from an early age. They sang with a music never heard in other parts of the city, where gulls and rats climbed over one for food and warmth, and crows leapt upon dead and dying people and animals for their dinner. It struck Suzanne how odd it was that this park, landscaped as it was in the French fashion, was nature made far more orderly than the jumbled, reworked, rotting, catch-as-catch-can man-made squalor that made up the rest of London. While the city built by men leaned against itself every which way and had been constructed according to whim for a millennium and a half, this sanctuary of the natural world, with its birds, grasses, shrubs, and trees, was as disciplined and organized as a Calvinist pastor's study.

Movement among the trees and shrubbery caught her attention. There cavorted men and women who thought themselves unobserved, or else didn't care that they were observed. Suzanne had a glimpse of one couple as they casually disappeared into a thicket, their shaded movements still visible from the lawn. For a moment she watched them fumble at each other until she was bored with it and she found something else to look at.

She saw peeking from another part of that same thicket a face she recognized, but couldn't quite place it for a few seconds. It was only a wide-eyed face she saw, framed with leaves and shadowed by trees. Then she realized who it was, and still didn't truly believe she saw correctly. William Wainwright peered out from between two low trees, watching the king and his escort stroll across the lawn. He crouched like a stalking cat, staring hard at Charles. Like the brazen lovers, he thought himself unobserved, so she had a good look at him. It was he, for a certainty. Though he appeared unusually pale, his lowered brow and pressed lips expressed his habitual anger. His gaze followed the king for a space, then he ducked back into the bushes and that was the last she saw of him, even when Charles drew much nearer to the thicket before veering off in his wandering.

Why hadn't William gone to France? Had he even intended to go as he'd said? She wished he had, and she tensed to realize he was still lurking about London. Her mind tumbled with questions, until she realized Daniel was talking to her and she'd not heard a word.

"I'm sorry, my lord. What did you say?"

He went silent for a moment, then said darkly, "How far back need I go?"

"Tell it all to me in short."

He sighed. "In short, I do wish you would refrain from coming to the palace. If you must see me, send a message and let me come to you. And please make certain the message is delivered discreetly."

"Whatever for? Puritan rule is over; there's no need to pretend you have no mistresses."

"Anymore, I don't have any mistresses."

"I no longer count?"

"We are no longer sleeping together."

"Thank you for letting me know. After last summer, I wasn't entirely certain."

He gave her a puzzled look, blinking and squinting. "I found you whoring at the Goat and Boar. I thought you were looking to earn some money. I know you needed it. I thought I was doing you a favor."

Shame reddened her cheeks. She wanted to walk away from him, leave the park, and never speak to him again. Instead she drew a deep breath and told him what she thought. "I was visiting with friends. When you invited me to sit with you, I thought you were trying to rekindle feelings."

There was a long silence as they strolled. Suzanne could hardly breathe, waiting for what he would say next. Finally he cleared his throat and said, "I don't dare."

She also had to cough to make her voice work. "I disagree. We're both adults. We've both matured these past years. I believe we could be together and be quite reasonable about it."

"Of course we could. And it might be nice. But it would also be unwise."

"In what way? Surely the king wouldn't judge you for it."

"Of course he would not. He's entirely reasonable about such things, and could hardly be anything but. Others, however, would judge me, and harshly."

"I doubt there's a man in London who hasn't his hand up the skirts of several of his friends' wives. Or isn't buggering the friends themselves. And nobody seems to care who knows who's banging whom. Such as those over there." She pointed with her chin toward the thicket where the couple she'd seen before was now emerging, straightening their clothing, and appearing inordinately pleased with themselves as they glanced around to see who had observed them. "Plainly those two haven't the least worry about who saw them groping at each other in the bushes."

"Ha! Those two are the worst kept secret in London. They would most likely strip naked on the lawn in broad daylight if they wouldn't be chastised for stealing everyone's attention from Charles and his growing brood. Less a mortal sin of adultery, and more a case of poor sportsmanship."

Suzanne chuckled, and leaned in close as if in conspiracy. "Naked on the lawn; there's an image to dwell on. That fellow's belly nearly touches his knees, and she's so tiny she can barely get her arms about his waist. Her size rather suggests his, don't you think?"

Daniel laughed. "So you see, though others may indulge in unseemly French behavior, I am far better off being more decorous."

"And how did you behave when you were in France? Just how French did you become?"

He sighed and shrugged, still smiling, but somewhat ruefully now. "I did make two daughters. I can't say I behaved particularly well."

"And now that you're once again by my side you've a sudden fit of conscience and will only be with me if you think it a charitable gift?"

"I've a sudden need to please my wife."

"She's being a bit unreasonable, I think. To expect you to behave differently from other men."

"Differently from other men whose fortunes are more secure than mine. Or who don't care much how their fortunes rise or fall." There was an edge to his voice now, but Suzanne ignored it and carried on the banter.

"I think you should—"

Daniel stopped walking and held her arm tightly so his fingers dug into her flesh. His voice had more than an edge of anger now. "Listen to me, Suzanne. You will do what I say, and never come to the palace again uninvited. Do you hear me?"

She pulled away and rubbed her arm, which was sure to bruise by tomorrow. Alarmed, she examined his face, hoping for humor but finding none. Coming here had been a mistake, that was plain. She said, "Yes, your *lordship*. I do hear you. Now, if you'll excuse me, I have a chair waiting to return me to my place." Without another word, she left him standing on the park lawn and returned to the palace gate with all the scant dignity left to her.

There she found Samuel and Thomas, still loitering by the palace gatehouse, hoping for a fare to take them in the direction of Southwark. They were quite pleased to see Suzanne, and gestured her into their chair most kindly and with wide smiles. Then they saw her flushed cheeks and lips pressed together as she stepped into the chair, and shadows fell over their faces. Samuel and Thomas said nothing, though they plainly wanted to ask what could be the matter. She sat back in her accustomed seat, ready to sulk all the way back to the theatre.

But a whim overtook her for the second time that day. After Daniel's behavior in the park, Suzanne wanted to see Anne Stockton, the woman who loomed so large in Daniel's life, whom Suzanne had never seen. The urge was suddenly all she could think about. She would lay eyes on Daniel's wife. Why, she couldn't say. But at that moment nothing would do but to catch sight of the woman who was privileged to spend her evenings and nights with Daniel, and who would prevent him from coming to the theatre to meet his son.

"Samuel. Thomas. Be so good as to take me around to the Pall Mall, would you?"

Thomas readily acknowledged the request, and the chair changed direction.

Pall Mall was a street near St. James's Palace, where the ruling class liked to amuse themselves with a game of that name. The place was open, almost parklike, and though there were yet few homes there, it was getting to be a place for the returning nobility to build new London residences. Daniel couldn't have chosen a more advantageous neighborhood to install his wife, which probably well suited the woman and her brother the duke. This was Suzanne's first sight of the area, for she'd never had occasion to come this way before. There had been little enough here during the interregnum, and never anything to interest her. Until now.

Daniel's house was not terribly far from the palace, amid a small clump of new houses, each one more beautiful than the last, each struggling to steal attention from the others. Though dwarfed by the palace itself, to Suzanne they were enormous. Her father's house, which she'd come to remember as astonishing luxury, was a hovel compared to these magnificent structures. And there was Daniel's house, which she recognized by his carriage standing out front, waiting to carry away someone from inside. The house was built of fresh-cut stone, spotless iron, and gleaming wood, all new and sparkling clean, free of vines or moss. The landscaping around it was still unsure of itself, its newly planted trees all saplings surrounded by fresh-dug earth and a lawn of barely sprouted grass. All around was fresh earth that showed little more than promise.

Samuel and Thomas set the chair down a distance from the house and across the street, and slipped their yokes to await further instruction. Suzanne sat still in the shadows of her seat and gazed across at the house. It was where Daniel lived. He'd built it for the woman who shared his life, and with no thought at all about herself or Piers. It had nothing to do with them, and was a world they could never inhabit.

A shadow passed behind the curtain of one window, then was gone. Had that been Anne? A maid? Anne wasn't with Daniel today, probably not even at Whitehall at all or Daniel would have mentioned it, so perhaps it was she. Although, Daniel had said Anne sometimes went to the palace to see other people, so perhaps this was a maid.

The carriage at the front of Daniel's house was surely there to take someone somewhere. Suzanne sat forward in her seat to see who might come out. Certainly not a maid. She couldn't imagine Daniel sending his carriage for a maid. Surely it was there for the use of the lady of the house.

A woman emerged. Suzanne's heart clenched, for she knew it must be the countess. The dress this woman wore was elegant and rich. It was the costume of a woman who had been born to enormous wealth and knew how to spend it and how to carry it. Someone who was secure in the knowledge there would always be silk and pearls to wear, rich and tasty delicacies to eat, and a thick feather mattress covered in fine, clean linen to sleep in every night. Her posture as she strode from her house was rod-straight and her gait smooth and graceful— the sort of natural grace Suzanne herself had struggled for all her life and never quite achieved. Her face was of radiant beauty, not merely "handsome," though she was the same age as Suzanne. Her hair, which peeked from under a fashionable hat adorned with white feathers, shone a bright red-gold. Suzanne had heard there was Tudor blood in her lineage, and now she believed it could be true. She imagined Queen Elizabeth must have looked very much like Anne did today.

Suzanne caught only a glimpse of her as she made her way to the carriage and the footman helped her up into it, then the driver cracked his whip over the horses and they drew the vehicle and its passenger off down the street, leaving Suzanne to stare after it with the bottom fallen out of her heart. She shored it up by reminding herself that she had something Anne never would. She had Piers.

She sat back in her seat and ordered Samuel and Thomas back to Southwark.

Not long after spotting William in the park, Suzanne had a visitor she had thought never to see again and certainly didn't care to see. That day she'd dismissed Sheila for the evening and was readied for bed in her bronze-colored brocade robe. She'd finished her nightly regime and had brought out the pen and ink to work on her writings at the desk in an alcove of her bedchamber. Some bits of diary, some snatches of poem, and among it came some ideas for drama. When or whether any of it might be useful was yet to be seen, but a kernel of a dream was forming in the back of her mind. It pleased her to think she might one day show her scribblings to someone and that they might be well received. In any case, she enjoyed the stories she invented and it was pleasant entertainment of an evening when the troupers were out at pubs and the theatre was quiet and dark.

Tonight the workmen had gone at sunset, but a few of the performers had spent the early evening in rehearsal, using whatever spaces they could find that were serviceable. Any clearing on a floor would do, for scenery was always evoked by the words and actions, created in the imagination of the audience by the actors' voices and bodies. Any given scene took up little space, so it wasn't necessary to occupy an entire stage just to rehearse. The small group was just then winding down, about to end their day. The rest had retired to their pallets while others went to their homes or wended through the few streets and closes to the Goat and Boar for some food, drink, and recreation.

It had been a long, frenetic day, but Suzanne was pleased with how well the work was coming. Piers seemed to thrive in his new occupation as master of the theatre, and it made her proud that the workers listened to him and followed his orders. Her quill paused, hovering over the page, as she thought how wonderful it was to watch him direct the work. So much like his father, and how unfortunate was it that Daniel didn't seem to have any interest in him. Never mind that he didn't care for her anymore, he should have some regard for his son.

"Suzanne."

She jerked alert and turned, but saw no one. The hair at the back of her neck prickled, for she thought she'd heard William. It was William's voice that had said her name, but that was impossible. How could he have gotten in here? And why hadn't he gone to France as he'd said he would? She whispered, hoping she hadn't really heard anything, "William?"

He stepped out from behind some gowns hung from the side of the armoire. Suzanne pressed a hand to her chest and gasped, for close up she could see his appearance was as shocking as his presence. In the past year he'd lost weight and looked quite ill, even like a scarecrow, with hollowed eye sockets, prominent cheekbones, and shoulders that seemed to poke out from his shirt. His eyes were rimmed in red, and his skin was as pale as paper. A wig sat awkwardly on his head, askew and unkempt. Random bits of straw clung to it, as if he'd been sleeping in a barn and hadn't even attempted to neaten himself. "Help me," he said with trembling lips. Then she saw he held a dagger in his fist.

She only gaped at him. Help? Why hadn't he fled England? She was almost impatient with him for his unreliability, which was so like him. Why wasn't he with his wife in France? But she didn't say these things out loud because anything she might have said would have been angry and pointless. Also, he looked like he might hurt her if she said the wrong thing.

"Suzanne . . ." He could see she wasn't happy to see him, and now whined at her. She'd once rejected Stephen Farthingworth for being weak, and the irony of ending up with this wheedling infant was not lost on her.

"William, why are you here?" She turned on her stool and laid a hand on her dressing table, struggling for some grace when she would have liked to throw something hard and heavy at him.

"They pursue me," he replied. His eyes darted this way and that, apparently searching the room for those who pursued him, whoever "they" might be.

"Who, William? What is the matter?"

He licked his lips, which were dry and cracked, nearly white for being so chapped. He wore only a shirt and breeches that were filthy, no leggings so that the hair on his unshaved legs appeared as dark patches on paleness, and his shoes had seen better days long before this one. They in addition to his wig appeared to have spent some nights in a barn, and Suzanne caught a whiff of horse manure. He said in a whisper, "They want me in the Tower. They will have me if I'm not cautious."

"Who do you mean? What on God's earth has happened to you?"

"They wouldn't allow me out of the country. I was prevented from going to France. They've taken my wife. She's gone."

"Gone where?"

His face screwed up as if to weep, but then he opened his eyes and took a deep breath. "I know not. I only know that she is gone."

"And who took her?"

"The king's men."

"How do you know this?"

"She's in the Tower. They've put her in the Tower."

"*How do you know?* Has someone told you she's been arrested?" Suzanne couldn't imagine William's shy, mousy wife holding enough interest for the crown that she would be placed under arrest in the Tower of London. Newgate, perhaps, if she owed money or had murdered someone. But never the Tower. She just wasn't important enough, and neither was William.

"They've got her, I know it. They want me, but they'll torture her in my stead." He clouded up to weep again, but overcame it. Again. He had always been awfully good at working up the tears.

"But why, William?"

"Because of my religion, of course! You must know it!" His fists clenched and he spoke through gritted teeth, in frustration that she wasn't understanding what to him was patently obvious.

She stifled a sigh. "That's absurd. Nobody wants to put

your wife in the Tower for your religion, least of all the crown. There are far too many Puritans in Parliament for that sort of nonsense, and if Charles were to persecute the religion, he would surely start with them. William, what have you been doing all these months? Why aren't you in France?"

"France?" He shook his head. "My wife wouldn't go. She denied the danger. She laughed when I said we needed to leave before the king began taking retribution for his exile. Poor naïve woman, she wouldn't come with me. And now it's too late! Oh alas, it's too late! They've taken her, and it's far too late!" Now he began to weep in earnest, hugging himself and retreating behind the hanging gowns once more. "Oh woe!"

She rose in an impulse to go to him, as once she might have when she'd owed him such comfort for their arrangement, but stopped herself. She was no longer his mistress. He'd abandoned her a year ago, leaving her to fend for herself in a new regime. She owed him nothing. But she took a soft tone with him, hoping he would calm down and go away. "William, you can't be sure your wife is in the Tower. In fact, I'm certain she's not."

"She is! They've locked her away from me, so they might capture me when I enquire about her!"

"You haven't asked anyone?"

"How can I? They would pounce upon me in an instant were I to show my face!"

"Whatever for? What have you done to incur his majesty's wrath?" From what she knew of Charles's character, it seemed terribly unlikely that William might do or say anything to annoy the king. Or even to attract his attention.

William's agitation grew so that he gasped as he spoke. "You know what I've done! You were with me the entire time! You know how guilty I am!"

Suzanne was aware of how easily guilt came to people like William. Their relationship had been riddled with it, and perhaps even depended on it, given some of his odd preferences in the bedchamber. Even as a base prostitute she'd had few clients who'd enjoyed "correction" as much as he had. "Guilty of what, William? What is it you think you've done?" Suddenly she wanted to smack his face and shove him out the door. But getting him out of her quarters would only put him in another part of the theatre, leaving him to do what he would in the 'tiring house. She thought of screaming for help, but was afraid of what William might do if she screamed. So she talked to him calmly, as if he were a growling dog or a fractious horse. "Tell me, William. What do you think you did?"

In his frustration at her lack of comprehension, William clenched his fists before him. "I did business with Cromwell! You know it's true!"

"Indeed. It's true of most of London. Hardly a man walking about in the streets is innocent of that charge."

"Then you understand!"

She felt as if she grasped nothing. "Understand what, William?"

"'Tis but a matter of time before they will herd us all together and hang us all!" He waved the dagger as if it were a brush, painting his words onto an invisible wall before him.

Suzanne sat on her stool again and gathered her composure. She eyed the dagger, though she was certain he didn't intend to hurt her with it. "Nonsense, William. The king and all his men have far more important people to behead, and he would have to work his way through most of London before arriving at you. And I think he might even be done with all that by now. Or at the very least he's dealt with all the serious offenders and is just finishing the last of the minor ones. You've nothing to fear, I assure you."

William brought himself up, insulted. "I do. I have much to fear. I was an important man in the Lord Protector's government."

Suzanne then finally grasped William's need to be persecuted. He couldn't bear to have been so unimportant to Cromwell that the king could let him live. "Ah, I see." She then saw an avenue to bring him back from this insanity, or at least convince him to leave the theatre in peace, by playing into his delusion. She could give him an address and tell him there were people there who would be willing to smuggle him out of England. He would believe that, and see it as refuge.

But William said, "Ah, you see! It's time you saw something, you ignorant slut!"

A sudden, perverse anger came over her. His inflated sense of self-importance and entitlement was what had caused him to abandon her. Something snapped in her at the thought of what he'd put her through because he could consider only himself in all things, and she just couldn't feed his arrogance anymore. Or any man's arrogance. No more could she simply smile and nod and hope things would work out for the best.

She took a deep breath and said in a low, angry tone, "But, William, you weren't important at all. You were a small influence and hardly noticed by Cromwell, let alone King Charles. Don't overestimate yourself. You were always good at that, thinking you are better than you actually are."

William gaped at her, shocked that she could think such a thing, and saying it was unimaginable rudeness.

"Yes, William, you always were a small, unimportant man. You left me without a farthing of support, convinced that the king would want your head for your involvement with the

Protectorate. And now you just can't face that you aren't important enough to kill. Not worth the hangman's fee, or even an old rope. I expect your wife has run off as well. Perhaps she's gone to France without you. Or she's gone to the country. Has she a relative to stay with? Have you enquired there? Or did you even think of that?"

His mouth opened and closed like a fish, his eyes agog.

"Nothing to say, William?"

"My . . . wife . . ."

"Go to France, William. Leave London, there's nothing here for you. Get out of England. You'll be safe, and you can find another woman to annoy. There are plenty of whores in Paris; you should be able to find one desperate enough for money to put up with you." She stood and went to shove him. "Go. Now." She shoved him again, then grabbed his dagger from him and threw it to the floor.

"You lay hands on me!" He made no attempt to recover his knife but took a step backward, startled.

"You've laid hands on me often enough, I suppose it's my turn. Now go!" She shoved him again, toward the door. "Get out before I scream and my son comes running. You've far more to fear from him than you do from Charles, I promise." Another shove, and William began to retreat toward the door.

"I came for help, and this is how you treat me." His voice faltered, for this was a development he hadn't anticipated.

"I've no help for you, William. Go to France if you're afraid of the king. Show yourself here again, and I'll make certain Charles knows exactly where to find you."

"Harridan!"

"Madman!" She shoved him once again, and he finally broke for the door. Truly angry now, she followed him, shouting, "Get out! Get out, you little man!" He scrambled through the rest of her rooms, knocking things over in his haste to get away from her. Sheila rose from her pallet by the hearth in the kitchen and gaped at him as he passed, her blankets held close about her. Suzanne's voice rose to a shrill scream as she chased him from the rooms. "Out! Out! Out! Out of London! Get to France, where they know how to treat your kind!" Suzanne was a Protestant herself, but just then was enraged and hateful.

Voices came from elsewhere in the theatre as the performers who had retired to their pallets in the common room upstairs rose to see what the commotion was about. William fled from Suzanne, but outside the outer door of her apartment he encountered two performers who tried to grab him. Arturo, one of the mummers, grasped an arm, but was a small man and William shook him off. Arturo staggered backward a couple of steps as William tried to bolt up the stairs. The other, one of Horatio's actors whose name was Louis, waved his arms as if herding a bull. Horatio approached from the stairs as he drew on a dressing robe and frowned like a thundercloud at the disturbance.

William turned to flee Louis, looking for an escape in the darkness, and was about to rush past Suzanne again when Horatio grabbed him by the back of the neck. When William attempted to twist free, Arturo and Louis lent a hand to control him, each grabbing an arm. William screamed like a girl, and his knees buckled so that the actors had to hold him up to keep him from collapsing to the floor. Horatio stood over him, his fingers dug into William's spine, and shouted, his voice reverberating from the walls, "What nefarious business is at hand? Who is this man?"

As she watched William struggle fruitlessly to free himself, Suzanne said, "He's nobody. Nobody at all." Her anger made her want to spit at him, but she refrained as she struggled for control of her rage. "Take him to the street and leave him there." Her tone was angry enough to keep Horatio from asking further questions, and the actors complied with her wishes.

On her way back to the dressing table, her foot knocked the hilt of William's dagger, lying on the floor, and it went spinning a few feet. She bent to pick it up and turned it in her hand to examine it. The thing was small and plain, and not particularly sharp. She set it on her dressing table, where it would not be stepped on.

Chapter Ten

Three weeks after the incident with William, Daniel came to the Globe to see after its progress. One misty morning when the fog was low over the nearby tenements, his carriage arrived at the entrance and everyone attended as he stepped out of it. The crew whitewashing the outside of the building stopped to gawk at the well-appointed blue carriage with its matched black horses. Suzanne saw it from the stage through the front entrance doors and knew well whose it was. The workers' enormous brushes dripped onto the cobbles and went unheeded. The muralist inside the theatre, painting the pale-blue, puffy-clouded heavens onto the ceiling over the upstage area, continued with his work, engrossed by it and uninterested in the outside world. He was the only one who didn't take the momentous arrival as an excuse for a break from work.

Suzanne hurried to meet Daniel and intercept whatever he might have to say to anyone. At the moment Piers was high in the third floor gallery, measuring various areas with a knotted string and calculating the number of new benches they would need. In a wealthier theatre, those galleries would have required folding chairs, but the Globe's anticipated audience might not be so gentle with expensive, fragile seating, so benches were thought to be the best choice for these galleries. Particularly since benches would increase the Globe's capacity of about three thousand by nearly a third, and that would make up for the lower admission price. The audience in the pit, of course, would stand as always, and for that they would pay even less than those on benches.

Somehow, the last time she'd seen Daniel slipped from her memory and she found herself happy to see him. It was as if he hadn't shamed her last they'd met, and his presence here made up for the embarrassment she'd felt then. She dashed through the entrance and came to a staggering halt next to the carriage as Daniel debarked. "Good morrow, my lord," Suzanne said, cheerful and a bit tongue-in-cheek as she performed an elaborate curtsey to the earl. It was easy enough to act as if their last meeting hadn't happened, for they were in her territory today. She was the one who would send him away if she chose. He was the earl, but she was the one who lived there.

At the moment she was attired in breeches and tights with a ruffled shirt she'd embroidered with flowers and butterflies to make the outfit just a little less masculine. With no stays tight about her midriff, it was a joy to breathe like a man, and her mood was light. Her hair hung down around her collar, utterly scandalous and only for the premises. Were she to venture outside the theatre she would want to change her clothes and restrain her hair, or be gawked at even in London, where it was becoming the style to never be shocked by anything.

But here in her theatre, where any sort of dress could be passed off as creative and eccentric, she greeted Daniel as she was and expected he would think her more interesting than scandalous.

Daniel grinned, apparently in a good mood also. He graced her with an approving look, and that made her glad. It made her feel interesting. "Good morrow, wench. I've come to see what my coin hath wrought." His glance took in the newly hung entrance doors, which were plain but solidly built and bound in good iron. He seemed to approve of the theatre as well.

"Very good, then. Come this way and I'll show you what we've accomplished."

He offered her his arm and she accepted it. They stepped through the open doors to the theatre interior, which had changed much since the days when she'd stopped by to admire it. She took him onto the stage, which was now entirely new, sloping just slightly from rear to front and extending into the ground-level, dirt-floor pit, exactly as it had done originally. The new-style stage was not for them. Rumor had it the new royal theatre stage would have a small apron at the front and the bulk of it would lie behind a frame-like arch called a proscenium, an innovation that was all the rage in Paris. The new plays, Suzanne had heard, were made to be seen from only one side, like a living picture with realistic-looking murals at the rear, which, unlike the small set pieces traditional theatre used on occasion, left little to the imagination and limited dramatic flexibility. Scenes were less fluid in the new plays because changing the scene involved changing a great deal of scenery.

However, the Globe's new stage wasn't entirely without innovation, for it boasted two trapdoors—one at center and one downstage—that gave access to the platform from the cellarage below. All else was as before. Steps at each side allowed entrance to the downstage apron. Upstage where the platform met the 'tiring house and its galleries, there were two large doors for entrance and exeunt.

Daniel's smile faded some. "This is as far as you've come on the work?"

Suzanne wasn't entirely sure what to reply to that. She'd thought the reconstruction was going wonderfully. There had been so much needed to make the place even safe for occupation that making this much progress in the amount of time spent was a miracle to her. "Well, my lord, the workers have been hard at it. You didn't see what it was when we started. Perhaps you should have, given the large amount of money you've invested." Anyone else would have inspected the place before putting up the money, but Daniel had waved off her offer to see the theatre.

"You know I've been terribly busy."

Right. Terribly busy wandering through the park with Charles. And there was that he didn't wish anyone to connect him to Piers. Suzanne warned herself to resist thinking that would ever change. This visit today might mean his wife was out of town, and so Daniel thought himself safe. But rather than dwell on that thought, she shook it off and reinforced the smile she presented.

As he looked around at the construction, he spotted Piers in the third floor gallery and a change came over him. Even at this distance, he could recognize the son he'd never met. He said nothing, but went silent and stared, as still as the foggy air. He'd never seen Piers before now. All the business and exchange of money had been in Piers's name, but Suzanne's messengers and Daniel's pages had been the ones to ferry the papers and negotiations back and forth. At the time she'd thought he was avoiding her, but now she understood why Daniel had done it that way. It wasn't herself, but Piers he'd avoided. She watched his face for a sign of what he might be thinking.

It was blank. He revealed nothing.

Piers, up in the top seating gallery, gazed down at Daniel, also with a blank stare, eerily like his father. Suzanne raised a hand and gestured he should join them there on the stage.

After a moment's consideration, Piers set down the papers in his hand, said something to the worker at his side, and headed toward the stairs.

Daniel watched the muralist above the stage while they waited, and appeared fascinated for the moment. It seemed to take Piers forever to descend the stairs. Suzanne and Daniel waited.

When Piers arrived, Suzanne opened her mouth to introduce them, but words failed her. Neither "Daniel, this is my son" nor "Daniel, this is our son" seemed right. Saying "This is Piers" seemed insufficient.

"Good morning, my lord," Piers said, and executed a token bow that was little more than a nod. "Piers Thornton."

Daniel turned, his mouth opened to say something witty, but when he saw Piers up close his voice failed him. Suzanne held silent as she observed. She'd once thought Daniel uncaring, callous regarding his only son, but just then she wasn't so sure. His wife had no children at all, and Daniel admitted to two daughters with French mistresses. As far as she knew, he had no particular affection for any of his three known children, but now as he saw his son for the first time she noticed a spark of interest. Maybe more than just interest; his gaze riveted on Piers's face.

The young man stood still, almost at attention. Neither did his face reveal his thoughts. Then he slowly bowed fully, and straightened. The silence continued. Finally Daniel said, "Greetings"—he coughed to clear his throat—"Piers."

Piers seemed a younger version of Daniel except for a wider mouth that resembled his mother's. The eyes and nose were so much like Daniel's it nearly gave the impression of a mask made to emulate his father's face. Daniel's hair was grayer, of course, and his bones more prominent, as age will do to a man. But particularly as they gazed, one examining the other, it was almost as if each were staring at a magic mirror that showed himself at another age.

Daniel broke the silence. "You appear well."

"I am, quite, thank you."

"I'm told you've become an enterprising young man."

"Time will tell." Piers wasn't terribly forthcoming with conversation, and a whiteness about his lips betrayed the anger he barely controlled in his curiosity. Suzanne wished he would say something worthwhile. Anything. She wished one or both would say something to end this draw, even if it were only something more honest than witty. But she expected they would not. Not here where everyone could hear and it would all certainly be repeated elsewhere.

"Let us all go have some chocolate!" she said, and loudly she called through the trapdoor to Sheila in the kitchen behind the cellarage that she should begin preparations.

"No, Mother, I think his lordship would prefer to see the theatre. It is, after all, why he's here." Piers addressed Daniel. "Is it not?"

They all now knew it wasn't really, but nevertheless Daniel nodded and said, "Certainly. Would you care to show me around? Piers?"

"Excellent idea!" Relieved, Suzanne reached for her son's arm. "Let us—"

"But, Mother, you said you wanted chocolate. I think you should have Sheila make you some. And perhaps some dinner." He glanced up at the sun overhead. "'Tis nearly noon. You know how you get if you don't eat on time. Go have some chocolate, and some meat as well, and allow me to show the earl the fruits of his investment."

Suzanne looked from Piers to Daniel, then to Piers again. Should she let them alone together? She had no idea what to expect from either of them, except that she knew Piers was likely to say anything in his youth and his anger. Daniel, knowing nothing about his son, might not know where not to tread in conversation with him.

But she had no choice in the matter. Piers was a man now and wouldn't be told how to feel about anything. She stepped away, and curtsied to Daniel. There was nothing for it but to trust her son to take a diplomatic approach with his father, no matter what resentment there might be. He was intelligent, and in spite of his youth and inexperience, he stood a good chance of not endangering his first business relationship.

"Go, Mother," he said softly. "Sheila must be waiting for you. She surely heard you through the trapdoor." He pointed with his chin toward the stage.

"Very well, Piers." She turned to Daniel and dropped another quick curtsey. "Daniel, enjoy the tour." With that, she gave an airy, carefree wave and retired.

But she went only far enough to let them think she'd retreated to her rooms. As soon as she was inside the 'tiring house, she turned back to peek at Daniel and Piers through the upstage right door. The men spoke for a moment, but she couldn't hear what they were saying. Piers gestured broadly, indicating the three tiers of galleries all around them. Then he pointed upward to where the muralist was on his back on a scaffold, painting clouds on the ceiling and focused on his work as if he were Michelangelo himself in the Sistine Chapel. Then the two headed upstage toward the backstage doors and Suzanne, who caught a glimpse of their faces before she ducked farther away into the 'tiring house. It was hard to tell what each was thinking, but in that moment she saw them both thin-lipped and with furrowed brow. Not the family feeling she'd hoped for.

In the darkness she lurked, watching from behind some costumes hanging from a rod attached to a rafter by ropes. Bits of disturbed feathers drifted down past her nose as Piers took a candle from a candelabra and the two men proceeded.

"Here are the 'tiring rooms, where the actors will prepare for their roles and wait for their time onstage. See over here . . ." Piers directed Daniel into a passage, where Suzanne could no longer hear what was said. Daniel appeared absorbed in the tour, and she took heart from that, but Piers's face was harder than she'd ever seen it. She followed them, hoping to hear more gentle voices from them.

Piers showed his father the chamber where more costumes hung from rods suspended in rows. There weren't a great many pieces in their wardrobe, and most belonged to Horatio. The troupe still needed a number of armor bits to costume the battle of Agincourt in their opening play. And weapons. The knights of Henry V would need pikes, crossbows, and swords. The wardrobe and properties seemed scant.

From there they visited the 'tiring room, freshly painted pale green because it was a calming color. Through the open door Suzanne could see the chairs and dressing tables were shoved to the walls to clear space, and a rehearsal of mummers was in progress. This short piece, intended to precede the main play on opening night, involved a man cuckolded by his wife, and though the performers weren't in costume at the moment, the man playing the husband wore a set of paper horns on his head, held by a strip of cloth tied at the nape of his neck. In performance the paper headpiece would be replaced by a more substantial one of stuffed, brightly colored cloth decorated with streamers and tipped with two tiny silver bells. The "wife," played by a skinny lad who was Arturo's son, wore a tight shirt sewn with enormous pockets stuffed with rags to represent a ridiculously ample bosom. He slung the false chest this way and that as no real woman would, which made the scene ever so much more comical.

When Piers and Daniel emerged from the room, Suzanne ducked again, this time behind some long boards leaning against a wall, but when she looked again she was glad to see Daniel's earlier cheer had returned, at least as a façade. Piers still appeared angry.

She followed them up the rear stairs to the galleries above the stage, which could be used either for privileged audience or for musicians or actors. Balcony scenes could be staged in these areas, though in such cases the actors were sometimes swallowed up by being so far upstage they were distanced from the audience. Suzanne hid just inside the stairwell to listen.

Secluded from the rest of the troupe now, Suzanne was horrified to hear Piers say to Daniel, "My lord, I wonder whether you might allow me to ask a question of you."

"Of course."

"Not to put too fine a point on it, but what are your intentions regarding my mother?"

Suzanne opened her mouth to intervene, but was torn between stopping Piers from interrogating Daniel and wanting to hear the answer to the question herself. In the end curiosity won out. She kept silent and hung back farther into the shadows. She couldn't see Daniel's face, but it was a long moment before he spoke and she could imagine his stunned expression. He replied, "My intention is to be her friend."

"What sort of friend?"

Piers! She rather wished he would mind his own business, but stayed put nevertheless.

"Piers, I understand that you might distrust me, and I suppose you have reason. However—"

"Your *lordship*, I've asked a simple, straightforward question. I hope for a response in kind."

Suzanne took a step forward, but still couldn't break up this conversation. Curiosity gripped her. More than anything, she would know the answer to Piers's question and couldn't bring herself to stop the answer.

Daniel said, "The question is not so very simple as you imagine."

"Have you feelings for my mother?"

"Of course I do. Within her limitations as a woman, she is honorable and as respectable as anyone could be in her circumstances."

"She's a whore, so 'within her circumstances' isn't very high praise."

"She's certainly nobody's wife."

"Thanks to you."

Daniel harrumphed like an old man, momentarily stalled while searching for a reply. "Not at all. I made no decisions for her. She understood the situation when she ran away from her father's house."

"You made it so she had to leave, but gave her nowhere to go."

Daniel had no argument for that, either, and only made a slow shrug of one shoulder, in grudging agreement. "It's true. I had nothing for her, and your grandfather would not have received you kindly."

"Neither has my father."

Daniel drew himself up taller. "Life is filled with difficulties. We can't always have things as we wish. In fact, complete freedom is so rare as to be nonexistent."

Piers's voice rose. "A fine excuse!"

Suzanne decided it was time to interrupt this conversation, so she stepped forward. "Oh, there you are!" The men both jumped a bit, startled that they might have been overheard. She continued, "Come! Sheila has some dinner for all of us." A lie, but she would make it up to Sheila later for having to chastise her for being tardy with the promised food.

Piers glared at Daniel, who received the anger with utter aplomb, as if he didn't notice. Then Piers guided Daniel back down the stairs. Dinner was a long silence, punctuated only by an occasional question from Suzanne followed by a short response from either Piers or Daniel. Like a Scottish call-and-response waulking song, she asked and they answered. The rest was only chewing.

After eating, Suzanne accompanied as Piers showed Daniel the house galleries. They circled the theatre along the third tier of seats, and Piers explained how improved the capacity would be once the benches were built. From there they went outside and around the perimeter of the property. The building was surrounded by clumps of tenements, some very old with upper floors overhanging, and the taller ones reaching far out over the street, blocking whatever sunlight might be had. Many had residents leaning out the windows to watch the work on the theatre or catch a glimpse of the Earl of

Throckmorton and his fancy carriage. Suzanne, Piers, and Daniel witnessed some boys loitering too close to it who were chased away by Daniel's coachman, and the boys ran just far enough so he stopped chasing them. He returned to guard the coach, and they sneaked back one by one to lurk and spy again.

Once Daniel's visit was finished and he mounted the steps to his carriage, Suzanne and Piers watched it make its way down Maid Street. Piers muttered under his breath, "Pompous ass." Then without further comment he turned to resume his work in the galleries.

Suzanne watched him go, and wished Piers's opinion of Daniel was more respectful. More like a son's.

After that, Suzanne's thoughts kept drifting back to Piers's query to Daniel. *What are your intentions regarding my mother?* He'd thought it a simple question, but even Suzanne knew the truth must be so complex as to make it unanswerable. Daniel's personal conflict of legal duty to his wife and moral duty to his son muddied those waters so horribly there was no telling what actually lay in his heart. Suzanne found herself passing through Pall Mall anytime she was in the vicinity, to gaze at the house and hope for a glimpse of its occupants. Those glimpses were few, and told her nothing.

One day in July she was in a shop near Whitehall, browsing some fabric that had just come from Paris, midnight-blue silk velvet that felt to her fingers like the fur of a newborn kitten. She longed to buy enough for a gown, but it was far too costly and she knew she would order only wool today, and flinch at the price for that.

The street door opened, and in came Anne Stockton, Countess of Throckmorton, a noble presence that made everyone in the shop turn to look. She was accompanied by her footman, who followed her like a stately shadow in blue livery, silent and unobtrusive but never far. Suzanne watched from under lowered lids, pretending to assess the silk velvet in her hand but seeing it not at all. Anne had a smile for everyone she saw, and nobody could resist her grace and charm. She asked after some fabric suitable for a dressing gown, and the merchant invited his lady to have a seat on the upholstered sofa nearby while he would bring her some possibilities.

Close up, Anne's beauty was undeniable. She wore little face paint and only one beauty mark, for on her enhancement was unnecessary. Her bright smile was infectious, and her cheeks were dimpled in spite of her age. Though the corners of her eyes were creased, it didn't seem to matter because the wrinkles were apparently caused by constant smiling. She appeared to have all her teeth, and the ones in front were still light colored and hardly stained at all. It made her appear more than a decade younger than her actual age, and Suzanne felt like a hag.

The fabric merchant returned with some assistants bearing several bolts of silk cloth. Rich velvets in an array of reds and golden yellow, some of which were nice but not for Anne, and others that were just plain ugly. Anne's reddish hair was tricky to complement, in some lights appearing blond and in others bright red, and the merchant wasn't seeing that.

On the sort of impulse that had always seemed to rule Suzanne's life, she reached for a nearby bolt of dark green. The silk was so dark as to appear nearly black, but it had a lustrous green highlight that flowed as the cloth moved. She carried it over to Anne and draped a short length of it over her hand to present it. "My lady," she said in her gentlest voice. "Perhaps you might try this. I was just admiring it over here, and I see that it sets off your hair magnificently. I assume the dressing gown is for yourself?"

Anne graced her with the sunniest smile Suzanne had ever received, and though she struggled to hate the woman, she found it impossible. "Why, thank you," Anne said. She accepted the length of fabric and held it against her skin. "Yes, it is. I'm having a new one made. I've tired of my old favorite and wish for a change." She eyed the color against her skin, thinking hard. It seemed to Suzanne that she'd never in her life had a new dressing gown before the old one was threadbare, never mind having more than one, but of course she kept that to herself.

"My lady, if I may say so, green suits your complexion perfectly."

"I quite agree." With that, she ordered a sumptuous yardage of it, and quite a lot of two other fabrics as well. The merchant, a thin-lipped fellow with a Mediterranean look about him, fairly vibrated with pleasure at the sale. He set an assistant to cut and wrap the yardage while he himself recorded the tab in a ledger book on a nearby table. "I thank you, my lady. Is there aught else you might like today?"

"No, I think that will do for the moment. Though I might send my girl when I've decided what sort of gown I'll want for my cousin's wedding in September."

"I'll be most happy to accommodate you for that, my lady."

"Until then, my man, and God bless you." She turned her brilliant smile once again to Suzanne and said, "And thank you also for your help, mistress . . ."

"My name is Suzanne Thornton, my lady." As she curtsied, she watched the countess's face. No flicker of recognition. Apparently the name meant nothing to her, and Daniel hadn't mentioned her at all. Anne was completely ignorant of Daniel's relationship with her and Piers. "Suzanne," said Anne. "How very nice to have met you. You've been a great help to me."

"It was my pleasure. The green will suit you well, I think."

"I think so, too. Good day, Suzanne, and God bless you." Then Anne went through the door held by her footman, who also carried the large package of heavy fabric.

Suzanne watched her leave and thought how wonderful—and how impossible—it would be to hate that woman.

THE work on the theatre continued through July and August, and it was late August when the work was finally finished on the Globe. The day before opening night The New Globe Players were fully rehearsed with fifteen plays by Shakespeare and twice as many mummeries and comedies. They would continue to rehearse in the days to come and increase their repertoire to the entire oeuvre of Shakespeare, but today they put a final polish on tomorrow's selection, *Henry V.*

The atmosphere in the theatre was charged like an approaching thunderstorm. The very air over the stage crackled with anticipation of opening. The scene at hand was in Act V, the courtship between Henry and Katharine, lightly played as denouement to the Battle of Agincourt by a young thief named Matthew and the whore Liza.

Liza was proving a remarkable asset to the troupe, for once she heard something, she remembered it verbatim and forever. Contrary to what Horatio had told her the day she'd auditioned, he did recite the plays to her. But only once. She now had all fifteen in the repertoire memorized as cold as a priest knew his rosary, and not just the female roles. Every word of every role, including the prologues, was committed to memory, and she'd only needed to hear them once. If one gave her a cue, she would respond with the next speech in its entirety, however long or obscure it might be.

The icing on the cake was that as an actress she was a natural, and well experienced at playacting in her life on the streets. Her coyness as the beautiful and unspeakably proper French princess Katharine amused those who had come to know her as a blithe, insouciant, and vulgar prostitute, but Liza played the role as earnestly as if she were the Virgin Mary herself. The other actors spoke of her talent in awed whispers, and with not a little envy.

So that afternoon during rehearsal, Liza and Matthew were going through their paces in full costume as king and future consort, with a rapt audience of fellow performers and musicians clustered in the pit and scattered throughout the galleries. Suzanne watched from the top gallery over the main entrance, her arms crossed and a flutter in her belly from anticipation. Goose bumps rose and she rubbed them down as she imagined the audience reaction to these fine performers. The revived Globe would be a rousing success, she was certain.

An adamant pounding came from the large doors to the street, and voices lifted, shouting to open up. The actors onstage fell silent. Before anyone could move, loud thuds rattled the doors and splintered wood. It sounded like a battering ram. Suzanne leapt to her feet and ran to the back of the gallery where a window overlooked the street and the entrance below. The view wasn't wide enough to reveal much, but she saw clusters of onlookers gawking, and three stories below her was a glimpse of madder red coats of infantrymen. A surge of panic made her gasp, and she turned to hurry down the stairs.

Horatio, standing in the pit, shouted to a boy sitting near the doors to open them up before the bolts were torn from the wood and made useless. Suzanne leapt down the stairs two at a time. But when the boy unlatched the doors and they flew open, Suzanne's concern became less for the doors and more for their troupe inside the theatre. For in rushed five king's men, wearing armor and carrying pikes and maces. They spread out to address any defenders, but the theatre was large and the five soldiers were not an overwhelming presence, and they didn't stray far from their sergeant. He shouted as Globe Players nearby scattered to avoid being bludgeoned.

"William Wainwright! Give us William Wainwright immediately!" The sergeant was short and muscular, like an English bulldog even to his teeth protruding from an underslung jaw, and his gravelly, commanding voice evidenced years of whiskey and shouting much like what he was doing now.

Suzanne burst from the stairs, hurried forward, and went straight toward the invaders while everyone else fell back. "What is the matter, good man? How may I help you?" She struggled to seem casual, for authority always smelled fear and suspected guilt for it. Just then she would not have butter melt in her mouth, so cool was she.

The sergeant turned to her and on sight faltered in his insistence on seeing William. He blinked at her masculine costume and smooth, confident air, but recovered himself and said, "We seek William Wainwright."

"What makes you think he's ever been here?" Of the very few who knew of William's visit, not one would have spoken of it to the authorities on his life.

"You're a known associate, Mistress Thornton. I'm charged with searching the premises for him."

"Whatever for?"

"We've a warrant for his arrest."

"Again I ask, whatever for?"

"I'm not at liberty to say."

"Surely the king isn't seeking vengeance from every Puritan in the realm."

The sergeant thought about that a moment, looking a bit confused, then went stern again. "I've no knowledge of Wainwright's religious leanings. All I know is that certain authorities wish to question him about some statements made recently."

"About him, or by him?"

The sergeant considered his reply, then said as if confiding a secret, "'Tis said he's threatened the king."

That took Suzanne fully aback. "Threatened? Oh no, it must be a misunderstanding. William is in terror of the crown. He would never utter a word against the king."

"Nevertheless, the crown wishes to interrogate him. If the charge is proven to be false, he will then be released and no harm." Except, of course, for whatever damage might be done during interrogation, but that went unsaid by both of them.

"Who made the charge?"

"I surely cannot say, even did I know." Then he was moved to add, "And I do not."

"His wife?"

The flicker in the sergeant's eyes told her she'd guessed right, but he insisted he didn't know. A lie, of course, and Suzanne had learned to expect nothing else from men in authority.

"He's wanted for interrogation, then? Pray, don't tell me Parliament has interest in what William might know about anything. His is as empty a head as any I've known. Pick his brain and you'll surely come away disappointed, whatever you're after. Pierce his skull and then watch it collapse as the air escapes."

The witnesses standing about all chuckled. The sergeant

caught himself in a snicker and brought himself up to attention, lest he lose control of the situation. Here on business, and nothing else, and he gave a stern glance to his men. He continued, with as much authority and superiority as he could muster, "If he's on the premises, you would do well to surrender him. We'll find him one way or another."

She held out her palms to either side to show she had nothing to hide and he was welcome to search the theatre. "By all means, sergeant. Be my guest, and best of luck to you. He's no friend to any of us, and if you find him, you're welcome to him." She gestured toward the surrounding galleries and the terrified Globe Players, including in her insouciant wave a few of the curious who had stepped just inside the entrance to gawk. "Have your men search. We've nothing to hide. William isn't here. In fact, we sent him on his way when he did come here. I told him to never show his face again. Were you to arrest him, it would be a blessing to us all." She looked to the rest of the troupe, who all picked up the cue and nodded and muttered in the affirmative, though most of them had never seen nor heard of William Wainwright before now.

"So you say he was here?"

"Months ago. There was an altercation and he was shown the door. To the best of my knowledge, he hasn't returned. But if he ever does, sergeant, I'll be ever so happy to alert you so you might come get him. I assure you we've had quite enough of him and wish to see him put where he will be less of an annoyance to us and to the rest of humanity."

Her attitude seemed unexpected by the sergeant, who likely was more accustomed to reluctance in this neighborhood than cheerful cooperation. His men remained still, one holding the small iron battering ram and the rest with their arquebuses and pikes at ready. The sergeant looked from Suzanne to Horatio, then he scanned the rest of the house, turning a small circle to see the galleries. He ordered his men, "Search the premises."

They obeyed. To Suzanne the sergeant said quite reasonably, "If you're telling the truth and we find no evidence of him, we will leave you in peace."

Suzanne nodded, knowing that the best one could ever hope for from any army was that they would go away. She took a seat on a nearby bench to wait. There were only four men searching the huge theatre; this would take some time.

Horatio said, "May we continue our rehearsal?"

The sergeant replied, "No. Your people will keep still while my men look around."

Horatio looked as if he wanted to say something angry, but at a glance from Suzanne swallowed whatever it was and it soured him even more. He eyed the soldiers as they disappeared into the 'tiring house.

Suzanne crossed her arms and continued to appear uncaring, but alarm returned and her stomach flopped over when she remembered William's dagger lying on her dressing table. A shiver took her as her skin went cold. God help them all if for any reason that dagger were recognized by any of the soldiers.

Chapter Eleven

Suzanne needn't have worried. The searching soldiers took no notice of the dagger, which lay in plain sight. Daggers were common enough, and there was nothing noteworthy about this one. As nondescript as it was, if any of them saw it, they most likely passed it off as Suzanne's personal knife, nothing more than an eating utensil. There was nothing special about it to identify it as William's, and apparently the crime for which the crown wanted him did not involve a weapon.

However, much attention was given to any papers found on the premises, and the soldiers whiled away an hour or so paging through Piers's accounting ledgers and some scribbled notes that were a germ of a play Suzanne fantasized she might write someday. The story was a purposefully innocuous comedy, and so elicited nothing more than a chuckle from the sergeant, who was apparently the only literate soldier of the group. In the end, none of it sparked concern, and it was all left scattered across a table in the corner of Suzanne's bed-chamber.

Once they'd gone, Suzanne was relieved to have the soldiers leave them alone, but was not happy to have been noticed in the first place. It left an uneasiness in her gut that felt a little like rumblings caused by bad food. Early on in life she'd learned that in this world undue attention from the authorities often brought more attention, whether warranted or not, and nobody in the kingdom was eager for authority to take notice of them. Suzanne prayed William would stay away forever, and hoped whatever trouble he'd gotten himself into would cause him to leave the country. If he showed himself again in her theatre, she thought she might like to knife him herself. That dagger could come in handy after all.

The next afternoon the play opened and William slipped from everyone's mind. The audience crowded into the theatre to fill up benches, until even the pit was packed with milling bodies. The luxury of sitting for the price the duke's new theatre charged for standing drew everyone in walking distance, and the neighborhood was overrun with people who loved a good play.

If the excitement among the audience was palpable, the mood in the 'tiring house was near hysteria. Joking and stifled laughter fed the energy until the littlest of the boys ran from the green room to vomit in a fire bucket. Laughter followed him and shamed him, though many had done the same thing once or twice in their careers and nobody was entirely immune to excitement. For most of them the thrill was what they lived for. The boy returned to the green room with a red face, patted on the shoulders by his elders.

In her quarters, Suzanne readied herself to watch the play, eager to see her new theatre through the eyes of its audience.

Through the cellarage window in the kitchen she could hear the voices of gathering spectators grow from scattered conversations to a low collective murmur to a roar of thousands trying to be heard amongst themselves. As she painted her lips she toyed with the idea of lurking in the pit to listen in on conversations, but decided she would enjoy the afternoon more if she went upstairs to sit with the musicians in a gallery over the stage. There she would be able to chat with Big Willie, Warren, and that Scottish fellow, and they would be as fine an entertainment as the play itself. She hurried with her beauty marks, eager to be finished and take her place in the audience.

The door from the stairwell opened, and she heard someone enter. She turned as Piers made his way through her rooms to her bedchamber. Though the day was cheerful and sunny, Piers's visage was not so. He glowered as he planked himself down on the foot of her bed, wrapped an arm around its post, and leaned his face against it. He was in a sulking mood, and Suzanne steeled herself for a bit of childish pique. For the most part Piers behaved as an adult, fully his eighteen years, but sometimes he slipped back into childhood, requiring to be nudged toward maturity again.

He said, "I would have thought Daniel might have been here tonight."

"I, on the other hand, would not have thought it." She examined her hair in the small hand mirror she'd wheedled out of William several years before. "And what makes you think he's not here?"

"I haven't seen him."

"You mean he hasn't come backstage."

"Surely you would agree that he should present himself on opening night. I think it's an insult to you that he hasn't."

"You mean he should have come backstage to wish me well?"

"Precisely. He should be here with gifts. Flowers and jewelry. But I see naught. He's insulted you."

"And by extension, he's insulted you."

Piers straightened his posture and shrugged. "That isn't the point."

"Oh, but it is. He's your father, and he should treat you better than he does."

"I have no father."

"You do, and I think he cares more for you than you think."

"He does not. He cares only about himself and his money. If he had any thought for us—for you, he would be here right now, wishing you luck in your venture."

"It's his venture as well, so wishing me luck would be a bit self-serving, don't you think?"

He thought that over for a moment, then reiterated, "He should be here." Piers said that as if it settled the entire question.

"Well," Suzanne said as she waved dry the glue on her star-shaped beauty marks, "We must remember that his help has enabled us to eat every day, which wouldn't be the case now that William has deserted us. If you wish to be angry with someone, William is a marvelous candidate. You should feel free on that account."

Piers grunted, unhappy with the entire situation. "William. If he returns, I think I should kill him."

"Don't say that. Never say that, even about William. He is mad, and can't be held responsible for his delusions. You should pity him, not hate him."

"But he's dangerous. Someone should gut him, I think." Piers thought about it a moment, then muttered half to himself, "Slit his throat." He thought some more. "Hang and quarter—"

"That will do, young man. Now go make certain the cash box is well attended by someone more trustworthy than the mummers' troupe. It's like setting a weasel to guard the hens' nests." Piers hesitated, so she waved him on. "Go. Before someone absconds with the proceeds and we've nothing to show Daniel for our first night."

Piers reluctantly rose from the bed and scuffed his boots in insolence all the way out the door. Suzanne made one more check of her coif, then set the mirror on her dressing table and left her quarters.

As the time drew close, Suzanne climbed the steps at the rear of the 'tiring house to watch the performance from the gallery directly above the stage, where the musicians sat. As she found a stool and settled in at the front, Big Willie, Warren, and the Scot played an old-fashioned tune that might have been played in this theatre during Elizabethan times. Suzanne's fancy toyed with the thought that Shakespeare himself might have listened to this very tune from this very gallery half a century ago. She looked around, and the idea made her smile. It was a fine, sunny day, and especially warm even for this time of year. Afternoon light bathed the stage, and there was no fear of a sudden rain from the pale-blue sky overhead.

In the third tier gallery over the theatre entrance directly across from the stage, she spotted several rather well-dressed men making their way to a vacant bench, and she thought one of them resembled Daniel. She hoped it was him. She would have liked to tell Piers his father had come after all. It was hard to say whether it was him, and the others with him—one very tall and one very short—she didn't recognize at all. They might have been former Cavaliers and were probably older men, though they dressed rather plainly and the tall one wore no wig. Beneath the plain green cloak were brown doublet and white collar. On the other hand, the wigless one wore an uncommonly large feather in his hat, more appropriate for a parade than for theatre in Southwark.

The men settled into seats, chatting among themselves. They appeared to be enjoying their outing, and Daniel— Suzanne decided it *was* him—did quite a bit of the talking himself. She peered at the others to see who they might be, but they were too far away and their hats made strong shade over their faces in the bright afternoon sunlight. Suzanne let it go and focused her attention on the stage below as performers entered from upstage.

That afternoon's performance began with a short *commedia* play, the one involving the cuckolded husband. The mummers had today's audience laughing well and quickly, and in a few minutes they left the stage with the entire audience of nearly four thousand people in a good mood. To Suzanne, this was the wonderful thing about the theatre: to have that many gathered together in one place and everyone having a good time. One could do that in a public house with alcohol, cards, and women, but a pub could host only a fraction of the souls a theatre could. A day at the theatre was like a party so enormous only the king might rival it as a host.

She looked across at Daniel and saw his smile flash. Yes, making people laugh could be a good way to live.

The play began, and Matthew lit up the stage as King Henry, young and eager to prove himself to the world as a ruler to be reckoned with. The audience was as caught up as she. They shouted advice to Henry, and in response Matthew invented bawdy asides in spite of the directive to keep to

Shakespeare's own words. Suzanne supposed so long as the asides were not political or slanderous they might go unnoticed. In any case, she hoped nobody in the house tonight was likely to go running to the king, tattling.

Then the battle of Agincourt. The French king and his dukes in desperation. The murder of the boys in the luggage. The horror of that cowardly act. Suzanne was caught up in the story as if she hadn't seen the play a dozen times before. Even as she gasped along with Henry and his dukes, she thought what a fine time she was having. For a moment she thanked William for leaving her and forcing her to find something so worthwhile to do with her life.

A scream lifted from the audience, and she thought how wonderfully involved everyone was. Then something thudded on the stage below like a sack of rags or flour. More screaming and confusion moved the audience, some surging forward and others falling back. Suzanne leaned over the banister for a better look, and saw a man lying on the stage, writhing and grasping at a crossbow bolt stuck in his neck. One brave boy ran forward to yank out the bolt, and a gout of blood poured over the stage. The pool spread quickly, and though two actors tried to stanch the flow with their hands, it was hopeless. The fallen man weakened and stopped struggling, finally going limp in the arms of those who tried to help him. The play had come to a halt.

Suzanne leapt to her feet and ran down the rear stairs to the stage. All the actors in the troupe were there, those not in the scene having emerged from the 'tiring house to see, gathered around the body, while those in the pit attempted to climb onto the stage for a look. The audience was abuzz, and some shouted advice to those on the stage as if it were all part of the performance. Suzanne shoved men aside and attempted to take charge, but all she could manage was to enter the circle to see. There, she cried out in shock.

The dead man was William.

He lay on her stage in a pool of blood, killed by a crossbow. His ragged clothing was turning red, his shirt soaking up the draining blood. The red stain slowly crept along the white fabric, and more of it enlarged the pool on the stage boards as it ran downstage.

She said to the boy standing by with the crossbow bolt still in his hand, "Go fetch the constable. Tell him we've found William Wainwright, but the crown is unlikely to have much information from him."

Chapter Twelve

By the time the constable came the next morning, most of the nearly four thousand people who had witnessed the murder had gone home. Suzanne supposed there would be no information forthcoming from anyone in the audience who might have chanced to be looking up when William was shot. Certainly nobody was likely to step forward for questioning. In her experience the appointed authorities could never be trusted and had no respect for the rabble they monitored. Everyone in Southwark was raised to understand that too much involvement with those who had the power to arrest was never a good idea. So the audience had scattered, and none but the performers would ever admit to having been there that night.

Performers scattered as well. The mummer troupe had packed up and disappeared during the night, and the constable's tardy appearance gave them plenty of lead in their flight. Only the Globe Players were on hand that morning, readying for rehearsal, and there was much speculation about who of the nonresident actors would show up that day.

When he finally arrived to ask questions, Constable Samuel Pepper appeared as by magic, standing on the stage and staring down at the bloodstain. He was a short, rotund man, rocking back and forth heel-to-toe in absentminded habit. His breeches were too long for fashion and too short for warmth, and his leggings were tight at the calf and sagged at the ankle. They bunched into his shoes as if tucked there hastily to hide excess length. The faded brown velvet jacket had bare spots at elbow and collar, and he wore an old-fashioned plain black hat that had not been meant to be worn over the constable's new wig and so was too small. It teetered atop the mass of gray hair and swayed with each rocking movement heel-to-toe, heel-to-toe.

The deceased was gone, William having been carried off to his wife for burial. There wasn't much left to see here.

Nobody had noticed Pepper entering the theatre, though when Suzanne caught sight of him as she happened to be walking through the pit, she saw that the large front entrance doors were slightly ajar. She wondered whether the battering that bolt had taken from the soldiers had caused it to come loose, or if someone had let in the constable, then wandered away without telling anyone there were visitors. In any case, if the bolt was broken, she'd want Piers to attend to it.

Pepper, of course, was familiar to Suzanne from her days as a prostitute, when she and her friends had often had bad scrapes with the authorities over one thing and another. But she'd spent the past decade avoiding him and had been mostly successful during the years she'd been with William. He had never paid her much attention even then, and now she reckoned he was unlikely to remember her. She knew him as not terribly trustworthy, and his laziness was legendary, evidenced by his late arrival to the scene of a murder.

"Good morrow, constable." She shielded her eyes from the sun as she looked up at him on the stage.

He started as if he'd been unaware of her presence until that moment. "Oh. Hello. Mistress . . . ?" He peered at her, with no light of recognition in his eyes, plainly expecting her to introduce herself. Good, he didn't remember her.

She came to the side of the stage and climbed the steps. As she approached him she adjusted her silk jacket. "Suzanne Thornton. My son manages this establishment."

He eyed her breeches. "Then your husband is . . ."

"A figment of the imagination, I'm afraid." She'd never been apologetic for not having a husband, for apology never got her anywhere.

He nodded. "I see. Is your son about, then?"

"I'm afraid he is meeting with a business partner across the river." Piers was at Whitehall, discussing the previous night's excitement with Daniel. Suzanne had wanted to go with him, but stayed behind in compliance with Daniel's decree she not show herself at the palace. Pepper's visit suggested it had been a wise choice for her to stay, but she still wished to be with them in Daniel's quarters.

Pepper turned to gaze down at the bloodstain again. "You were here last night, then?"

"I saw the entire thing."

He heaved a sigh of satisfaction. "Ah, then, I expect my job here is finished and I can return to my office without delay. If you saw the whole thing, you might tell me who shot the bolt." He said it with a smile, so she understood it was a joke, but underlying the joke was perhaps a wish she could have saved him a bit of trouble after all by revealing the culprit herself.

She didn't think him very funny at all, but she chuckled just to make certain he understood the humor was nothing more than that and she had no idea who the murderer was. But then a puzzled look crossed his face and she realized he hadn't been joking at all. He'd seriously thought she knew the name of the murderer and could tell him whom to arrest. He was too lazy to investigate. "Alas," she said, "I never saw the bolt or where it came from. We were all attending to the players on the stage, you see, which of course is what one does during a play. I doubt anyone on the premises could tell where the murderer stood when he fired."

"There were several on the stage with crossbows, I expect. The play was *Henry V*, yes? You staged a battle last night and the players were armed."

"Some were. Four or five, I think; that's how many crossbows we own. But nobody goes onstage with his weapon cocked. It's far too dangerous; the trigger mechanism too easily could unlatch and send the bolt God knows where."

"Which might have been the case last night. The weapons are all functional, yes?"

"Except that, as I said, we never allow them to be cocked. Nobody onstage had a cocked crossbow."

"You're certain of that?"

The despairing feeling grew that Pepper was looking for a quick solution to the crime so he could go home. If the thing were found to be an accident, there was no murderer to catch and no more work to be done on this case. William might have been a thoughtless lover and a dangerous madman, but surely even he didn't deserve for his murderer to go free. She lowered her chin and gazed straight into his face. "Yes, I'm certain. Nobody wants to risk the accidental death of a fellow player, and besides, it takes great time and effort to cock a crossbow; it never happens inadvertently. That's why long-bows, which are easily and quickly drawn, were so loved by Edward Longshanks, whose armies darkened the skies with arrows all over the kingdom. William surely was murdered, by someone who intentionally shot him with an intentionally cocked crossbow."

Pepper threw her a cross look, then put a hand to his chin, thinking. Suzanne waited patiently for his next question, wondering which way he would leap in his logic. He said, "May I speak to the actors who carried bows onto the stage?"

"Certainly." She looked upstage and saw several faces peeking from the doors there. "Matthew! Have the five who carried crossbows last night come for a chat with the constable."

Matthew ducked away, and a moment later several others came forward from the doors, quickly enough that they must have all been listening from behind. Five men who had populated the stage the day before as soldiers in King Henry's army at Agincourt made their way downstage toward Constable Pepper and Suzanne.

While four of them came on with a straightforward gaze at Constable Pepper, the one boy in the group, whose name was Christian, looked as if he wished he were anywhere but there. He hung back and had to be urged to join the others on the stage before the constable. His gaze never left the boards at his feet. Suzanne watched him, and wondered whether they'd found their culprit. She'd never seen anyone look so guilty. But why on earth would Christian have shot William? As far as she knew, Christian had never laid eyes on him.

Constable Pepper asked the actors as a group, "You each had a crossbow onstage?"

The four men nodded. Christian said nothing, and never

indicated he heard the question. Suzanne saw this, but also saw that Pepper didn't seem to take note of him at all. As if his youth made him beneath notice. Pepper's next question seemed to ignore the lad and he addressed the men. "Did any of you have any quarrel with William Wainwright?"

Christian, who had never met William, still said nothing, and Suzanne wondered why. Pepper didn't appear to notice him. She fell silent, stepped back, and availed herself of the luxury of observing reactions to questions asked by another without being observed herself. The actors were alert to him and ignoring her, so she was able to see little behaviors that told the meaning beneath their words.

The men all shook their heads. They had no quarrel with the victim. One of them was Louis, who had helped restrain William the night of the intrusion, so at least one of them was lying. "No, sirrah," said Louis. His hands were clenched into fists, though he let his arms dangle loose in an attitude he surely hoped appeared more insouciant than it was. His chin rose in defiance. Plainly he had something to hide, and Suzanne wondered whether it was only that he'd thrown William from the theatre, or if he'd had some other conflict with William he didn't want known. Suzanne wanted to ask, but unfortunately his willingness to speak made him the specific target of the constable, who focused on him. She would have to ask later. "Tell me your name, young man."

"Louis."

"Your surname, Louis?"

"I've none."

Pepper grunted and muttered to himself, "No surprise there."

Louis glanced over at Suzanne and blew out his cheeks

impatiently as he awaited the next question without seeming to care much what Pepper thought about anything.

The constable said, "Where were you standing when the body dropped to the stage?"

"Bloody near under it, sirrah. I jumped back when it landed, afeared for me life."

"So you stood directly beneath the victim?"

"Yes, sirrah."

Suzanne, standing next to the bloodstain, looked up and again shaded her eyes from the nearly noon sun overhead. Directly above was the stage right gallery, which had been unused last night. The musicians had occupied the stage left gallery.

"Where were you looking when it landed? Did you see it fall?"

"As I've said, I never seen the sod until it made a big, bloody noise at me feet. I was looking at Matthew, who was speechifying as Henry." He gestured vaguely upstage, where Matthew once again watched from one of the doors. "*Once more unto the breach*, and all that."

One of the other men spoke up. "No, it was later. *Well have we done, thrice valiant—*"

"That far along?" said Louis. "Are you certain?"

"At least. Maybe later, even."

"Or perhaps *I was not angry since I came to France until this instant?*" He called back to Matthew at the upstage doors. "Oh, Matthew! What line was it—"

"Never mind!" Pepper shouted. "The dialogue is not important!" He again addressed Louis. "And your crossbow was pointed where?"

"I expect I had it pointed at the stage, sirrah. I believe we all did." He gestured to the other four, and each of them nodded in the affirmative, except for the boy. Christian looked up at Louis, as if searching his face for the correct answer. Not finding it there, he gave a quick glance to Matthew upstage. Then he glanced at Pepper and gave a slight nod before returning his attention to the stage. He stared hard at it, as if he'd spotted a snake about to strike and didn't dare take his eyes off it.

Pepper seemed to take the testimony without question and nodded sagely as if he'd known it all along. Suzanne began to feel as if he were wasting their time and wondered whether he was merely filling his. There were a few more questions, none of them addressed to the boy, then Pepper announced he was finished with his interviews and dismissed the five actors.

Suzanne said, "I suppose you'll want to find and question the mummers next."

"Mummers? Whatever for?"

She opened her mouth to reply, but for a moment was quite stunned. "Why . . . on the face of it, one might wonder why they departed so hastily. Thinking a mite deeper, one might wonder whether they had seen anything or if one or more of them might have a conflict with the deceased. As I see it, asking questions is always worth the effort."

Pepper's face reddened, his eyes narrowed, and his chest puffed out, looking like an offended rooster. "I'll thank you to not presume to tell me my job, mistress. I've been constable here for a number of years and know quite well how to accomplish it."

"I was only—"

"As I said, do not tell me my job. Now, good day, I must be on my way." With that, he trundled off the stage, across the pit, and out of the theatre without another word to them or to Suzanne.

Suzanne looked at the men, who looked back at her, and she shrugged. "I suppose that's all he needed from us."

They all shrugged, and the four men headed toward the backstage. Suzanne looked to the entrance doors, where the constable had just disappeared. That couldn't have been all there was. Surely Pepper couldn't believe he would ever find the murderer with the scant information he'd just obtained. Suzanne called after the four. "All of you! Bring me the crossbows you had onstage last night."

They glanced back at her, nodded, then went to comply. She said to Christian, "Boy, come speak to me." Christian didn't move, and he blinked at her as his face paled.

He watched the others return upstage to disappear through the doors to the 'tiring house. Then he glanced at her sideways, unwilling to look her in the eye.

"Your name is Christian, yes?"

The boy nodded.

"Christian, where is the crossbow you had onstage last night?"

"I had none, mistress." The quaver in his voice betrayed his terror.

"Why are you so afraid?"

"I cannot find the weapon, mistress. I had it in Act III, but for the battle I couldn't find it to carry it back onto the stage. I went without it. Did some arm waving and shouting as if I still had it. I'm small enough, nobody noticed I wasn't armed."

"Someone had taken it?"

"Yes, mistress."

"Why didn't you tell the constable this?"

Christian became agitated. "Because I was afraid he'd accuse me of doing the murder myself."

"He would think it because you *didn't* have the weapon?"

He thought about that for a moment, realized her point, then said, "It was all irregular and everything. You know how them folks in charge of things always jumps on anything irregular, then they work things around so's they can make an accusation no matter what actually happened. What if he said I got rid of the thing? What if he said I shot the fellow and then threw away the crossbow like you does a knife when you've done a murder?"

"One would think you speak from experience."

Christian blanched, and Suzanne patted his shoulder.

"Fear not, young man. I only tease you."

"Yes, mistress. So you see why I fear the constable."

It was a bizarre sort of logic, but it made sense to anyone who grew up distrusting authority the way she had. And apparently Christian had. She said, "No blood on a crossbow, even when it's killed someone. You would have had no reason to throw it away."

He blinked at her, and his cheeks flushed red at his error. He mumbled, "Even still . . ."

She said, "Well, someone has done away with William, and I don't know about you but I'm intensely curious as to who it was. Where was the thing when you saw it last?"

Christian pointed toward the 'tiring house. "'Twas in the green room, mistress. I had it leaning against a table leg in order to adjust my costume. My leggings was all a-falling down and I had to pull them back up under my tunic and tie them all proper."

"You were right there when the crossbow disappeared?"

Christian lowered his gaze again and shook his head just

barely. "No, mistress. I left it there to go into the dressing room."

"I see. Was there anyone in the green room when you left it there?"

"Of course there was. Otherwise I could have yanked up my drawers all in privacy, and maybe had a good scratch while I was at it without being chastised by Master Horatio. There was nearly everyone who was ready to go on for Act IV, a-waiting for their cues. Every eye in the play, almost. I had to go elsewhere or show them all my bum."

"Very well, then. You left the crossbow leaning against the table leg. Was the bolt in it?"

Christian nodded.

"Was it cocked?"

Christian shook his head.

"Thank you, Christian. You may go."

The boy took off running, up the stage and through one of the doors.

Suzanne frowned into the middle distance as he went.

Then she looked up at the gallery from which William had fallen. He'd been directly across the stage from her. If only she'd been looking across instead of down at the stage, she might have seen him and prevented his death. Or at least she might have seen who killed him.

DAYS later, before rehearsal Suzanne took Horatio with her for a shopping trip in Cheapside across the river. She wanted to replenish the paper and ink she'd been using so much of lately in her newly found passion for writing, and Horatio was a comfortable companion on such walks, as well as a handy bodyguard for a moderately well-dressed woman out and about by herself. They stopped in at a shop and she asked for a ream of writing paper and a bottle of the darkest ink available.

As the shopkeeper wrapped her order in brown paper and twine, he noticed Horatio idling by the door. His eyes narrowed, and he said, "I've seen you somewhere before, I think."

Horatio spoke up in his strong stage voice, "I imagine a successful merchant such as yourself might see a great many people in his shop over the course of time."

"No," said the shopkeeper, remembering now. "Not here. 'Twas in the theatre. You're that actor fellow, used to have a troupe that performed about town."

"I am that fellow, indeed." Horatio beamed with pleasure at being recognized. "You've attended our street performances?"

"I certainly have."

"You frequent the playhouses, then?"

"As often as I can. I love a good drama. Did you hear of the great excitement over to the Globe, then? A murder, it was."

Suzanne cut Horatio a sharp glance that he should keep quiet, and Horatio made a slight gesture with his hand to let her know he understood, though his expression never changed. To the shopkeeper he said with just the right measure of regret in his voice at an unfortunate event, "Right. Bad business, that. Poor fellow was shot with a crossbow. Entirely an accident, from what I've heard."

The shopkeeper shook his head. "Ahhh, but it wasn't. Not by the lights of the constable."

Suzanne's attention sharpened, though she never showed it, as she examined a bottle of ink in her hand.

"A friend of Constable Pepper, are you?" said Horatio. "How did you hear of this?"

"A good friend of the constable likes a bit of gossip."

"Don't they all?"

"Indeed. I don't rightly understand nosy folk who can't mind their own business, but there you are. He comes here often to swap stories. There's not much worth knowing that doesn't come through this shop."

"So tell me all that's worth knowing about the murder of William Wainwright."

The shopkeeper leaned forward and lowered his voice, as if he were protecting his secret from others in the shop and this information was strictly between himself and Horatio. "Word is, he's decided 'twas not an accident, but rather a murder. By all accounts, 'tis believed the woman who lives there done it."

Suzanne paled, but did not flinch. She took interest in some quills standing in tall glasses on a nearby shelf. Horatio asked the question she could not without giving herself away. "And why does the right honorable constable happen to think that?"

The shopkeeper shrugged. "Not entirely certain, I'm afraid. It appears, though, that she was caught covering up evidence of some sort."

What evidence? It was what Suzanne wanted to shout, but she let Horatio say it.

"What evidence?" said Horatio.

Again the merchant shrugged. "They say she hid the fact that she was the victim's lover. They say it was a triangle, and she killed him out of jealousy."

Suzanne could barely hold in her astonishment. Calmly she fingered the feathers, while inside she seethed. Her chest rose and fell in even, controlled breaths though her body craved air and wanted to gulp it in panicky gasps.

Horatio questioned further. "Who was the theoretical third party?"

"I couldn't tell you. Couldn't even tell you the name of the woman who done it. I just know she lives at the theatre, and that she was the man's mistress until she left him for it. Left him high and dry, by all accounts. I expect she's one of those new actresses they've got now. The king, it seems, has taken a fancy to seeing women on the stage and is encouraging the practice." The shopkeeper's tone was dark with disgust. "Women on the stage; it can only lead to evil and the decay of mankind, I say."

He finished wrapping the package for Suzanne, offered it to her, and bade her good day. She thanked him as gracefully as she could and gestured to Horatio they should leave. On their way out, the shopkeeper called after him, "Keep a sharp eye out for that woman at the Globe, if you're in the theatre, my friend. I hear she's handy with a crossbow."

Horatio nodded acknowledgment, and they hurried from the shop.

Once outside, Suzanne allowed herself several deep breaths that might have been taken for gasps. "Horatio! Pepper thinks I did it!"

"No, my niece. If he thought that, you'd be arrested already. Pepper is known to be a lazy man. Were there an easy way to make a convincing case against you, and had he any interest in you, he'd have detained you yesterday. What we heard was rumor, nothing more, and most likely corrupted a great deal on its route to you from Pepper."

"But how did it start? What was said that germinated and blossomed into this?"

"I' faith, I cannot say. But let us hurry home, and there we might gain some insight as well as a modicum of safety."

"No, I must go to Daniel. I must go to Whitehall where I will be safe."

Horatio held her arm against any attempt to see Daniel. "Oh no! Anywhere but Whitehall. Once in, you might never leave except as cargo to Tyburn."

In a weak attempt at humor, she said with a wry smile, "Not the Tower?"

"Don't be silly. You could only wish to go to the Tower."

Suzanne had to grin, though her stomach flopped horribly. She continued as Horatio hustled her through the crowds on the street, urging her toward the bridge and home, "I must alert Daniel of my predicament."

"Then send him a message. Send that little fellow, Christian, with your plea for help."

"And if the note is intercepted?"

"Well, after all, you needn't unburden your heart in the letter. You are clever enough to communicate subtly, without giving yourself away. Simply let him know you require his assistance, and he will come. He cares about you, I can see it."

Suzanne glanced sharply at him and wondered at the truth of it. Could Daniel have a care for her? If so, he certainly didn't wear the sentiment on his sleeve. There was no telling whether Daniel would come to her aid if she were accused by the constabulary. She took a deep, settling breath and returned with Horatio to the Globe, hoping her friend was right.

Her message to Daniel, scribbled quickly on the paper she'd just bought, read simply: "Need assistance immediately. Urgent." She folded the page into an envelope packet, wrote Daniel's name on the outside, and handed it off to Christian, who ran away with it as if in a race.

Daniel's response was immediate. In less than two hours he arrived by coach and disembarked, and Christian escorted him to Suzanne's quarters straightaway. The relief of seeing him was like a cool breeze wafting over her. She greeted him with a hug, which he returned. Tears welled and her heart clenched. For a moment she remembered how it had been when she was young and had believed he would be her protector in life, and she grieved for the loss of that time.

"Daniel, that evil little constable is spreading it about that I killed William." She drew him to a chair near her writing desk, then sat herself in her work chair.

"You didn't, did you?"

"Didn't what?"

"Kill him."

"Daniel!" She choked a little and swallowed her terror. "Daniel, how can you think I might? After all, I haven't murdered you yet, have I?"

He laughed, and that seemed to make everything a little lighter. Even Suzanne had to chuckle some and she found it easier to breathe. "So," he said as he settled back in his seat and crossed his legs, one arm draped across his lap and the other hand fiddling with a tassel on the hilt of his dagger. "What is being said, and by whom?"

"It's bandied about I murdered him out of jealousy."

"Bandied about? It's mere rumor, then."

"A friend of a friend of the constable."

Daniel gave his head an equivocal tilt. "That could mean something, or it could mean nothing at all."

"It is said there was a third party involved."

"William was cheating on his mistress? With his wife, I suppose. He was, after all, a Puritan and therefore a right stick. Perhaps she killed him?"

"Hardly. She was as surprised as anyone to learn he'd died. Further, Constable Pepper didn't even ask what we'd done with the body and didn't appear terribly concerned about us having let her take the corpse. As far as I know, she's suspected of nothing. And by her past behavior, I'd say she had no interest in him at all beyond his support of her household."

"Most wives are like that."

His bitter tone alerted her. She thought he might have meant his own wife, and that made her curious. But instead of asking, she fell back on her habitual attitude. "Having never been one, I would have no idea."

The edge to her voice likewise caught his attention. His tone sharpened in his reply. "I was already married when you met me."

Suzanne sighed, for it was true. For a moment she closed her eyes to calm herself, then continued. "In any case, William's wife cannot be involved. I, however, am. Apparently it's all over town that I'm the murderess, and it's but a matter of time until Pepper has me apprehended. You've got to help me, Daniel."

"What can I do?"

"Tell the king I didn't do it!"

Daniel snorted. "The king doesn't give a damn who killed William Wainwright."

"Well, I do! And I must be cleared of it!"

"You haven't been charged with it."

"I will be."

"And then, perhaps, there will be something I might do. But until then, bringing this excitement to the attention of Charles will only run you the risk of him deciding you did do it. He might say, *The lady doth protest too much, methinks.* You will defeat your own purpose."

"Daniel, you were in the audience that night. You saw what happened, and you know I didn't do it."

He went silent for a moment, taken by surprise. His mouth opened as if to speak, but he said nothing and shut it.

"I know you were there, Daniel. I saw you. I would know your form from half a mile away, so don't try to deny it. The way you move, your every gesture, are as familiar to me as . . . as Piers's. You and your friends sat in the third gallery, directly over the entrance doors. You must have seen William fall."

Daniel thought for a moment, deciding whether to admit he was there, then finally said, "Very well. I was there. But I saw nothing. At that moment I was talking to a friend who sat next to me. I wasn't even looking at the stage, never mind the rest of the 'tiring house."

"But before the fall. Did you see him before? You sat directly across from the stage galleries. Did you see William at stage right before he was shot?"

Daniel shook his head. "I can't say I did. To the best of my recollection, the gallery opposite the musicians' seating was empty. However, inside it was dark and I wasn't paying any attention to the shadows across the way. My friends and I were attending to the play, as it was quite enjoyable indeed. Your little troupe does well, and I would hardly have missed a moment."

Suzanne thanked him somewhat distractedly, mildly surprised at the compliment in the midst of her distress. Then she had an idea. "Come, Daniel. Come with me." She leapt to her feet and hurried from the room with Daniel behind her.

They climbed the backstage stairs to the stage level and went to the green room. At that moment it was occupied by the three musicians, who were going through their paces, cue to cue, for that afternoon's play. Another corner of the room was being used by actors rehearsing. The mummers had gone for good, so their part of the program had to be filled in temporarily by humorous skits the rest of the actors already knew. Small roles filled by Arturo and members of his family would have to be covered by other actors or simply left out. Big Willie and the others stood in the presence of the earl.

Suzanne addressed Willie, who set his fiddle on his three-legged stool to listen. "Dearest Willie, may I ask you something? In fact, all of you. None of you were watching the play. Did any of you see William fall from the gallery?"

All three shook their heads without having to think about it. Willie said, "I saw naught, Suze. Near as I could tell, he wasn't even in the gallery. That is, when I did look, which was a bit before he fell. If he were there, he weren't there long, I'd say."

Suzanne looked at the other musicians, and they both agreed.

"Perhaps he was running from his killer? Could he have been fleeing, found himself cornered, and fell over the banister when he was shot?"

The musicians all shrugged, and Willie said, "That sounds as good an explanation as any, Suze. As I said, I never saw him until I heard that great crash and screaming from down in the pit."

"Thank you, fellows," said Suzanne. "I'll leave you to your rehearsal now."

They all gave awkward, nodding bows to the earl, then waited for him and Suzanne to move toward the door before seating themselves again.

Just outside the door, Suzanne stopped to think. She looked around at the narrow corridor that led in one direction to the stage and in the other toward the staircase that connected all three stories at the rear of the 'tiring house. A question was rising in her mind, and she found herself drawn toward the stairs.

"Come," she said to Daniel. "I want to look at something." She grabbed his hand and pulled him along with her.

He grunted with a bit of impatience, but followed her, probably out of curiosity more than anything else. She led him up the stone spiral stairs two levels to the rear of the stage right gallery. The bright afternoon sun lit up every corner of it. There were no benches here, for this area had not yet been prepared to seat an audience. The space was open, occupied only by a few pillars down the center holding up the roof. Suzanne went to the railing and looked over it to the stage below, where a short pantomime was being performed, heedless of the ever-darkening bloodstain that still marred the boards. Suzanne made a mental note to have that sanded clean.

She examined the railing and the floor alongside it.

"What are you looking for?" asked Daniel.

"Nothing."

"Then why—"

"I mean, I think I'll find nothing."

"Should you find something?"

"If there were someone here. There's no indication that anyone was ever here."

"The place was recently restored. Of course there were people here."

"The area is clean. The workers cleaned it up, and there's nothing to indicate anyone has been here since."

"Again, I ask, should there be?"

Suzanne thought hard. "Well, I suppose William could have fallen over the side without leaving a mark, but I don't see any blood."

That piqued Daniel's interest, and he came to look at the railing and the floor beside it. "No blood?"

"I don't see any. Do you?"

"Indeed, I do not. I find that disquieting. Wainwright was

pierced in the throat with a crossbow bolt. There should be blood everywhere. I don't see even one drop."

"It couldn't have spattered out over the stage?"

"Dear Suzanne, I've been in battle, and have seen many men's throats cut or pierced. The force of blood leaving a body from such a wound sends it in a spray that would not only have reddened the entire area, but would also have marked the killer, were he standing within the confines of this gallery. I've spat out enough of my enemies' blood to know it can't be avoided."

Suzanne looked down at the stage and its dark stain, then around at the floor beneath her feet. "Not a drop up here. Not anywhere."

Chapter Thirteen

The very next afternoon they had another visit from Constable Pepper. Again he appeared as if from nowhere, and nobody noticed his presence until Suzanne came across him poking around in the 'tiring house. Some costumes hanging outside the stairwell interested him, and he was examining some moth-eaten wool that had been put back together with tiny stitches.

"How may I help you, constable?" Suzanne was breathless with terror that he must have come to arrest her, but she held her voice even. She could fake calmness. Panic would only make her appear guilty.

He fingered the fabric, and said, "This cloak is filled with holes."

"Moths. They're a scourge for the costumes. They make holes in the wool. Much cheaper to sew it than to replace it, and nobody more than a few feet away from the stage can know the difference, particularly if the fabric is a dark color."

"Illusion is your business."

"We're here to tell a story."

"Tell lies."

"To entertain, if you please. The difference between a lie and a story is that when one tells a story the audience is in on the fiction. A story can have holes, like this cloak, so long as they're small, not obvious, and the audience is willing to overlook them. Just as with the cloak. A lie, on the other hand, unravels completely the very instant the listener detects a single, tiny flaw. A lie is much, much harder to construct, because it must be perfect or it's worthless. I far prefer telling stories to lies, for lies require far more effort than I generally care to spend."

Pepper peered at Suzanne, thinking. Then he said, "You've thought this over."

"Not really. I should think it would be patently obvious to anyone with any sort of intelligence."

Pepper's lips pressed together, as if he'd been insulted, and Suzanne realized he may very well have felt she'd meant to insult him. She bit her lip, realizing a perverse impulse may have caused her to unintentionally insult him. She now worried she'd annoyed him. Not for the first time in her life, she mentally kicked herself for saying too much.

He let go of the cloak and turned to face her directly. "Remind me where you were when the body of William Wainwright fell to the stage."

"I was in the stage left gallery. I sat with the musicians that night."

"Was anyone else with you there?"

She blinked, wondering whether he had even heard her mention the musicians. She answered the question again. "The . . . musicians. Big Willie, Warren, and the Scottish fellow."

"Are they willing to vouch for your presence in the gallery at the time of the murder?"

"I expect so." They would be foolish to tell him anything other than what she'd told them, for she was their employer.

"Are any of them gentlemen? Landed, perhaps?"

"They're musicians. I believe Warren also has a position with St. Paul's Cathedral. Keeping books, or some such, I believe. Each is an upstanding Christian, and as honest as anyone, but not landed, I'm certain." Suzanne knew "honest as anyone" to be faint praise, for most people she knew were habitual liars. But at least she didn't lie when she said it, for Big Willie and the others were no worse than most people.

Pepper made a disappointed face Suzanne didn't believe in the least. He'd surely known none of the musicians were gentlemen, and couldn't have been disappointed at the news. "Terrible shame. Hardly an adequate alibi. Had a person of repute seen you there . . ."

"Why ever should I need an alibi? Am I under suspicion?"

"You had motive."

"I wished him gone, but never dead. He was once my lover; I couldn't hate him enough to kill him."

"He was your lover? You didn't tell me that last time we spoke."

"You didn't ask. In fact, you asked me no questions at all. Had you done so, I would have told you exactly what I saw and from whence I saw it, and why I could not possibly have killed William. A good Christian woman could not wish any man dead for any reason."

Pepper tilted his head and peered into her face as if examining her eyes for a lie. "Good Christian woman? How do you reconcile that with your long history of prostitution? Your years of fornication with Wainwright? Your"—he glanced around him at the theatre building—"your current occupation as a purveyor of . . . fiction?"

"Plays are how we communicate our culture, constable. I do a service to England with my troupe. Stories are how we teach each other who we are, and who our ancestors were before us. Have you read Genesis, constable?"

He let out an offended harrumph. "Of course I have."

"Have you really read it, and not just browsed bits of it during church?"

Pepper declined to reply and merely looked at her as if disgusted with the entire thread of thought.

She continued, "If you read the whole of the book of Genesis, you'll notice that it's a string of stories that tell where the Jewish culture originated."

"Where we all originated."

Suzanne nodded once and allowed as that was true. "And so each story tells us who we are and where we came from." She gestured toward the stage. "Our plays are not the word of God, but they nevertheless tell us things about ourselves that help us to understand our place in the world. They serve our culture and bind the society together." Pepper's mouth pressed into a white line of disagreement, and she said somewhat tartly, "Also, constable, our plays keep the riffraff off the streets of an afternoon and give them something to do with themselves other than stealing from or injuring each other."

"Well, apparently you've failed to keep the riffraff from murdering William Wainwright."

"Knowing William, I'd say there must be a great many people who would have loved to see him quieted for good."

"Such as whom?"

Suzanne suddenly wanted to kick herself for saying that, for she could think of no names.

"Such as yourself, I suppose?" said Pepper.

"His wife, I expect." She knew little about his wife, but had no allegiance to her and was quite willing to send Pepper off to question her. "By all accounts, she was not particularly enchanted with him."

"Neither were you, by all accounts."

Suzanne burned to know who had been talking to him. "Not I, constable. As I said, I would wish no man dead, let alone actually make him so." Then she had a sudden thought and blurted it. "You might look to the mummers who left so precipitously the night of the murder."

Strangely, the look that came to Pepper's face was almost one of disappointment. Certainly of irritation. "Ah. The mummers."

"We had the troupe of them here for short commedia dell'arte bits and tumbling. They left so quickly, and without taking their money for the night, I thought it terribly suspicious."

"And do you know where one might locate them?"

"I'm afraid I don't. They packed up and left the night of the murder. Quite suddenly, and I can't imagine why."

"You didn't tell me of this."

"I did."

Pepper's eyes narrowed, and he looked as if he might want to argue the point, but then he only sidestepped the issue. "Surely you understand the implications."

"Indeed, I think it relevant, but had doubts you thought so, too."

Pepper went silent for a moment, clearly annoyed with her and unhappy to have these things pointed out to him. He said, "And you have no way of learning where this troupe went?"

"No. I don't. They may be long gone from London by now."

Pepper's lips pressed together in irritation, and he eyed Suzanne for a moment, as if struggling to decide something. Then he said, "If you hear anything of them, do let me know."

"I certainly will, constable. You can count on me." This was a fine example of the difference between a story and a lie, for she was certain Pepper didn't know she had no intention of ever telling him anything of the sort. If he wanted to arrest Arturo and his mummer troupe, he'd have to find them himself, without her help. If she ever had any knowledge of their whereabouts, she would speak to Arturo first, then determine whether Constable Pepper should know where to find him.

He nodded, confident he would be obeyed. "Then I'll bid you good day, and return you to your lawful occasions."

"Thank you, constable. Good day." She watched him exit the 'tiring house to the stage, then went to the door to see him continue on his way out of the theatre, threading his way between the actors in rehearsal. Her heart raced still, and she dreaded ever seeing him again. She resisted the urge to have the main entrance doors closed against him, for she knew it would do no good.

THE theatre that night was packed, as it had been every night since the murder. Every seat sold before the show began, and the groundlings elbowed each other for space in the pit. By the time the actors took the stage for *Henry V*, the overspill from the house galleries filled the standing room in the stage galleries. The fortunate ones who bought their tickets late were treated to the opportunity to stand in the spot from whence the victim had fallen, and peer over the rail at the death stain below. Hardly anyone saw or heard the play for the chatter of speculation about how the murder had been done and who had done it. By the end of the performance when the audience had gone and only the resident actors remained, removing paint from their faces and cooking supper on the green room hearth, Horatio had risen to a fine temper at the audience behavior. He paced the floor, shouting and gesticulating.

"We've lost our audience! We're no longer a theatre, we're a curiosity! They were only interested in seeing the bloodied stage! None of them came for the play; it was only the murder that had their attention. This is a disgrace, I tell you!" He paced back and forth and his booming voice reverberated from the green walls of the 'tiring room.

Suzanne's voice was as calm as she could make it, though she was nearly as annoyed as he and would have liked to have joined him in his tantrum. But she knew from past experience that someone had to stay calm when he was like this or the fabric of the troupe would continue to tear and become a rag. "Here, Horatio. It matters not why they came; what matters is they paid their admission and had a good time. Perhaps we should charge a premium for seats in the stage galleries, where the view of the bloodstain is excellent. Would that satisfy your pride?"

Horatio stopped his pacing and brought himself up to his full, considerable height. "We should charge a premium regardless, for we are the finest actors in London! And the quality of theatre in London has surpassed all of Europe for a hundred years!" One finger rose toward heaven to punctuate his speech. "'Tis a given that we should have the house full every night, for aught but interest in the play and eagerness to witness greatness!" He fairly shouted the word "greatness," then continued in intense sotto voce as he leaned close to Suzanne's face, finger still in the air, *"Attendance as curiosity is not success!"*

"Horatio, please calm down. You're upsetting the players."

He looked around at the frightened faces in the room. Louis sat perched on the edge of a table laden with pots of paint, brushes, and powders, his arms crossed over his chest. Christian stood in a corner, looking sideways at Horatio like a dog about to be beaten. Others by the hearth chewed slowly on sausages and bread. Horatio seemed to deflate, all the air sighing from him as he realized he was once again alarming people.

"Very well." His tone was now reasonable. "We shall rejoice in our lucre and not care why we are popular."

The room relaxed at once, and everyone began to breathe again, except Suzanne. She didn't care much what the audience thought of William's murder, nor was she all that concerned about Horatio's temper, but she did still wonder what was going through the mind of Constable Pepper.

Horatio said brightly, in a tone of false cheer, "And even better, we can be glad we're no longer paying the mummers."

Louis muttered, "But we have to fill in their bits, don't we? I rather wish they'd stayed, myself. They pleased the audience." They also had a daughter who was fourteen and beautiful, and everyone knew Louis had set his eye on her. Since the mummers left, Louis had been keen to find them again.

Big Willie, parked in a corner and cleaning his fiddle, said, "They had to leave, or Pepper'd be all over them in a heartbeat, he would. One of them had a to-do with Master William not long ago."

Suzanne frowned to learn this and came to sit beside him. She leaned her elbows on her knees to listen closely. "What did you say, Willie?"

The fiddler shrugged and shook his head as he rubbed the sound board of his instrument with an oiled cloth. "Weren't nothing, Suze. One night a few weeks ago, one of them mummers—Arturo it was, I believe—had a fight with Wainwright. Came to fisticuffs, it did."

"A fight? An exchange of blows?"

Willie nodded.

"Did you see the fight?"

Willie shook his head. "Nah, we all just heard about it after. Arturo was a-telling it about at the Goat and Boar. Said Wainwright came after him for something or other. Said he wanted his knife back, or somewhat. Seems he was a mite forceful about it, shouting and poking and such. Arturo told him to shove off, or he'd show him his own dagger. Wainwright insisted he'd have his knife back and then he'd cut the throats of everyone who'd disrespected him. That was when Arturo presented his weapon and told Wainwright to leave off or he'd be the one to die."

"So Arturo threatened William's life?"

"He did. But it was defense. Arturo didn't look for it none. And as far as I know he never meant to do it. 'Twas only a threat."

"And where did this take place?"

Willie pointed with his chin in the general direction of the stage and said, "Out in the pit, when most everyone had left, he said."

"There were no witnesses?"

"None as Arturo mentioned. But he took his mummers and left after the murder, seeing as how he'd told the story around so much and Pepper was bound to hear of it." On his fiddle he found something invisible that he removed with a hard, moist puff of breath and a scrub with his oiled cloth.

"So, William backed down and left without a fight?"

"Well, he was a madman, but not so far gone as he'd fight

a man with a knife on him, I expect." He held his fiddle up to the candle to assess its shine, and seemed satisfied. Then he began to tune the strings, plinking with his fingers, then stroking with his bow.

That someone in the mummers' troupe had fought with William just before his death, then they'd all departed so quickly, looked bad for Arturo and might not be good in actuality. Particularly if Constable Pepper caught wind of it and decided to arrest him. Suzanne liked Arturo and couldn't imagine him doing cold-blooded murder, but even she had to wonder whether he had killed William that night.

"What do you think, Horatio, that Arturo and his group left so precipitously that night?"

Louis said, "I think he done it."

"Arturo?"

Louis nodded. "That Arturo is a mean, sly bastard. He'll stab you in the back as soon as look at you, and never with the slightest conscience. He's got no conscience. Them foreigners is all like that."

"He's not a foreigner. To the best of my knowledge, he was born right here in London. At least, he speaks like a Londoner."

"His people are from Italy. Or Greece. Italy, I think. They're all oily foreigners, and can't be trusted."

"Except for their young girls."

"Well, of course except for the girls. Girls ain't all ready to knife you like that. You can trust a girl. But the men, they all stick together and anyone who isn't one of them can't trust 'em as far as you could throw this here theatre."

Suzanne made a humming sound as a fit of melancholy came over her. "Yes, they're loyal to their families. I think there's something to be said about the ideal of familial ties.

Never having had family ties of any kind, I am rather awed by it. I envy them."

Horatio opened his mouth to say something, but didn't in the presence of the others. Suzanne knew he thought of himself as her family, and she appreciated the sentiment, but she wished for a real blood tie and knew she would never in her life find it with anyone other than Piers.

But she shook off the sad thought and said, "All that aside, Louis, I asked Horatio whether he thinks it's significant that the mummers departed without a 'Fare thee well' the very night of the murder. Horatio? What do you think?"

Horatio grunted noncommittally and shrugged. "I couldn't say, for a certainty, except that they surely were afraid of something. Whether their fear related to the murder or not is a mystery. Perhaps they fled for the sake of escaping punishment for another crime. Even a minor one. They are thieves, after all. After we took them on, I had to take Arturo aside to inform him that he was not to send members of his troupe through the audience to relieve them of their valuables. For that, he would need to attach himself to the royal companies and victimize the gentry."

"And what was his response to that?"

"He said that robbing the grubby sort who are likely to attend our theatre would net his men little more than buttons and lint, and that we shouldn't worry about gaining a reputation for harboring cutpurses. In fact, he suggested he put his group out to identify known thieves in the galleries so they might be ejected."

Louis laughed. "'Sblood! Were we to eject every thief who came into this theatre, we'd have no audience at all!"

Everyone chuckled at that. Suzanne said, "But still, though Arturo is an honorable thief in his own clannish way, perhaps there's reason to believe one or several of the mummers could have involvement in William's murder."

Horatio said, "I wouldn't completely discount the possibility."

Louis nodded and said, "You never can tell with them. 'Tis the simplest misdirection to let folks believe in an honor system that may or may not exist. The most skilled liars will tell you they're liars and let you think that they only lie to *other* people."

Thoughtfully, Suzanne said, "I think I would like to know where they went. And why. Louis, you know people in all the right places to hear where Arturo might have gone."

"If they're still anywhere near London, I can find them." He seemed eager to bolt out the door to that very end at that very moment.

"Good. Do that, won't you?"

"I'll have Arturo back here in a trice, mistress." Louis gave a large, flourished bow.

"Oh, that won't be necessary. Just let me know where they are, and we can go speak to them. No need to send them all into a tizzy by abducting anyone. We should be civilized about it, I think."

"As you wish, Mistress Suze. I expect we can be civilized even when they might not be."

"We'll see how it all turns out, Louis."

SHE didn't have long to worry about Arturo. Three days later, after two more performances with sellout crowds, the feeling during rehearsal that afternoon was of pleasant confidence in a full house. The company had come to expect it, and even Horatio's wounded pride was muted in the wake of the public attention given to his new troupe. And the money. Money had a way of healing many sorts of wounds, and was especially effective on wounded pride.

His fine mood soured again when his instructions to the players were interrupted by thunderous banging at the entrance doors. He turned and glowered at the noise, saying nothing. Everyone else in the theatre stopped to listen and watch, for they all knew it was the sound made by men with intent to enter whether invited or not. Someone was looking for someone to arrest. Suzanne's heart leapt to her throat, and she had to suppress the urge to flee. Running away would help nothing. Instead she strode across the pit to the entrance and ordered the huge doors to be opened before the men outside did damage to them. Two men of the Globe Players complied and lifted the bolt.

In swarmed soldiers in dark red coats and wielding pikes, some with arquebuses. At their head strode Constable Pepper, and Suzanne's alarm edged toward panic that he'd been given charge of so many heavily armed king's men. He was only a local official and shouldn't have command over any part of the army, but there they were, obeying his orders as if he were Lord and Commander. She hitched a little, resisting the urge to run away from him, then forced herself to address the pompous little man, who gazed about at the place as if he owned it.

"What is meant by this?" She bluffed as smoothly as her talent as an actress would allow. "I thought your investigation of my theatre was finished." Not true, but she thought it sounded strong and she meant to discourage further disturbances. "The king shall know of this."

"Indeed he shall," said Pepper with a knowing air. Now she

wondered what had already been said to the king, and by whom. Her bluff wobbled, but she held her chin up.

"We're rehearsing, if you please. We have a performance in two hours and haven't time to spend on interruptions."

Pepper's eyes narrowed at her, then he said to the men behind him, "Take her."

Two men with pikes stepped forward to grab her by the arms. Her composure crumbled and she resisted, tried to yank free, but they held her and she realized a struggle would only make things worse. She then relented and stood as calmly as she could, but trembling, and addressed Pepper with all her dignity and half her voice. "How dare you!"

"By the king's authority, I place you, Suzanne Thorn—"

"I did it!" Piers's voice cut through the commotion as he called out over the heads of those clustered around his mother.

Suzanne turned to see her son approach through the players, who parted before him, astonished. He shouted and waved a fist. "Arrest me! I killed William Wainwright!"

"Piers! No!"

He ignored her, and kept his eyes on Pepper. They were alive with his habitual anger, and his nostrils flared with heavy breaths. His cheeks flushed dark red, and his clenched fists seemed ready to strike out at whatever might challenge him.

Pepper peered at him. "You?"

"I killed William Wainwright. I took a crossbow from the green room, found him in the gallery, and shot him."

"No, Piers! You did no such thing!"

But the light in Pepper's eyes told them all he liked the idea of being able to arrest a man rather than a woman for the murder. He gestured to the soldiers to release Suzanne, then said to Piers, "Why did you shoot him?"

"I've always hated him. He deserted my mother in a time of need. He used her when it suited him, and was never particularly good to her in any case. I've always wanted him dead, so I killed him when I saw a chance. It's exactly that simple."

"That's not true!" Suzanne felt the world distort, and suddenly it seemed she was shouting across a great distance to her son. "No, Piers! Don't do this!" Then she burst into tears as the soldiers shoved her aside and grabbed Piers by his arms.

As the soldiers hustled him away, he looked back at her, and she saw for a moment the little boy he had once been, afraid and hoping for his mother to help him. Then he shut his eyes. When they opened, he was once again the grown man who would sacrifice himself for his mother. He went peacefully with Pepper and the king's men.

Suzanne screamed and Horatio caught her as she collapsed, sobbing.

Louis, Christian, and Horatio helped her into the green room, away from the others. Rehearsal resumed for the rest of the troupe, for there was nothing for it but to continue with that afternoon's performance. Loss of revenue was one thing, but turning away a full house of patrons eager for a show and a look at the murder scene was a prospect more risky than dealing with a platoon of redcoats. Outside the green room voices rang out here and there as performers readied themselves. Suzanne sat on a stool and leaned against the face paint table behind her.

To Horatio she said, "Not Piers. Anyone but Piers." The image of her son in a dank cell rose and choked her so she couldn't take breath. She clutched the front of her shirt in both fists and bent nearly double in her chair. Liza put an arm around her shoulders, and so did Christian. Horatio stood to the side, silent and wide-eyed. Silent Horatio was even more frightening than angry Horatio, for the rarity and strangeness of it. Suzanne's sobs came harder. "We've got to do something, Horatio."

"Perhaps the earl will have him out soon."

That hope washed over Suzanne, cool and fresh, for it was a reasonable one. It was something to cling to, a rock in a flood. She blinked and stared at the floor as she realized it. "Yes. Daniel will help. Now that there's something for him to take to the king, he can help. Surely he will." But though Suzanne was able to straighten and breathe again, hands still shaking, a small, cold terror remained that Daniel might not want to help his son.

Horatio dispatched Christian at a run to Whitehall with a message, but two hours later the boy returned without Daniel. Suzanne received Christian in her quarters, where he reported, sweating from his exertions and wide-eyed with apprehension. She grasped his shoulders and made him look at her. "Did you see Throckmorton?"

Christian nodded, then looked at the floor.

"What did he say?"

"He said naught."

Suzanne blinked and let go of the boy's shoulders. "Nothing at all? Tell me from the beginning."

Christian stared straight down at his feet and fidgeted. "I was allowed into the palace, and admitted to the earl's quarters. His page at first claimed Throckmorton wasn't present, but upon pressing my mission was an emergency, the earl came from the inner rooms to speak to me." He shrugged, a little apologetic. "I was a bit loud, and I suppose he'd heard me, well, shouting."

"And you told him what happened?"

Christian nodded. "I said Master Piers had been arrested."

"And what did he reply?"

"Nothing, as I told you." The boy's voice took an edge of impatience, and he looked at the floor, then glanced sideways at her to gauge her reaction to it. When she showed no reaction to read, he continued in a more subordinate tone, "He only sat in a chair and stared at me for a spell. Soon I began to wonder whether he'd forgotten I was there, though his eyes looked right at me. I dared not speak until spoken to, and he weren't speaking to me at all. Then finally he dismissed me."

"Dismissed you? With no explanation? No answer for me?"

"None, mistress. He only said, 'You may go.' Just like that. And then he rose from his chair, retreated to his inner rooms, and left me there for his page to show me the door."

Suzanne sat, for her legs quite failed her and her knees buckled. Daniel wasn't going to help. She'd been left alone once more to fend for herself. Tears rose, and she choked them back, for crying never solved anything. She'd done enough of it to know. So she took deep breaths and struggled to clear her mind. No Daniel, and no Piers to help her through this. Horatio was sweet and she knew he supported her with all his heart like an uncle, but he was unsuited to the task of freeing Piers from gaol, and especially he hadn't the power to save him from the gallows.

Oh, the gallows! Once more panic gripped her hard and there was no breath to be had. Her fists pressed to her chest, and she leaned forward so her forehead almost touched her knees. Oh, the gallows! For several minutes she sat there, unable to speak or move.

Horatio said softly, "Fear not, my niece. Piers has his mother to protect him."

Through the panic, Suzanne heard this, and it touched something deep within her. Piers had her to protect him, just as he always had as a child. She sat up and found her breath, and her head began to clear. Piers would be all right, for she would make sure of it. It was up to her now to save her son.

"Horatio, do you know where Piers was when William was shot?"

The big man shrugged. "I cannot say. I was behind the entrance door, awaiting my cue. I saw nothing, not even the falling man."

She turned to the boy. "Christian, was he in the green room when the crossbow was stolen?"

Christian shook his head, certain of his answer. "No, not at all. Master Piers never goes into the green room, mistress. He's not a trouper, and there's precious little enough room in there for them as are supposed to be in there during a performance, what with all the guests there always is. Folks who want to be backstage but never onstage; he never cared for them. Had he gone in there for any reason, it would have been an oddity noticed by all. There weren't no Master Piers in the green room at all that night, not any night, not for any reason."

Suzanne would have thought the same thing. Piers could not have taken the crossbow. Without that crossbow, it was impossible for him to have killed William. The thing to do now was to go to Constable Pepper in the morning and make him understand the truth of it.

The office of the constable in Southwark was a tidy little building on a more or less quiet side street near the bridge but not on the bank. The office itself was so quiet and stuffy, its atmosphere sludge-like, Suzanne wondered what might ever get done there. She thought it likely not much did. It smelled of old wood, dust, and cheap ink, and the floors appeared to have gone a long time since they'd been scrubbed.

A clerk sat at a writing desk, absorbed in recording numbers, with a stack of notes at his elbow and a pot of ink just under his nose, which pointed straight down as he bent over the ledger like an ice-laden tree. A half-eaten loaf stuffed with meat sat at his other elbow, and as Suzanne watched he took a slow, massive bite from it. His manner was lethargic, and it took a moment for him to even realize someone had walked into the room. Plainly it was a struggle for him to focus, and he peered at her for a moment before lowering his glasses and addressing her, his cheek still full of bread and beef from his last bite. "May I help you, mistress?"

"I wish to speak to the constable, please."

The clerk's glance at an inner door that was ajar told her Pepper was in, but he turned back and said in a voice muffled by food, "I'm afraid that's not possible."

"Are you saying he's not in, or he's in and not available?"

The young man had to think about that, and Suzanne waited patiently for a reply she knew would be a lie. Finally he swallowed enough to be intelligible and said, "Not in, mistress."

"Please don't lie to me. If he's in but not available, simply say so."

It was with relief that the clerk said, "Oh, then. Not available." He returned his attention to his work, as if that settled the matter and she was now to leave him in peace.

And so she did. Without further discussion, she marched through the inner door and found the constable sitting behind a desk, in the company of two other men who lounged in chairs and held fine, clear glasses filled with dark brownish-purple liquid that appeared to be brandy. A bottle with a label in French stood on the desk between them, and it held only an inch or two of the stuff. From the flushed cheeks all around, Suzanne guessed these good fellows well met had been at it the better part of the morning.

"Good morning, constable," she said brightly, as if she'd been invited in.

He peered up at her, apparently unable to focus well. It took a moment for him to recognize her in a dress, but when he did he replied appropriately. "Mistress Thornton. What a surprise."

"I can't imagine why you should think it surprising. You have my son in custody; I am, in fact, tardy in responding to this outrage."

Pepper set his glass on the desk before him, glanced at his companions, and said, "Your son has confessed to a heinous murder. Your outrage will be of no help to you or him, and I'm told there will be no help from your friend Throckmorton, either."

Suzanne's cheeks warmed. She wanted desperately to know what Pepper could have learned about her and Daniel, and what had been said that made Pepper think Daniel wouldn't help her. But she ignored Pepper and continued, "Piers did not murder William."

"And what makes you say that, other than that you don't wish to see your son hang?"

"Constable Pepper, nothing about his confession meets with what we know to be true. He was nowhere near the stage right gallery when William was shot. He could not have been the one to have taken the crossbow that night, for it was stolen from a room he never enters and nobody in the room at that time saw him."

"So you say. Am I to believe the word of the mother of a murderer? If every mother who came forward to exonerate her son told the truth, Newgate Prison would be empty and I would be out of a job." That brought a chuckle from the two other men with their brandies.

228 ❧ *Anne Rutherford*

"Even so, Pepper, it is by all accounts that Piers was not in those places at those times. There is no reason to believe Piers killed William."

"Oh!" Here Pepper gave his friends a sly glance. "I see now I'm to be taken in by the testimonies of *actors*!" The smirky grin on his face angered Suzanne, and her cheeks flushed darker, but she held her temper and forced herself to draw deep, even breaths.

"Yes, indeed, constable," she continued. "If you're to find the man who did this, you must take into account the testimonies of those who witnessed it. And I would add that had you come to the murder scene in a timely manner instead of waiting for all the witnesses to go home and the body to be taken away, you might have found someone who actually saw the murder. If the only accounts are from actors, you've only yourself to blame."

That also brought a chuckle from Pepper's friends, but not from Pepper. His look was sour as he replied, "There is one eyewitness account more important than all the rest. I have a confession from your son. And in fact, I have it in writing." He reached over and lifted a corner of a page that lay on his desk. Suzanne stared at it and wished mightily for the nerve to snatch it up and run away with it. But that would accomplish nothing in the end, so she held her hands in fists and tried to reason with this stupid man.

"He only wished to keep me from Newgate. I'm certain you know that, and you must understand that for that reason his testimony is as self-serving as my own."

"It's true I was prepared to press a case against you for the murder, what with your history with the victim, but I find it much easier to convict when I have a confession than when

I must build a case against one who protests. And I have no
reason to believe your son a liar."

"God forbid you should ever actually do your job."

A stung look came over Pepper, and Suzanne wondered
whether she'd gone too far. But he said evenly, "I'm a busy
man, Mistress Thornton. Any happenstance that enables me
to ease my day is a benefit not just to me but to the City of
London, for it frees me for other, more important work."

"Such as drinking with friends." She glanced at the
other men.

Pepper gestured to his companions with his glass. "I have
important friends." Now those friends, quite entertained with
this exchange and enjoying Pepper's performance, looked to
Suzanne with the eagerness of a paying audience awaiting her
response.

Suzanne hated such use from these men, but continued to
press. "You must want to find the real murderer."

Pepper shrugged. "I wish to have the case closed, to the
satisfaction of the king, for that is the extent of my job: to make
the king and the magistrate happy. I have no reason to believe
I haven't. And in any case, in the greater scheme of things, the
matter is not so terribly important. William Wainwright was
neither a weighty nor well connected man. Your son, though
he might be important to you, is of no significance to anyone
else. Since Wainwright was a rather vocal and annoying Puritan, the king wishes the case to be closed as quickly, quietly,
and neatly as possible. I cannot imagine a solution more quick
and neat than a full, written confession. Your son has done us
both enormous favors, Mistress Thornton. In one gesture he's
not only saved you from the gallows, he's also enabled me to
please my sovereign and my immediate superior. Now good

day, and on your way out tell my clerk I wish to see him, to know how you were able to enter the office and annoy me today." With that, he poured himself more brandy and resumed his conversation with his friends. Suzanne was dismissed.

Chapter Fourteen

The walk back to the Globe was not a long one, but Suzanne took it slowly and hardly saw where she was going. A fine rain drizzled over the city and a mist spilled from the river that made London a dream world, unreal and uncontrollable. People in the street, adults and children, vendors, prostitutes she'd known for years, drifted past as if incorporeal, silent in the muting fog. She'd neglected to bring an umbrella, and as the rain became more than a light softness she pulled her cloak around her and ducked her head.

As she walked she cast about in her mind in search of what to do next. Fantasies of breaking into Newgate with armed men to rescue Piers from his captors danced in her head. She imagined a sea of friends carrying knives, swords, and maces storming the gates of the prison, shouting and laying about them, then carrying away her son to safety. She imagined Pepper getting in their way and falling beneath their charge, trampled and finally bludgeoned to death. She pictured herself leading this charge, carrying an axe with which she would break her son's shackles and free him. She wanted enough for these fantasies to be true that she thought through the strategies and laid out in her mind the plan to accomplish them. But in the end, as she approached the theatre she came to her senses and understood her thoughts were only the product of desperation. Impractical and impracticable. With a sigh she let them go, and they dissolved in the damp air like ghosts.

When her vision cleared, she looked up and saw Daniel's carriage standing outside the theatre. His driver had thrown blankets over the waiting horses, so she knew he'd been there a while and didn't expect to depart soon. She picked up her skirts and hurried inside, her pattens clacking and wobbling on the cobbles.

"Daniel?" He wasn't in sight, in the house or on the stage, where rehearsal was in progress. She went straight to her quarters, where Throckmorton awaited her. He'd been given a cup of ale and was sipping it patiently when she burst in. "Daniel." She wanted to hug him for being there but refrained, afraid she'd mistaken his reason for coming, and further concerned that he might misinterpret her reason for wanting a hug. She stood still for a moment, got a grip on herself, and began calmly to divest herself of her dripping cloak and headdress. Sheila came to help her out of her pattens and to take the cloak. Then she brought a towel for Suzanne to dry off. At first she tried to leave her hair intact, but as it drooped she gave up and removed all the pins so Sheila could dry it all and brush it out.

When Sheila was finished and dismissed, Daniel set aside his ale, stood, and took her hand. His was warm and strong, while hers was very cold, wet, and trembling. He held hers in both of his to warm it. "Suzanne, where have you been?"

She retrieved her hand and stepped farther into the room to make space between them. "Speaking to the constable. He was no more help than you."

He made a disparaging noise and set his hands on his hips. "That fool is no good to anyone, even himself. I don't know why you went there."

Anger rose. If he couldn't help, then at least he could refrain from criticizing her for attempting to help Piers herself. "I had nowhere else to turn. You weren't forthcoming with a solution."

"My hands are tied, I'm afraid. I can't be of much use to you." He spread his palms, and to her his hands didn't appear so very bound.

"Your son's neck will be tied if we don't do something." Her own words choked her so she had to stop speaking for a moment. She stepped farther away, and he went toward her until she had to walk past him to keep from being cornered in the small room. He turned to follow her.

"You don't think I would help if I could? You don't think I would storm the very prison if I thought it would help my son?"

For a moment Suzanne had an eerie feeling that Daniel had read her mind and was using her own thoughts against her. Then it touched her heart that he'd been thinking the same thing as she had. But she recovered herself and said, "Your son? Daniel Stockton, do you know that's the first time you have ever referred to him as your son?"

He thought for a moment, surprised. "Well, he is."

"Only by blood."

"Which, as they say, is thicker than water. I'm here to offer my support, for what it's worth."

"After thinking long and hard."

"Of course I gave it some thought. Only a fool acts without

first considering the consequences." He drew her to sit, and he sat next to her. "I couldn't give an answer just then, when you sent the messenger. I needed to think through some things. And I still don't know what I might be able to do."

"What is there to think through? How can you be his father and not want to give everything you have to save his life? Why shouldn't you storm Newgate to free him?"

"Suzanne, you don't understand everything. There are things you don't know and I can't tell you. It's not just me who has a stake in the situation. As I said, my hands are tied by things not under my control."

"Such as . . . ?"

"Things I don't care to talk about."

That stung. "Daniel, you can tell me anything. Why don't you trust me? What secrets have I ever betrayed?"

"None, my dear. You've done nothing. But this is how the world works. Only when one has nothing to lose can one traipse off to rail at the constable, or whatever remedy comes to mind. There are people involved in this case who carry more weight than Samuel Pepper, and I must keep my own counsel."

"Tell me who."

"Suzanne, you know who."

"Anne."

"And others."

She stood. "Daniel, I must ask you to leave. You come here to offer your support, but it's only talk. You do nothing."

"Suzanne, you must believe me." He stood and reached for her hands again, but she held them behind her back to keep away from him. If she allowed him to touch her, she might fall into his arms and her cause would be entirely lost. He straightened and drew his chin in, angry now.

"And why? How do I owe you my faith? And why should you care what I believe or don't believe?"

His voice took on a sharp edge. "You wouldn't have this theatre without me."

There it was, the age-old control. She owed him money, so she must owe him whatever he might ask. Not for the first time in her life she was aware that the only freedom was to not care. "I would hand it back to have my son restored to me. I care nothing for this theatre, and everything for him."

There was a long pause as Daniel considered his next words, then he said them. "Without me you wouldn't have him, either."

Again she saw the "you owe me" trap, and declined to step into it. "Exactly. He's your son, too. No matter what you let be known publicly, he's your flesh and blood and there's no denying it. Help me save him! *You owe him that!*"

Daniel's frame sagged in defeat. "I simply don't have the power. The king thinks he's guilty, and there's no persuading him otherwise."

"Piers didn't steal the crossbow. He wasn't in the green room that night. He's almost never in the green room."

"That may very well be true, but you can't prove it. Suzanne, to convince Charles there must be more than just a mother's word that your baby boy wouldn't have done such a terrible thing."

"Surely you can convince him, Daniel. Nobody would ever accuse you of having too much affection for Piers."

Daniel blinked at the barb and didn't reply immediately. Then he swallowed, as if getting rid of the insult, and said, "They would. They surely would. But that's neither here nor there. I simply don't have that kind of influence, for it's a matter

236 *❦* Anne Rutherford

of larger things that cannot be controlled. Take my word on this, Suzanne. I would save him if I could, but I can't." For a brief moment his face dissolved in a mask of grief, but he overcame it and continued. "I simply cannot."

There was a long silence. She gazed into his face and he into hers, and she realized there was nothing more to be said except, "Please leave, Daniel."

"Suzanne—"

"Leave now." She called out, "Horatio!"

The large man plainly had been listening outside the door, for it opened immediately and he filled the doorway. "My lord," he said to Daniel in his gentlest voice, which nonetheless commanded attention, "I require thy compliance with my mistress's request, if thou will't." He gestured with an open hand for the earl to take his gracious leave.

Daniel looked over at him. "And if I decline?"

"I wouldn't care to 'compass the consequences, my lord. It wouldn't be pleasant at all, I'm afraid."

Daniel gazed blandly at Horatio, as if weighing those consequences against his desire to stay. Then he looked back at Suzanne. "I wish you would trust me."

She replied, "I wish for my son not to hang, and further I would you wished it. I'm appalled that you don't."

There was no possible reply to that, so Daniel straightened his jacket and allowed Horatio to accompany him to his carriage.

THE play, of course, went on that afternoon as usual. Still *Henry V*, though the next production would open the following day. Suzanne went to watch from the third floor gallery directly over the entrance doors. She liked to watch from there, though it sometimes made the dialogue hard to follow if too many patrons nearby chatted amongst themselves. The house today was full once again, but Suzanne found a wide enough space on a bench near the front of the gallery and settled in to watch.

She'd seen this play many times, of course, and had performed it as Katharine in earlier days when she could convincingly fill the role of a young French princess. She watched the play unfold on the stage below as her mind wandered to that night when William had fallen from the stage gallery, across the way and a bit to her left. She looked across, with a mind to what a witness might have seen. So many spectators, and not one had seen William before the fall.

This day was cloudy, and so she was able to see into the dim gallery without any trouble. She observed how well she was able to see inside the gallery today, but on the day of the murder the sun would have made deep shadows. Nobody outside it would have been able to see in. Today it was full of people who had paid dearly for the "murder seats," some of whom leaned over the rail to gaze at the stage below. Some were still there to see the bloodstain, which remained though several attempts had been made to clean it. Now she considered leaving it, at least as long as people were willing to pay extra to see it. Once the novelty wore off, then she would consider replacing the boards.

The play progressed, and she found herself moving her lips along with the lines in French spoken by Katharine. How difficult that had been to memorize, since she spoke so very little French, and now she rattled it off without thinking. She'd thought Katharine a silly girl, and had played her as such, which quite amused her street audience. Today Liza cavorted across the stage in that role, having memorized even the French with no effort at all. Suzanne envied that perfect memory, and might have hated her if the girl hadn't also been so free of problems common in performers and therefore a treasure to have in the troupe. She drank, but not to excess, and could stay sober as a minister. She maintained her former clientele, but never brought them to the theatre. She was smart, funny, pretty, and popular with the audience. Suzanne couldn't help liking her.

Further into the play, when Suzanne had nearly let slip from her mind her fear and had become absorbed in the story, a line leapt out at her. *"Go with my brothers to my lords of England: I and my bosom must debate awhile, and then I would no other company."*

At first she didn't know why the line struck her. It was King Henry, speaking to Sir Thomas Erpingham, one of his officers. The king wore a cloak borrowed from his subordinate and was about to go incognito amongst the men of his army on the night before the battle of Agincourt. It touched something in the back of Suzanne's mind, but just then she couldn't tell what. She looked to her left, at the bench on which had sat Daniel and his Cavalier friends the day of the murder, and the feeling grew stronger. The play went on below as she cast about for a reason that the scene of King Henry incognito should excite her so.

Then she remembered it. In her mind's eye she saw the man sitting next to Daniel that night, and now she recognized him. It had been Charles. The king, dressed as one of his own Cavaliers, had gone unnoticed among the street rabble and other commoners in that night's audience. And the third with them had been among those she'd seen in the presence chamber several months before. He had been the one who liked cows.

Her heart leapt, but she didn't know exactly what her realization could mean. Daniel had said that anonymous others had been involved the night of the murder. Was this what he'd meant? That Charles had been in the audience that night was an enormous thing, but the implications were unknowable. The only sure thing she could be reasonably certain of was that it might be the reason Daniel couldn't help Piers. But why? Was the king so afraid of anyone learning he'd attended their modest production of a very old play that he would allow Piers to hang for a murder he didn't commit? Surely that couldn't be the thing that kept Daniel silent. It made no sense. But many things men did made no sense. Particularly ruling-class men, who in her experience were often barking mad.

For now she tucked the information into the back of her mind to chew on it for a while, then bring it out to look at it some more. The coincidence of William and the king both being in the theatre on the same night seemed more significant than it might ordinarily.

The next morning at breakfast, Suzanne found herself thinking hard about Anne. If not for the fact that Daniel wished to keep the secret of his illegitimate son, he could acknowledge Piers, who then would be Daniel's heir. Then Pepper wouldn't have dared arrest him on such flimsy evidence. Piers would be a noble, and his word would mean something. If not for the countess, Piers might become the next Earl of Throckmorton rather than a dead convict dangling at the end of a rope.

The injustice of Pepper's actions and Piers's circumstance shocked her, and would have shocked her even had Piers not been her son. It simply was not right that any man's life should end this way. Anger hardened her heart, and she stopped caring about what Daniel needed or wanted. It was time to stand up for herself. It was time to have it all thrashed out and the stink aired. She dressed and hired a cab to take her to Pall Mall. There she exited the carriage, marched to the front door, and knocked on it, fully prepared to tell the countess all about Piers and remove Daniel's reason for not going to the king.

The footman came to the door, and by the disdaining look on his face Suzanne suddenly felt foolish. Like a beggar asking for alms at the front instead of the back. Her gown was the best she had, but it appeared a rag on this magnificent property. It made her know she was a retired tart, hopelessly worn, aged and . . . "handsome." It was a struggle to hold up her chin and boldly request a visit with the countess, but she pressed on with her mission.

The footman said, "I'll see if she is in." His tone told her the countess was in but would probably not want to visit with an uninvited commoner. He shut the door and left her waiting outside, an affront even to one of Suzanne's status. Anger once more burned her cheeks, and her resolve to reveal Daniel's secret to his wife returned. Whatever this might or might not accomplish for Piers, she was going to take away Daniel's easy excuse for his behavior and perhaps know the real reason.

The minutes felt like hours, but in reality it wasn't very long before the footman came to the door once more to invite her in. He escorted her through an entry from which a stairway rose, to a small back room where Anne Stockton sat with a book in her hand. She appeared comfortable, wearing an unadorned robe of dark brown silk, and matching silk slippers. The morning was yet early, and it appeared her habit was to relax with a book before dressing for the day. Suzanne didn't know whether to be offended that Anne hadn't dressed to receive her, or flattered she'd received her at all during this private time of her day. Anne did not rise to greet her, but set the book aside and folded her hands in her lap. Neither did she invite Suzanne to sit, but that was not expected.

"Good morning, Suzanne. You look well today."

Suzanne curtsied, in deference to Anne's rank. She glanced at a nearby chair, but soldiered on while standing like a servant. "Good morning, my lady, and thank you. You are radiant today, I must say."

Anne was. So early in the day, and so obviously not prepared for visitors, she nevertheless shone with pleasant good cheer. Her dimples enhanced a slight smile, and her bright eyes evinced a genuine interest in whatever Suzanne might need or want from her. She said, "How may I help you this fine day? I hope nothing is the matter."

Suzanne was momentarily at a loss to know how to approach her subject, whether to circle it carefully to avoid misunderstanding, or to get straight to the point and have the upper hand as in an ambush. Finally she said, "I know your husband, Daniel."

A puzzled light came into Anne's eyes, but no anger. No distrust. Only curiosity. "Do you? Well, it's a small world, then, isn't it?"

It was, and to Suzanne it was shrinking fast. Closing in. Daniel was going to be apoplectic when he heard she'd been here. "Yes, it is. Obviously I knew who you were when we met in the shop the other day, and I should have mentioned it then. It was thoughtless of me not to; I hope you'll forgive me."

Anne waved away her concern. "It's nothing. In fact, I can't imagine that is why you've come here today."

Suzanne opened her mouth to say the thing, but was interrupted by a man's voice from the doorway.

"Where in bloody hell are my gloves, Anne?"

The countess turned her attention to someone behind

Suzanne, who turned around to see. "I'm afraid I've not seen them, James."

"It's that slut of a maid you've got upstairs. I'll lay odds she's stolen them." James something or other, Duke of someplace. Suzanne couldn't remember his surname or title, but knew he was Anne's brother. He looked a bit like her, but younger. Slender and handsome, as blond as she, with a full, self-indulgent mouth and an ungenerous cast to his eye. Suzanne knew his lands were on the outskirts of London, and guessed he was staying with his sister and brother-in-law as a guest today.

Anne's reaction to her brother's insult was mild. "I can't imagine what Floria might want with your enormous black gloves."

"Why, to sell them, of course. Those people are all thieves; you can't trust a one of them."

The brightness of Anne's eyes waned some, and she said, "If you say so, James."

"I think you should fire her."

"I'll take it under advisement. Meanwhile, why don't you ask her where they are? Perhaps she put them somewhere they might be safe after finding them lying about on the floor. I see them there more often than I see them on your hands."

He laughed. "Somewhere safe, all right. Safe in her quarters."

"It wouldn't hurt to ask."

"Very well. I'll ask." He then left the room and Anne and Suzanne to their conversation.

Anne seemed to deflate as soon as he was gone. For a moment she stared at the middle distance, looking at nothing. Her shoulders slumped, and Suzanne could see pain in her eyes.

"Are you all right, my lady?"

Anne nodded, then looked over at Suzanne. "Do you have brothers or sisters?"

Suzanne nodded. "Both. Older and younger. There are five of us, but I haven't seen my family in a great many years."

"Do you miss them?"

That was difficult to answer, and in the end Suzanne had to shake her head. "No, I'm afraid I don't."

"Then you know how difficult it can be. Having close family ties is a two-edged sword. They can be a magnificent support, but the more one depends on them the more vulnerable one becomes to hurt. I'm sorry you had to see that."

"It's quite all right, my lady." Suzanne gave a slight dip of a curtsey, more as emphasis than protocol.

"I hope you'll keep it to yourself. It would mean a great deal to me to not have it bandied about that my upstairs maid is thought a thief. Particularly since she isn't, and doesn't deserve to be so ill-treated."

"Of course, my lady."

"Thank you." She now focused on Suzanne's face. "Now, you were saying about my husband?"

"Well, my lady, as I was saying, I know him and have known him for many years." Here Suzanne faltered as she realized that what she was about to say would be devastating to the woman before her. She didn't know Anne well, but the little she'd seen in these two encounters gave no indication that she was the hateful, vindictive harridan Daniel had painted her to be.

"Indeed," said Anne. Still nothing but curiosity, encouraging Suzanne to proceed.

"Yes. In fact, I knew him before he left with the Cavaliers." The revelation she'd come to make danced on the tip of her tongue. The words to tell Anne her husband had a grown son were right there for the saying. She opened her mouth, then found she had no voice for it. She couldn't utter the thing that would be so hurtful to someone she didn't know, who didn't deserve the heartache. She closed her mouth, at a loss for something to say.

Anne said, "That's quite a long time ago. You've known him for twenty years?"

Suzanne nodded.

Now a slight edge came to Anne's voice as she struggled to cobble some sense out of what Suzanne was getting at. "And what is it I can help you with today?"

Besides that Anne didn't deserve to be hurt, there was also that telling her Daniel had a third child, here in London, would not solve Piers's problem. It certainly would not move Daniel to go to the king to help Piers; he would only deny the relationship, then never speak to her or Piers again. The only thing Suzanne had hope of accomplishing today was revenge. It would hurt Daniel, who deserved it, but it would also hurt his wife, who did not. At the heart of it, she would be wrong to tell Daniel's secret.

Finally Suzanne found words she could say. "I'm not here for help, my lady. Your husband did me a good turn those many years ago, and I wish to return the favor."

A blink of pleased surprise, and Anne's face lit up with a smile.

Suzanne took a deep breath, her mind scrambling for something likely to tell her. She said, "My son has a theatre in Southwark he's renovated. He's installed an excellent theatre troupe to perform there."

Anne nodded. "The Globe. 'Tis a wondrous thing your son

has done; so much wonderful English tradition is there and he's preserved it. You should be proud."

Suzanne's heart lifted. "Yes, I am. And so, I would like to invite your husband and yourself to come see the plays at any time, without charge. Come early or send a messenger, and we can reserve a stage gallery for your exclusive use."

The countess's face lit up with a sunny smile. "How very lovely! I adore the theatre! What a thoughtful offer! I thank you for the invitation." She held out her hand for Suzanne to take it. "Daniel and I will be pleased to take you up on this, and soon. What play are you performing this week?"

"Shakespeare's *The Winter's Tale,* my lady."

"Not his best, but I'm certain your troupe will put a shine on it. What a joy! Well, then, I expect we'll be seeing you before very long."

"I look forward to it, my lady. And now I must take my leave, for there is always much to do at the theatre. Good day." Not that she expected to be invited to stay for breakfast, but she wished to be on her way and away from Daniel's home.

"Very well, Suzanne. It was lovely to see you this morning. Have a pleasant ride home, and I look forward to seeing *The Winter's Tale.* My man will see you out." She called for her footman, who appeared too quickly not to have been listening.

Suzanne curtsied once more, then followed the footman in silence to the exit. She hurried to the waiting cab and settled into the seat, and as the carriage lurched forward she burst into tears. Piers would certainly be convicted, and there was nothing she could do about it.

Chapter Fifteen

The following morning, Suzanne dressed for a trip to Whitehall, to take her knowledge of the king's theatre visit to Daniel and see his reaction. Never mind that he'd asked her to stay away from the palace. It was risky, but this was important. This might just be the poke needed to get him to take more interest in his son's plight. The next thing, if it came to that, would be to confront the king himself, if possible, and ask what he'd seen that night. If she couldn't storm the prison, she might storm the palace and get results.

But just as Sheila was buckling on the pattens for her, there was a knock at her door and Horatio burst in without waiting for summons. "Suzanne, my niece, I have dire news for thee."

Oh dear. Horatio was speaking in thee-thou. His news would be dire indeed.

"Come in, Horatio." Once Sheila was finished with the pattens, Suzanne received her vizard and was ready to leave for the palace. "Would you care to accompany me to Whitehall today? The king isn't expecting us, but we can't let that get in our way." Her words were far more insouciant than she felt.

Horatio shook his head and seemed quite agitated. His usual placidity rippled like a pond too full of hungry fish. "No, my niece. And you have other work to do as well. The mummer troupe has been found. Louis tells me he has heard from an acquaintance, whose mistress's other lover has knowledge of that very troupe giving performances on the outskirts of the city. We should go speak to them, and today, lest they slip away once more."

Suzanne's heart raced. This was good news. "Truly? Is Louis certain of this?"

Louis bounded from the stairwell and through the open door of the quarters, and it was apparent he'd been listening in. "I am, Mistress Suzanne. May I come along with you and Horatio? May I please?"

Horatio nodded, with a sly grin that was not the usual for him, looking like the cat who swallowed the canary. "Those mummers are ours, my niece."

Suzanne said to Louis, "I suppose you may." Then she wondered if perhaps this wasn't such a good idea after all. "What will we ask when we get there? Should we march up to them and say, 'Do tell, kind sir, did you, perchance, happen to murder William Wainwright?'"

Horatio replied, "Certainly we will not, for he certainly did not. William was shot with a crossbow, not cut with a dagger. And if Arturo were inclined to kill Wainwright he would have done it when he had the chance to do it easily and with justification. He wouldn't have waited to do it in cold blood with an unfamiliar weapon. But we will go speak to him because perhaps there is something to be learned by asking questions of the man who engaged in the fight. And if not, then sending

Pepper after them might distract him for a spell and give us time to pursue another avenue."

Suzanne shook her head and waved away the thought. "Pepper is far too lazy for that. He's got Piers and needs no other suspect. He'd never bother to question anyone else, even were the entire troupe to march into his office and offer all they know."

"Then, my dear, it would behoove us to gather the information for him and use whatever we find to best advantage, yes?"

Suzanne considered that for a moment, then nodded. "We should go. Let us hurry." She drew the hood of her cloak over her coif and led the way out the door.

So, rather than have Thomas and Samuel carry her alone to Whitehall, she hired a coach to take herself, Horatio, and Louis far out on White Chapel Street. The drive took an hour. From Maid Lane and across the river, they passed through teeming London streets filled with carriages jockeying in traffic, pedestrians wandering this way and that, vendors hawking prepared foods and all sorts of durable wares.

Then northeast along White Chapel Street where the abutting buildings gave way to less crowded ones before it all fell away to open countryside. Cattle and sheep outnumbered people in these precincts. Suzanne wondered how a troupe of performers could survive this far away from London. Surely she was lucky to have found them before they moved on too far.

Somewhere past Mile End, in a field off the road they found a makeshift stage, and Louis's knee began to bounce with excitement. His neck craned to see out the window, no doubt looking for Arturo's young daughter he'd found so sweet and nonforeign. Horatio directed the driver to follow a new track of trampled grass across to the mummers' camp. Brightly colored streamers flew and flapped from poles at the corners of the stage, and the camp tents clustered behind it were bright blue-and-yellow stripe, faded with age and use, but quite visible against the surrounding green. Some figures among the tents could be seen as they approached, but when the coach arrived at the stage, every living soul had disappeared like a mist before a slight breeze. By the time the driver reined the horses to a halt, there was no one about.

The festive colors of the tents, flags, and pennants now seemed strange, lonely as they were and appearing deserted. The flags beckoned to nobody, and nobody enjoyed the loud colors meant to attract attention.

It was not yet noon. A whiff of the food being prepared for sale to the audience drifted from the tents. Suzanne took a deep breath. Meat pies, she discerned from the scent of grease, onions, and pastry. This early there were no crowds of audience, and the ones who had been in rehearsal on the stage a moment ago were nowhere in evidence. She couldn't remember any names but Arturo's. As she descended from the coach, she looked around. Nothing moved except the streamers. They waved in the gentle breeze, slowly like seaweed in the tide.

"Hello?"

No sound or movement came from the tents.

Suzanne walked toward the cluster behind the stage. "Hello?"

Still no sound. The camp was still.

"Tell me, is Arturo about?" She called out, for her voice to carry to all the tents. A brown, shaggy mongrel dog came from behind one of them to stare at her, but he made no sound and only watched her with a slowly wagging tail as she proceeded through the camp.

More silence. This was beginning to irritate Suzanne. She

halted, folded her hands in front of her, and called out, "It's quite all right. I only wish to ask him some questions, then we'll be on our way." She looked at Horatio, whose neck was reddening with annoyance, and soon the flush would reach his face.

He also called out, his deep, carrying voice expressing both authority and threat, "My niece would speak to Arturo, and you all know she nearly always gets what she wants."

Suzanne wished with all her heart that were true. She smiled and added, "Please. I'll wait here until you decide."

Suzanne and Horatio waited. And waited. Somewhere in the distance a sheep bleated. Suzanne waited some more, and eventually the sheep bleated again. Amusing itself, she imagined. She wondered whether the mummers would all simply wait in the tents until she gave up and went home, but knew they all knew her well enough to understand it would be an absurdly long wait.

Eventually Arturo appeared at the tent flap and stood quite still in the shadow as he looked out to see if she was still there. His disappointment at seeing her was apparent even at this distance. He withdrew for a moment, disappeared inside the tent, then came out to face her, clearly unhappy at having to do so but struggling to put a good face on it.

"Good morrow, mistress." His voice was carefully modulated to express pleasant cheer and respect for a superior, neither of which he likely felt at that moment, and he bowed to her as if she were royalty. Or at least as if she were nobility, far above her true station. Suzanne sensed a bit of sarcasm, but ignored it in hopes of learning something helpful.

"Good morrow, Arturo." She nodded pleasantly to him, then drew back her cloak hood so he could see she meant no harm or subterfuge.

Louis stepped forward, his neck craning to see what he could find among the tents. The girl was nowhere in sight.

The mummer was an extremely small, spare fellow, wiry and thin to the point of emaciation, but tough and strong despite it. He had the ideal body for a tumbler, and he was a master, still able to leap, flip, and bend himself into a knot at an age when most men sought a warm fire and soft chair to ease their aching bones. Of Italian extraction, he bore a long, hooked nose that, with his thinness, gave him the profile of a scythe. He wore only tights and a tight-fitting shirt with no sleeves and no collar. Beneath those leggings he was bound with a cloth, and the sheen of sweat on him was further evidence he'd been in rehearsal that morning.

His black eyes gazed at her with a deep perception that pegged him as one whose life depended on knowing all that went on around him and understanding all it meant to him. Catching Arturo unawares was never likely. He said, eyeing her like a crow waiting to pounce on a fresh carcass, "What can I do for you this afternoon, Mistress Suzanne?"

Louis moved closer to the tents, letting go of any pretense he was there for any reason but to see Arturo's daughter. Arturo said to him, "She's in the cook's tent, Louis. Go to her before you burst apart. She will be happy to see you."

Louis needed no further permission and bolted for the tent from which the odors of cooking food wafted.

As Suzanne watched him go, she said, "I wonder, Arturo, why you and your family took leave of us so suddenly the other day. Have we offended you somehow?"

The reply was immediate and practiced, the better to masquerade as truth. "Greener pastures, mistress." His tone suggested that was the long and the short of it, and enquiring

252 of Anne Rutherford

further would be fruitless. Which might very well be the case, but Suzanne wasn't going to take his word for that.

She gave a glance about the area. This far away from the center of London, traffic was slow. All that could be seen from this spot were orchards and fields where cattle and sheep grazed. "Pastures, indeed, my friend. And green . . . maybe so. However, I think they can't be nearly as lucrative as Southwark, where your audience was much larger than it could possibly be here. Unless, of course, the sheep are paying admission." She paused to let that sink in, and Arturo did not reply. She added, "I wish you would be truthful with me."

Now that they understood each other, that there could be no pretense of belief the mummers' departure had been anything but flight from authorities, Arturo shrugged and said, "If not greener, mistress, then safer."

"To be sure, I can't find blame in keeping out of arm's reach of the constabulary."

"Then you answer your own question and you needn't bother us on the subject." He bowed to her again and turned as if to retreat to his tent. "If that is all, mis—"

"If we could speak of just one matter?"

Arturo paused, considered for a moment, then faced her. "Very well, mistress. I've no reason to think you'd wish us harm."

Suzanne nodded. "Indeed not, Arturo. I would always want you to feel our doors are open to you whenever you might deem it safe to return. You and your family are crowd pleasers, and as such are always welcome in my theatre. Furthermore, I expect to do whatever I might to make it safe for you to return."

A gratifying light of trust came into the tumbler's eyes, and he seemed to relax some. Tension eased in his shoulders, and he faced her straight on. He said, "What would you ask, mistress?"

"I hear tell of an altercation between yourself and William Wainwright shortly before his untimely death."

Arturo went stiff and alert once more. He only nodded in reply.

Suzanne continued, "You saw him after the night he came to my quarters."

"Yes, I did. I helped him to the exit."

"He threatened me before."

Arturo's eyes went wide with genuine surprise, and he quite lost his restraint. "He threatened you? The snake! He *threatened* you?" His olive complexion reddened and his bushy black eyebrows gathered in a knot. "How did he threaten you?"

"With a knife. I took it away from him."

A single finger jabbed the air as Arturo spoke, and Suzanne had to remind herself he was angry at William and not her. He fairly shouted, "Had I known it, I would have slit his throat on sight of him!" The finger made a line across his own throat in a slitting gesture. "The man would never have left the theatre that night! I swear I would have murdered him when I had the chance!"

"But you didn't."

"I now wish I had. I wish I had cut him with this here knife." He produced a dagger from his belt, an ordinary knife for eating and everyday utility. The handle was roughly carved by someone with little skill in it, though Arturo was deft enough in handling the thing. He twirled it in his fingers, then slipped it back into his belt. "I didn't kill him when he returned, nor did I kill him when I saw him in the green room the day he died."

That struck Suzanne speechless, and she blinked. "The

green room?" she finally was able to say. "You saw him in the green room that night?"

"I did indeed. 'Twas during the performance I caught sight of him, and surprised I was in it, for I thought I'd let him know he wasn't welcome around that theatre. To see him again so soon after warning him off . . . well, it angered me, it did. 'Twas in the green room he appeared. All brassy and arrogant, coming in where he wasn't welcome and didn't belong. Acting as if he owned the place and didn't have a care in the world for what I'd told him earlier."

"And did anyone else notice him?" Suzanne wondered why this was the first she'd heard of William in the green room.

"I think, mistress, that I was the only one who recognized him and knew who he was. There's a crowd of guests for every performance, and those who wish they were guests, who fill the 'tiring room so there is hardly space to breathe. A stranger in the green room is barely noticeable, there be so many of them. I didn't see that anyone paid him any particular attention. More than likely I myself would never have taken notice had I not fought with him shortly before."

"Very well. Then tell me what you did when you saw him."

Arturo continued, "I was like to kill him then, right there in the green room, but my better sense kept me from it. I could kill a man in a fight, but never in cold blood. And later, when he fell to the stage, dead, I had no sorrow for it and might have danced a jig if the celebration wouldn't have brought the attention of Constable Pepper. The simple fact of having drawn a knife on him shortly before was enough for me to make a strategic retreat with my troupe when he was murdered. I've been in the gaol, mistress, only once, and I don't care to return whether innocent or guilty."

"I see." Suzanne did see. Nobody, including herself, wanted

to encounter the constable even when innocent. Coming to the attention of any authority too often resulted in hanging, and that made it advisable to cut and run at the first hint of trouble. Then she asked, "Did you happen to see the crossbow in the green room?"

Arturo nodded. "There were several crossbows there."

"Did you see the one carried by the boy, Christian?"

Again the tumbler nodded. "He set it down. Left it beside a table."

"Did you see who took it?"

Arturo shook his head.

"Did you see William leave the room?"

Again Arturo shook his head. "I was needed onstage, and so I went while he was still there. I never miss my cue."

"Of course not."

The coincidence of William's presence in that room and the missing crossbow that was last seen there set up more echoes in Suzanne's mind. Too much coincidence. She knew by experience that chance was usually anything but. All of this had a fishy smell; she needed to find out the reasons for these things, then she might know what had really happened.

ALL the way back to the theatre in the hired coach, Suzanne sat silent, frowning at the floor before her. Horatio kept his thoughts to himself as well, staring out the window with narrowed eyes and thin lips as the carriage jostled over ruts, holes, and finally cobbles. Louis looked out the window on his side, his eyes half-closed in a dreamy stare, and Suzanne knew William's murder was the last thing on his mind. It had been a struggle to tear him away from Arturo's daughter. There seemed a real possibility Louis could run away from the Globe

Players to join Arturo's mummers. They would need to keep an eye on him and hope his terror of foreigners would keep him in London. The way his knee bounced with its nervous tic, he looked as if he were already running away in his daydream.

Suzanne's mind tumbled, barely aware he was even there. Questions rose and submerged like potatoes in a rolling boil, bobbing up to show themselves, then diving to be replaced by others. Why had William gone into the green room? Where had he gone when he left? Who had taken the crossbow, and why? Had someone recognized William and followed him out with the loaded bow? Where had they gone after leaving the green room? Exactly when had William left the green room? Who had been onstage at that time?

Had Arturo even told the truth about not picking up the crossbow himself? She asked Horatio his opinion, and the big man thought hard and stared skyward as he sorted out the story. Then he said, never taking his eyes from the carriage ceiling, "Well, he said he left to be onstage. To the best of my recollection he was assigned as one of Erpingham's men in Act IV, Scene III, a nonspeaking role. Though he wasn't onstage when Wainwright fell from the gallery, he's told the truth that he had to leave the green room earlier to be onstage. And I should think there was hardly enough time for him to make his exit after the scene and steal the crossbow before Christian could retrieve it and make his own entrance. They must have passed each other at the upstage doors. And it was but a few moments afterward that Wainwright was killed. I believe Arturo's testimony is honest; he did not kill Wainwright."

"The scene was the Agincourt battlefield, crowded with men. Who, then, was not onstage who might have shot the crossbow?"

Horatio looked once more out the window at the passing streets of London, and sternness hardened his voice. "Do not ask that, my niece, for your son was one of the very few who were not busy at that moment."

Suzanne went silent and focused her attention on the middle distance. She struggled to keep herself from screaming or weeping.

The performance that evening was the opening of *The Winter's Tale*. Suzanne sat through it, barely attending, her thoughts sorting through the things she'd learned these past couple of days. William in the green room. It made no sense. The king and William on the premises at the same time. That made even less sense, given Wainwright's terror of the crown. Plainly he hadn't known Charles was there. Which raised the question of why Wainwright was there. What had brought him to the theatre and sent him upstairs to the stage right gallery? And who'd had cause to follow him there?

The sun was low in the sky when the performance finished and the audience began to file out, abuzz with commentary on the show. Suzanne remained in her seat in the stage left gallery, thinking, even after the crowds had left and the actors were all in the dressing room. She gazed across at the stage right gallery, thinking hard but getting nowhere.

Nearly entranced, barely knowing where she was headed, so deep in thought was she, she rose from her seat and walked around back and to the other gallery. A murder had occurred here, but she looked around at the now empty space and couldn't see how it had happened. She knew it had, but couldn't visualize any of it. She looked down at the stage below, at the blackened bloodstain on it, and still couldn't imagine how William had been shot. Something was quite wrong, and she struggled to put her finger on it.

Then she tried visualizing the event as she had seen it rather than as it was said to have happened. In her mind's eye she saw the body lying on the stage, in the position indicated by the bloodstain that had spread across the boards when the crossbow bolt had been removed from William's throat.

His throat. Suzanne frowned. The bolt had been lodged in his throat, pointing downward into his chest. Nearly straight downward, the angle being very strange. She remembered seeing the fletching in front of his face, and the direction the boy had pulled when he removed the bolt had been past William's head rather than straight out from the throat. The gush of blood, as shown by the shape of the stain below, had been toward stage left rather than straight downstage. Only after the blood had surged that direction did it then begin to run down the boards toward the pit. Suzanne realized the bolt could only have been shot by someone standing above William. Almost directly above. She looked upward, to the heavens so painstakingly painted with clouds and cherubs.

The roof of the 'tiring house, on which the heavens had been painted, overhung the gallery by ten or fifteen feet. For someone to have shot William from up there they would have had to dangle from the eaves, an awkward thing that would most likely have resulted in two bodies falling rather than just the one. And still it would not have resulted in a wound like the one that had killed William.

Nevertheless, Suzanne was moved to have a look at the roof.

The 'tiring house stairs ended at the third floor and went no higher, but at the back of the stage right gallery was a ladder that led to a trapdoor above. It was composed of rough wood, of slats nailed to two wall supports. Suzanne rolled up the sleeves of the man's shirt she wore and climbed up. The slats were widely spaced and she was not tall, so she had to haul herself up by her arms with each step. She tried to imagine someone climbing this with one hand while holding a loaded crossbow and stalking a victim in the same, otherwise empty room. It just didn't seem plausible.

The trapdoor overhead was not easy to open. The thing was heavy and seldom used, and it resisted her attempts to shove it upward. Again, it would have been even more difficult carrying a crossbow, but she allowed it might have been possible for a man.

She considered going back downstairs for help, but disliked the idea of telling anyone where her thinking had taken her. So she persisted, put her shoulder into the effort, and shoved hard. The door creaked and complained, but finally it budged and she was able to shove it high enough for it to fall back onto the floor of the room above with a dull thud and a cloud of dust. Once more she thought of the victim supposedly in the gallery below and supposedly oblivious to being stalked by a man with a crossbow. She found it highly unlikely, but pressed on because the angle at which the crossbow had pierced William's throat would have been impossible unless the murderer had shot from the roof.

She climbed through the hole and into a storage room above. As scant as were the property stores of The New Globe Players, this room was nearly empty and held nothing more than some ends of cloth bolts left over from the recent costuming. They were stacked in a corner and covered with an oiled cloth to protect them from temperature and dampness.

Windows in the room overlooked the roofs of two gables over the rear of the 'tiring house. The roofs formed a valley between their peaks, immediately outside the windows. They were not terribly large and were much taller than they were wide, shuttered with frames stretched with animal skins shaved thin enough to let in light. Suzanne pulled them open. The flimsy frames wobbled on their leather hinges as she climbed through and onto the roofs outside.

All the shingles out here were new, for the old roofing had been so rotten that none of it had been salvageable. Each piece was attached solidly, with new iron nails, and she trusted the support beneath. Nothing shifted as she went to the front of the gables where they joined the heavens, which overhung the stage. There she paused.

The view of London from up here took her breath away. Just at sunset, the light threw shadows sideways and shone redly against the bridge, St. Paul's, and other of the taller structures. The river a few streets over shone blue and silver, and many boats bobbed on it. Barges floated slowly past, stately in their importance. For a moment Suzanne forgot her mission and marveled at the city that had been her home for more than three decades.

But then she returned to her purpose and moved across the roof of the heavens to her right, and thence to the inner eave of the theatre roof. She headed toward the spot that overhung the gallery from which William had fallen. When standing on the stage it was hard to see that the gallery roofs and 'tiring house heavens weren't just one continuous overhang, for all three sections were painted with blue sky and fluffy clouds.

Suzanne made her way carefully toward the edge of the stage gallery roof, and her boots slipped dangerously on the shingles. She put out a hand to steady herself, but here the pitch wasn't steep enough for her to put her hand all the way down. A dizziness of vertigo gave her a fear of toppling over the edge if she came too close, and for a moment she had to stop and get her bearings. The slant of the roof made it hard to tell which way was truly up. If she trusted her visual orientation, she was sure to tip sideways and hurtle to the stage. Trusting the horizon was no help, because it wasn't visible here. She paused, collected herself, then crept most carefully toward the edge to look down. There was a rain gutter there, but she didn't trust it to hold her up, so she kept to the shingles.

With utmost care to keep her balance, she peeked far enough over to see the bloodstain. It was directly below her, and she stood right at the spot where the heavens' roof met the stage gallery eave. The disparate angles of the two roofs were dizzying all by themselves. Anyone venturing up here might have fallen and died just for that.

Then she saw something that seemed to have nothing to do with William's death, but at the same time must have had, for Suzanne didn't believe in coincidence. Everything that was had a reason to be, and so this must have meaning for anything to make sense. She noticed that the spot where she was standing overlooked the third floor gallery over the main entrance doors. The very spot where the king had been sitting the night of the murder.

She sat down on the shingles at the edge of the eave and stared in that direction. Those particular seats were the only ones visible from this vantage point. The lower galleries were too low to see from here, and the rest of the third floor gallery was hidden by the roofs that rose to either side. The seats where Daniel, Charles, and the man who loved cows had sat were framed by the roofs surrounding the stage. Suzanne stared, unsettled by this, though she didn't know why.

Then she saw a sag in the gutter directly below her. It had somehow become broken and hung awkwardly from its moorings. A quick look at the rest of the gutters told her they'd all been replaced during the renovation, like the rest of the roof.

All were new, and so they shouldn't be broken anywhere. But this one had been damaged recently. There'd been someone up here after the work had been finished, and Suzanne was beginning to think she might know why.

She looked from the king's seat to the broken gutter. Then to the king's seat again. She turned to look up at the valley between the gables, where it met the roof over the heavens. Then at the king's seat again. She stood, took a step forward, then turned to have a good look at the gutters all along the eaves and heavens. In this area, near the broken section, they were covered with a spray of blackened spots. Blood? Could be. They were as black as the stain on the stage boards. They had the appearance of the spray Daniel had said was missing from the gallery below, which he'd said was inevitable with the sort of wound that had killed William.

Then she saw it. The missing crossbow.

Like seeing William's face in the shrubbery of St. James Park, when she'd been looking but not seeing, then suddenly saw, Suzanne saw the crossbow lodged behind a downspout. She caught her breath, though she didn't really feel surprised. It was excitement and hope that made her heart pound. With great care not to hurry and perhaps become clumsy, she crab-walked down to the heavens' roof and rolled over onto her belly to slide as close to the eave as she could get.

The bow was hung up on the downspout where it joined the gutter and curved back under the overhang. It pointed upward, but she could barely reach it. Her fingers touched the bow, but she couldn't quite get them around it. She scooted farther, put more weight on the gutter, and it sagged danger-ously. She held her breath as she stretched as far as she could and hooked the tip of her middle finger over the bow. The gutter sagged and bounced with each movement. With intense care she tugged on the bow. At first it didn't come, but she insisted and it began to move. After each movement, she reseated her grip and pulled again, and soon she had two fingers around the bow. Then three. Then it was close enough for her thumb to join them, and she pulled hard. The weapon came free and she scooted back onto the eave before the gutter could break under the extra weight.

She looked over at the broken gutter and figured she knew how it had given way. She sat up and held the crossbow in her lap as she considered what she knew.

The crossbow had been stolen at about the same time William had been seen in the green room, where it was also last seen. Someone else could have stolen the bow and followed him out, but no names had been put forth as possibilities. It was reasonable to consider that William himself may have taken it.

William did not fall from the stage gallery, but from the roof, as evidenced by the splatters of blood and the location of the crossbow. That was why whoever had taken the bow to the roof could do so without alarming anyone in the gallery. The gallery had been empty.

The only thing visible from that part of the roof was the bench where Daniel and Charles had been sitting at the time.

The crossbow was not wielded by a second person, who would have removed it from the scene in his flight after killing William, rather than stopping to wedge it in an inaccessible spot. Far easier to simply drop it onto the roof and escape.

This crossbow was certainly the one missing from the theatre properties. She recognized it from rehearsals. And there was no bolt; she figured the one Christian had put in it had killed William. The angle of the stock where it had lodged in the crook of the gutter told her that any bolt that happened to be in it would have shot upward and in the direction of the broken gutter over the stage right gallery. She figured she knew exactly what had happened the night William Wainwright died. And why.

As quickly as she could without toppling over the edge as William had, Suzanne carried the crossbow into the storage room, down the ladder, and down the stairs, calling for Horatio. "Look! Horatio! I've found—"

"Suzanne!" The big man was also looking for her, and she heard him call from her quarters at the bottom of the stairwell. He climbed up to meet her at the stage-level landing, distressed, with Louis, Christian, and Liza behind him. "Suzanne! Come! Christian has brought terrible news! Oh woe!"

Suzanne, coming down the stairs, met them all near the green room. She tried to show them all the crossbow, excited to have solved the mystery, but they ignored it in their urgency that she hear their news. Horatio continued, in a voice quavering with grief. Great, streaming tears made their way down his face. He took her by the shoulders, his fingers digging hard into her flesh. "Suzanne, Christian has brought news from the Goat and Boar. The magistrate has convicted Piers and the crown means to hang him!"

Chapter Sixteen

Suzanne and Horatio went directly to talk to Constable Pepper, to beg him to consider the new evidence, but found the building locked and nobody about who might know where Pepper lived. Panic rose.

Horatio said, "We must wait until the morning to speak to him."

"According to Christian, Piers is set for execution at noon tomorrow." Saying it out loud made it real, and she had to clap her hand over her mouth to stifle a sob. "Why so quickly? Why so soon?"

"It was the way the schedule fell at the Old Bailey. And the hanging days are all set. He was one of twenty tried today. He tried to send a message to you, but was unable."

"Piers must withdraw his confession."

"Yesterday that might have been useful, but he's been convicted and sentenced."

"Nevertheless, 'tis his best hope, and 'tis the only thing that can be done before morning."

She thought Horatio might be right, so they set out for Newgate in hopes of talking to Piers. She hired a carriage and took Horatio with her across the river.

Suzanne had never been to Newgate Prison, and until now had avoided even looking at its walls from the outside. All her adult life the place had stood like a monument to death and grief, a place where friends went in and were never seen again. Or if they returned, they came back changed. They walked the streets again, but with dull eyes that saw nothing, or too-alert ones that tried to see everything but couldn't. If one spent enough time in Newgate, skin and hair grayed, lesions grew, hair thinned, and any happy sensibility was quite leached away. No prison was like a mansion in the country, but Newgate had a reputation that made even those who were never likely to go there fall silent or speak of something else.

But Suzanne had to see her son immediately, and couldn't care what might happen to her in that place. The carriage deposited Suzanne and Horatio before the forbidding stone structure that stood several stories high and so wide as to dominate the street. Hundreds of years before, it had been no larger than the gatehouse that had given it a name, and now was an enormous, ghastly monument to misery. She and Horatio went through the entrance to the keeper's house. She hoped to appear as if they belonged there, but not too much. Deep down she harbored a fear that once inside she would not be let out.

There they found two men on guard. They wore the king's livery, but not very well. The taller one wore breeches slightly less filthy than the shorter one's, but neither was particularly presentable. Pikes leaned against a nearby wall, and the two were playing dice at a wooden table near them. Each man wore a large ring of keys hung at the waist, the keys dangling from the hip and nearly touching the stone floor. They both looked up at the entrance of their visitors and stood in unison, neither in any particular rush.

"What do you want?" said the shorter one. They were both startled enough to suggest they weren't accustomed to unannounced visitors this late at night. Little wonder, since most people avoided the place if they could.

Horatio did the talking, the better for the guards to take their request seriously. Suzanne stood, silent, hoping her expression was as neutral as she thought. He said, "We wish to see a prisoner."

"You'll need permission from a magistrate or constable, or someone higher up."

"We have no paper from such a person." He drew a gold pound coin from his purse and showed it to the guard. "Regretfully, we have only this."

The guard looked at the coin and sighed, as if about to decline. He said, "I'm sorry, but you can see there's two of us here. I couldn't let my associate go without."

Horatio grimaced and felt at his nearly empty purse. "I've only this one, I'm afraid."

"Then you'll not be seeing the prisoner today, I'm afraid."

"If you could see your way to—"

"I've got another, Horatio," said Suzanne. She reached through the slits in her skirt and petticoat, into the pocket beneath, and withdrew a single gold pound. She had several there, but was careful not to let them clink. She handed one to Horatio, who passed the two coins to the short guard, who then passed one of them to his tall associate.

They pocketed their enormous bribes, and the short one

said as he fingered the huge key ring dangling from his belt and turned to lead the way, "Very well, then. Which prisoner is it you wish to see?"

"Piers Thornton."

Both the guards burst forth with guffaws. The short one looked back at Suzanne and said, "He's set to hang. And soon, I think." He looked to the tall guard, who nodded in concurrence. "Next hanging day's tomorrow, if I've got it straight."

"We've got to see him immediately. It's terribly important."

"Important enough for you to hand over the other coins you've got under your skirt, mistress?"

Suzanne pressed her lips together. Could he smell them? With a bit of reluctance, she reached under her skirt for the other two coins she'd brought with her. Four pounds. A raging fortune, but she would have paid twice that to see her son that day.

The guards were right pleased with themselves to have extorted half a year's wages so easily from this pathetic woman. The short one chortled and grinned, nearly drooling at his good fortune. "Right this way, if you please, mistress." He handed over the tall guard's share to him.

Suzanne said, "Horatio, please wait for me here."

He went wide-eyed, shocked she would consider entering the prison without him by her side. "My niece! I cannot allow you to place yourself in jeopardy and leave me behind!"

"Horatio, it's for my protection that I ask you to stay. If I don't return in a timely manner, you're to find out why and engineer my release."

He thought about that, then nodded. "As you wish, cousin. I'll await you here and come for you if you don't return by dawn."

The short guard then picked up his pike and led the way into a passage and up some stairs.

The prison was old and stank of filth. Stench of rotting wood, rotting food, excrement, and standing water choked her as she was led into the bowels of the dank stone structure. Off in the distance a man screamed, a high, thin wail. The sort of despair that wishes for death and expects it, but not soon enough.

They came out on a gallery lined with thick wooden doors bound in iron. The spacing between them suggested cells. Then through another passage, and they were in a large quadrangle littered with loitering men. The prisoners lounged about, talking in low voices, playing cards or dice, and monitoring the passage of the visitors from the corners of their eyes. They were shadows within shadows, the only light provided by two torches in wall sconces. Guards stood by with truncheons, ready to keep order. At the other side of the large room, the escort guided Suzanne and Horatio into another passage. It came out to a small enclosure from which only three doors opened.

"This here's where we keep the condemned," said the short guard. Suzanne's stomach turned, and she felt light-headed. There were other distant shouts and carryings-on in the areas that held debtors and ordinary felons, but here, deep inside where resided the most dangerous prisoners, the cells were quiet with terror of the gallows. Everyone here was either accused or convicted of a capital crime, and nearly all of them would hang soon.

Another man in filthy livery sat on a three-legged stool at the end of the enclosure. He stood at sight of the escort. "What's the occasion?"

The short guard said, "We've a special request for visitation. This here's a friend dear to the king, who has allowed as she should see Master Thornton today."

"She got a release from the crown?"

"Don't need one." The short guard spoke as dismissively as any baron. "'Twas the king gave permission, and he sent no paper. I'd run back and request one for you, but besides being a waste of my time, 'twould be an annoyance to his majesty. I don't expect you want to be the one to explain to him why he should be bothered with this twice in one evening."

The guard of the condemned shrugged and rose from his seat. "No skin off my nose if the sod's got visitors. Just so long as he's still in his cell when they come to get him tomorrow, that's all I'm charged with." He sifted through the several keys at his waist, chose one, and unlocked the door at his elbow. "Here you go, mistress. Enjoy yourself. I'll be a-waiting for you when you're through here and wish an escort back to the keeper's house."

She nodded and entered the cell, her heart pounding.

The corridor had been lit by torches, but inside the cell was only one candle, stuck to a table by its own melted tallow. Beside the table stood a chair, where Piers sat just inside the tiny circle of light, leaning against the back of it with his arms crossed over his chest. Suzanne's heart clenched when she saw his face swollen with bruises and his lip split so badly she could see a tooth. His arms were crossed because one had been injured and he was holding it up with the other. Blood stained his shirt to his elbow. When he saw his guest was his mother, his face went slack with surprise. He leapt to his feet and came to hug her. "Mother!" He flinched from the pain in his arm. "What are you doing here? You shouldn't be in this place."

She held him tight and fought the tears that burned behind her eyes. The terror of what would happen to him made her shake, and it was all she could do not to collapse into a quivering pile on the floor. "Piers, what did they do to you?"

He looked down at his arm as if he'd just then realized he'd been injured. "I . . . well, when I heard the verdict and the sentence, I'm afraid I didn't take it very well. When I protested the trial was unfair, I rose from my seat and approached his honor the magistrate."

"You rushed him and tried to shake some sense into him. I know you well, Piers."

"I would have, had I reached him. As it was, the bailiff prevented me from it. Then he beat some sense into me. I am far wiser now than I was this morning."

Suzanne laid her fingers aside his cheek to examine his split lip in the candlelight. "I came when I heard the verdict. And the sentence."

He guided her to the chair, then sat on the edge of the bunk that contained a straw mattress and a wool blanket crusted with what may have been dried blood or vomit and was jumping with fleas. Seeing the look on her face, he fingered the blanket and said, "I'm told an anonymous person paid for me to have a more comfortable cell. I wonder what I would have had otherwise."

"Anonymous?"

"Daniel, I suppose. Unless you're as ashamed as he is to admit being my parent."

Suzanne shook away that thought and continued, her urgency not to be denied, "You must recant your confession."

"I killed him, Mother." He glanced at the door, and she understood that the guards must be listening, and they would offer to the crown for sale anything they heard. What went unsaid by him was that he would not recant, in order to keep Pepper from arresting his mother.

But she shook her head and said, "You did not. I know you didn't."

"Of course I did. I hated him, I hated the way he treated you. You know that much is true; he was a horrible man and there's no denying it. When he came around to threaten you, that was the last straw. Had I been there that night I would have throttled him with my bare hands." He stood and crossed his arms over his chest again and held his chin up, daring her to contradict him. "I had to kill him. So I stole the crossbow from the green room—"

"You were never in the green room. You almost never go into the green room."

He leaned toward her. "*I stole the crossbow.* Then I found him in the stage right gallery."

"What made you think he was there?"

"I followed him."

"From where? Had he been in the green room?"

Piers hesitated. All his life he had been no sort of liar, and was now no better at it than he had been as a child. He blinked, then continued with his original thread of story. "I followed him to the stage right gallery."

"He was never there."

Again Piers was thrown from his confession track. He backed up and went down it again. "I followed him to the stage right gallery, and shot him with the crossbow."

"He fell from the roof."

He glanced over at the door where the guard was eavesdropping, and his agitation grew. "Mother! I killed him, not you! You had nothing to do with it!"

"You're right, I did have nothing to do with it. It was an accident. I can prove it."

Piers's face went slack once more. "What sort of proof?"

There was no belief in his face, only doubt and a conviction that she was making things up so he would recant.

"I found the crossbow on the roof. I also found blood splattered on the gutters."

"That only means he wasn't shot in the gallery."

"This is how it happened, Piers." She settled herself into the chair and placed her hands on the table near the candle, then took a moment to sort the facts in her mind. Carefully she began the story. "The crossbow was stolen from the green room, and I was told by Arturo—"

"The mummer?"

Suzanne nodded. "He said he'd seen William that night in the green room. He didn't witness the theft, but he saw William was there."

"Why didn't anyone else see him?"

"Arturo was the only one in the room who would have recognized him. He, Louis, and Horatio are the only ones other than myself who have ever seen him, and the other two were already onstage at the time."

Piers nodded in understanding.

Suzanne continued, "So, William stole the loaded crossbow. He took it upstairs and up the ladder to the storage room, and out the window to the roof."

"Why?"

"To assassinate the king."

Piers took a moment to absorb that. "The king? Charles was there?"

"He'd accompanied Daniel to see the play, incognito. They sat in the third floor gallery, directly over the entrance."

"If he was on the roof, why didn't they see him from where they were sitting?"

"For the same reason nobody knew William didn't fall

from the gallery: Everyone who might have seen him was looking down at the stage. It stands to reason that William would have known that, and he thought he would get away with shooting the king by slipping away down the ladder from the storage room. Or even by hiding in the storage room until the danger was past and he could leave the premises at his leisure.

"In any case, he went to the roof, ready to kill Charles, and steadied himself on the sloping shingles with one foot on the rain gutter. But the gutter wasn't strong enough to hold his weight. It broke. He fell, and as he fell, he dropped the loaded, cocked crossbow and twisted around in an attempt to grab the gutter behind him and stop his fall. The falling crossbow lodged in a crook of the downspout, which set off the trigger and loosed the bolt upward and into William's throat. Blood sprayed over the gutter. Having been shot, he missed his grasp of the gutter and fell to the stage three stories below. Not quite dead yet, but he was finished off when someone pulled the bolt from his throat and he bled to death."

Piers thought hard some more, then said, "You can prove this? How can you be certain he wasn't followed from the green room to the roof instead of the gallery?"

"Two reasons. First, the angle of the wound was wrong for any scenario in which William was shot by anyone not directly above him. Since, by the splatters of blood, we know he was on the roof and not in the gallery below, we also know it is impossible for anyone to have shot him from above.

"In addition, I found the crossbow lodged in a spot where I had to hang over the eave of the roof to reach it. A murderer is unlikely to have stopped in his flight from the scene to oh-so-carefully hang over the eave and place the bow where I found it, thus risking someone looking up and seeing him there. You'll remember we all looked up in search of a murderer during those moments after William fell. Nobody saw anything, not even the crossbow, which was behind the downspout."

Piers was silent, lost in thought. Finally he said, "You didn't kill him, then?"

"Of course not. I would never kill anyone, though I've wanted to murder dozens in my time."

Her son hesitated for a moment, then said, "I would. I would have killed him to save you, without a moment's hesitation."

Suzanne had mixed feelings about that—on one hand pleased her son cared for her, but also not liking the idea that he could do murder. Or even that he thought he could do it. She said, "But you didn't. You must recant, Piers, or they will hang you."

He slowly shook his head. "It's too late, Mother. I'm convicted. They will hang me no matter what I say."

Chapter Seventeen

Suzanne stayed with Piers as long as she dared, but finally had to tear herself from him and ask to be returned to the keeper's house and Horatio.

Immediately on arrival at the theatre Suzanne sent for Daniel, then waited by the fire, staring into it and praying he would heed her summons, terrified he might ignore her completely. Daniel was the only one who could help her now. He must. Her body ached with tension and terror. Piers in that horrible place was too much to bear, and every time she closed her eyes she was visited with a nightmare vision of him carried to the gallows in a cart, his hands tied and his neck bared for the stretching. She saw the terror in his eyes, and knew what it would be in his heart. It was her job to keep him safe, as it had been since the day he was born. If he died, her life would be over as well.

She wished she could go to Daniel at his house in Pall Mall. A part of her relished the idea of an ugly, theatrical scene in front of his wife. Or even her brother. Surely that prospect would be sweet revenge for abandoning her. To have Anne and Piers punish him where Suzanne could not, and hand James the power to give Daniel grief with his wife and disgrace him in Parliament at every opportunity for the rest of his life.

But she refrained, for the same reason she hadn't done any of that already: Making a further mess out of things just wouldn't be helpful. Hurting Daniel for revenge wouldn't save Piers. She needed better grace than that.

Daniel arrived quite late that evening—nearly midnight—in a timely manner but still in no particular hurry, and somewhat impatient at having been bothered to come. His attitude frightened her, for she had no power to save Piers and neither did anyone she knew except him. He was her only hope. But she took heart in that he did come and didn't simply send a return message. Perhaps it meant he had a thought about how to proceed.

She presented him with the crossbow, holding it out to him laid across both hands. "Here is the crossbow that killed William, Daniel. When I tell you where I found it, you'll know our son is not a murderer."

Daniel gave the bow an unconcerned glance as he folded his gloves and tucked them into his belt. "I don't think he's a murderer. I think he's protecting you. In fact, almost nobody actually thinks he did it, and nearly everyone knows he's protecting you."

She blinked and her jaw dropped. "You believe I did it?"

He grinned and handed his hat and cloak off to Sheila, then settled into the sofa and crossed his legs to be comfortable. "Of course not. I don't know you all that well, but I know you well enough to be certain you haven't a murderous bone in your body. But Pepper thinks you did it, and as stupid and

278 ✿ Anne Rutherford

lazy as he is, he's the one who matters in this. He would see you hung if he didn't have Piers for it. He would rather see a man go to the gallows, because any woman, even a whore—"

"Former whore."

He tilted his head side to side in equivocal agreement. "That may very well be, and I'm enchanted you've turned over a new leaf, but Pepper won't ever see you that way. He neither knows nor cares whether you're virgin or whore or my old Aunt Fanny. Regardless of how you make your money these days, or who might be welcome or unwelcome in your bed, Pepper would prefer to hang a man than a woman. Onlookers are far more accepting of a questionable hanging if it's a man, and if he can get Piers executed, the case will be closed and stay closed. Pepper will then no longer fear questioning after the fact."

She ignored his irrelevant point, for she had faith in the rightness of things and had evidence of the truth. All she needed was for Pepper or the king to know what she knew. She sat in a chair nearby and leaned forward in her excitement, her hands on her knees. "There will be no hanging. William's death was an accident. What we need is for the right people to hear it."

Daniel let out a bark of a laugh. "Oh, won't Pepper be amused! What he'd said all along, and now it's you saying it! Of course, it has nothing to do with wanting to get Piers off the hook. And now he'll be ever so pleased to give you grief for making him actually investigate the mystery. Which, I suppose, may be why he picked you out of the crowd to take the blame in the first place. God knows it couldn't have been because of the evidence he couldn't be bothered to discover."

She was frustrated with Daniel's refusal to hear what she was telling him. "The death was an *accident*; I have proof."

"What proof is that?" Daniel still sounded unimpressed.

"I found the crossbow lodged behind a downspout beneath the eave of the heavens. William was never in the gallery, as you said. He was shot when he fell and dropped the crossbow. It jarred when it hit the downspout, loosed the bolt, then it struck him in the throat before he toppled over the eave and landed on the stage."

"You mean you wish to present one of your several crossbows as the murder weapon?"

Suzanne sat up, feeling as if he'd slapped her face. "Pardon me?"

"You're Piers's mother. And you've had days to think of a way to prove he didn't do it. Far better that someone else had found the bow, other than you. Nobody will believe you."

Suzanne's face flushed hot red. She said, "There was blood splatter on the roof, just as you said there should be where William was murdered."

"Sheep's blood, then?"

Again Suzanne was caught up short. "You're accusing me of manufacturing the evidence?"

"I'm only saying the things Pepper would tell you. He dislikes you, is naturally vindictive, is as lazy as the day is long, and is unlikely to simply swallow your story whole."

"Then you must convince him of the truth." She leaned forward in her urgency. "Pepper has got his conviction. The crown will hang Piers *tomorrow* if something isn't done quickly!"

That took the wind out of Daniel's sails, and all breath left him. For a moment he appeared to struggle for words, then said, "So soon? He's been convicted?"

She nodded. "I can't say what sort of trial he had, but I can't imagine it was fair at all." More tears rose, and it became hard to find her voice. "I would that it were myself rather than he, because you're right. The crown would sooner hang a man than a woman." She narrowed her eyes at Daniel. "Even a whore such as myself might languish for months, or even years, in prison before hanging. They would put an end to Piers at the very earliest opportunity."

Daniel still struggled for words, and ultimately said nothing.

Suzanne pressed on, knowing he would flinch further at what she would say next. "Daniel, I think I've worked out the scenario. I've reason to believe William was on that roof because he was trying to assassinate the king."

Daniel went from pale to flushed in an instant. Plainly what would come out of his mouth next would be a lie. "No, he was not."

"I think he was."

"The king was not there."

"He certainly was, Daniel, and that is why William was there. He was terrified of being arrested by the crown. He thought his life would be over when Charles returned from the Continent. When he abandoned me, he told me he was fleeing the country, afraid the returning king would have his head on a spike. Then last spring he came to me again, ranting some nonsense about the crown being after him, and wanting to hide here in the theatre. It was madness, of course, and quite a lot of delusional self-importance, but he truly believed he was being hunted. He also believed Charles would ruin the country with his libertine thinking. He thought of French ideals as Catholic evil, and was terribly unhappy that the king didn't expect people to continue to hide their mistresses in shame. I think he was mad enough to take action against Charles. William was insane enough and had enough conviction to make right everything he deemed wrong by killing the king."

"Then why go to the roof of the Globe?" The tension in Daniel's voice betrayed his growing apprehension. "What has that place to do with Charles?"

"You and I both know that the king was one of the men with you on opening night."

The long silence that followed told her she not only was right, but she had touched on something terribly delicate. Daniel was unhappy the king had been found out. Finally, he said, "I'm afraid you're mistaken."

"I'm not, and I wish you would stop saying that, for I know it's true, you know it's true, and I dislike being lied to. So many people are such liars, it shows no originality and I find it quite tedious. The king sat to your left. He was disguised and wearing a plain, old-fashioned outfit more suited to one of his Cavaliers than to a monarch. I'm guessing the suit he wore was yours. It may have been his own, but I doubt it."

Daniel's eyes flashed with anger, though Suzanne couldn't imagine what she'd done to warrant it. She'd only told him what they both knew to be true. What any alert person might have known. His voice was low and tense. "How could William have known the king would be here?" So much for pretending Charles hadn't been there, and Suzanne viewed that as progress.

"Surely William followed him."

"Rather fanciful, I'd say." Daniel's tone derided her, which put Suzanne's hackles up. It was a form of bullying she'd long ago learned to despise. "You have no reason to believe—"

"Oh, but I do." She bit her tongue and didn't call him a fool, but her tone probably conveyed it. "I saw him following the king in St. James's Park that day we were there. I'm certain it was William, lurking a short distance from Charles, for I saw him clear as day. He never saw me because he was so intent on watching the king. William was stalking Charles as if he were a hart."

Daniel spoke slowly, carefully, as if trying to get across a simple concept to an idiot. "Again, your credibility as a witness is wanting. If what you just said is true, you should have pointed him out to me at the time. You've become so desperate, now even I am hard put to believe you."

"I didn't know at the time I was going to need corroboration of my word. And I take exception that I need it from you."

"Alas, hindsight is too perfect."

"Daniel, you're not very much help."

"Nonsense. I'm being quite a lot of help. I'm saving you from embarrassment and frustration, and possibly wrecking your own case when you rush over to see Constable Pepper in the morning and insist once more that your son is not a murderer. And let me add that if you try to tell him Charles was in the theatre that day, you will have a public statement from the crown that he was not."

"Why would Charles lie?"

Daniel blinked in mock surprise. "Why, because he can, of course. And he's very good at it. I often marvel at his skill in making things up. But there is also that he can't have everyone in London knowing he likes to walk among them as a commoner whenever the mood strikes him. Besides leading to many false sightings, it would also make it impossible for him to do it ever again if the entire city were on the lookout for him. He values those outings. He believes them to be helpful in understanding his subjects so he might govern well. Or at least keep his head, as his father did not."

"He values the outings more than he values the life of an innocent man?"

Daniel looked her straight in the eye and said with heavy regret, "Of course he does. As I just said, *he wishes to keep his own head*. Surely he values his own neck more than he does Piers's. As he should, actually, for he is, after all, the king. There are few in the realm who would suggest our son's life was worth more than Charles's."

Cold panic washed over Suzanne as she saw how little hope she had of freeing Piers with her proof that William's death was an accident. Her voice would only come in a whisper. "But you're a peer. Why would the king let your son hang? You're of high enough rank to influence, and your word is valued."

"Charles doesn't know he's my son."

Suzanne fell silent, not daring to speak lest she say something ugly and irretrievable. The silence stretched like gut on a violin.

Finally Daniel added, "Charles has no reason to believe Piers didn't do the murder."

"I found the crossbow."

Irritation rose, and Daniel's voice was sharp with impatience. "You should have left it where you found it. Had you sent for Pepper and shown him the bow where it had lodged, you might have had a chance of convincing him you didn't put it there yourself. But now the crossbow is just another one of your theatrical properties."

"The blood . . ."

"The blood." Daniel gave a slight, rather Continental shrug, as if to allow she had a point, but only a small one. "He might take that a little more seriously, but if he really wants a body to hang, he'll discount it as sheep's blood."

"Arturo said—"

"Is Arturo here to give his story?"

"No."

"Is he likely to be talked into coming back by morning to testify to Pepper?"

Suzanne sighed. "No."

"Then anything Arturo said to you is worthless."

Suzanne was silent, thinking hard and struggling not to cry. Finally she sat straight as a rod in her chair and said, "Your word could set Piers free."

Daniel said nothing and fiddled with the fingers of his gloves as if he wanted to don them and leave. Suzanne waited. Finally she asked, "Daniel, why won't you ask the king to pardon him?"

"I don't wield that sort of power."

"You mean you don't wish to squander your goodwill with Charles."

"If that's how you would put it, then yes. I have other concerns that require political coin, and haven't any to spare."

"How can you think that way? How can you toss your son to the lions?"

"My wife's family would stand against me vigorously were I to go to Charles and ask for a pardon for my son. Even if I committed everything of myself to Piers's cause, I would more than likely fail to save him. They would make certain of it."

"And you the coward would let them. Shame on you! Shame on you for not protecting your flesh and blood! You are a coward, Daniel Stockton, and I'm ashamed to have ever thought otherwise!"

Daniel said nothing in argument, and his eyes betrayed his belief she was right. He said, "I'm afraid I can't argue with that. I am a coward. And I am powerless to change the situation. My brother-in-law carries a great deal of weight in Parliament, and Parliament has a nose ring on Charles. He depends on them for money."

"And Piers is so unimportant to you that you will allow your wife's family to use him for political purposes?"

"Nobody is using him, Suzanne. He's simply landed in a bad spot and I am prevented from helping him because I am at the mercy of Anne and her brother. They don't care for the fact that she is childless due to my long absence, and they especially don't care for the fact that I have children by mistresses. And they only know about the daughters. Piers being the only male has sealed his fate. James would be ever so pleased to punish me with whatever he might use against me, particularly where his sister is concerned. He's made my marriage impossible, and is breathing down my neck in Parliament. Anne wants retribution for her childlessness, and if she knew I had a son, she would like to see him dead because it would hurt me. James would give her that wish, and relish it."

The countess had not struck her as the sort to be so vindictive, but Suzanne pressed her lips together to keep herself from saying so. It would not do to let Daniel know she'd gone to see Anne. Neither would it make a difference, since Daniel was certainly right about the brother.

She felt as if a band of steel were tightening around her chest. She couldn't breathe, and was panicked to be free of it. She stood and went to the door, thinking she might leave, but instead turned and walked toward the door at the other side of the room. She stopped, unable to retreat to the inner rooms. There was no escape from the situation. "Daniel, I've got to do something!"

"There's nothing you can do. Our hands are tied."

"So easy for you to say! He's your son, too! How is it so easy for you to give him up?"

He watched her pace for a moment, then said in a voice that had softened, "I never had him, Suze. He was never part of my life. He was always just yours, and you clung to him like a raft in a storm. For the rest of us, there's no entering that magic circle. I realized it when we spoke that day at the Goat and Boar. I'd thought we might rekindle the old fire, but all you could talk about was Piers. All you ever talk about is Piers. There's nothing of you left to know. Only Piers.

"And you seemed quite happy with that. It appeared to me that you could have gone on the rest of your life all wrapped up in him. In fact, I'm stunned you were able to bring yourself to send him away for an apprenticeship with Farthingworth. It must have killed you to let him go. I should have thought you'd keep him under your skirts until he was worthless for anything but petty theft. I must hand it to you; as a mother you've quite succeeded."

That mollified her and took the edge off her panic, but only the fine edge. Was she that wrapped up in Piers? Was there really so little of herself apart from him? She couldn't imagine a life without him. It seemed natural for every thought to be about him, to feed, clothe, teach, and protect her child. How could that ever be wrong? Furthermore, how could that have prevented a caring father from being a part of that life? What was so "magic" about the bond between mother and son that it couldn't accommodate a father who wanted to know his son?

She turned to him. "You could have been his father. You could have been part of his life. You *should* have been."

Daniel shook his head. "No, that was never possible. Anne and her brother would never have stood for it, and Charles needed me during the war."

"Then it's not our fault you didn't know us. More than there being room for you, there was a gaping hole in our lives where you should have been. We needed you far more than he did."

"But my previous commitments took precedence. I had no choice in the matter."

"Your wife is more important than we."

"In many ways, she is. In other ways, not at all."

She thought she might regret asking this, but curiosity made her do it. She folded her hands before her and braced herself to hear something she might rather not. "In what ways is it not true?"

He considered his reply for a moment, then said slowly, "You know ours was not a love match. I married Anne for her father's influence. My own father believed an alliance with a Presbyterian family would be advantageous, regardless of his own loyalties and beliefs, given the religious climate at the time. Were he alive now, he would be shocked at how mistaken he was and how unyielding they can be. How *unaccommodating*."

"You married a Presbyterian?"

"You didn't know that? Her father converted when she was a little girl, and I was unable to convince her to convert back to the English Church after our marriage. Nor would she even budge after her father's death. Her brother was raised Presbyterian, but is as zealous as a convert and as hardheaded and straitlaced as any pastor in the Marches. There's no talking to him once he's made up his mind, and he hates me for my illegitimate children as much as Anne does. Perhaps more, for he views it as a sin and she sees it only as a personal insult. They wish to punish me for my daughters' existence, and would ruin me if they knew of Piers."

Icy cold crept up Suzanne's spine as she realized the true meaning of his words. Her voice shook as she said, "So you would see Piers dead. That's why you won't take his case to the king."

Daniel's eyes went wide. "No!"

"You do want him dead. He's an inconvenience, and you want him dead for fear of your wife and her brother. So you can become a proper Presbyterian toady, so holy and free of . . . sin!"

He stood, and his voice rose, desperate to convince her. "No, Suzanne! Don't think that!"

She went to stand toe-to-toe, her face upturned and her own voice as strident. "It's true. You can deny it all you like, but what you've just told me is exactly that but coated to appear as if you have nothing to do with our fate, and no responsibility toward your son."

His hands were fists at his sides. "I have no power in this. There's nothing I can do."

"You mean there's nothing you can do that won't cost you anything. There's nothing you can do that won't make you vulnerable to someone who hates you. And you'll be backed against that wall so long as Anne lives. As long as she and her brother have your tender bits in a vise, your interests will never be other than theirs. You're spineless! I despise you! I despise everything about you! Get out!" She waved him toward the door. "Leave me; I don't want to see your face ever again!"

"Suzanne—"

"Get out!"

He stared at her a moment, then slowly drew his gloves from his belt and donned them. Sheila brought his hat and cloak, and he put them on. Then he made his utterly dignified exit without any more comment.

Chapter Eighteen

Suzanne sat up all that night, unable to even consider sleep.
Piers was to die at noon the following day. How could she
sleep, knowing that if she didn't do something she would never
see him again? The fires dwindled and candles guttered. Cold
crept into her bones, the sharper as she began to realize she
could see no avenue to take that might save her son. If Piers
were to die, she would have no more need to live. Her life
would be a failure. As her mind cast about for possible avenues
of recourse, and found none, hope dwindled like the fires until
she was in danger of descending into eternal darkness. Without Piers, there could be no light. No joy.

She lay on the sofa, her fists tight against her chest, her
fingernails dug into her palms, unable to move and barely able
to breathe. There had to be something. *Something.* She thought
of going to the king, but there was a great deal of truth to
what Daniel had said. Charles didn't want to be bothered with
the small concerns of unimportant people, and it would be

only too easy for him to dismiss the pleadings of a convict's mother as fiction. Daniel was powerless because he believed himself to be, and would not put himself forward and risk the ire of his wife's family. The only other man in London with any power in the situation was Pepper.

Constable Pepper, that vile, lazy, stupid man. Well, certainly vile and lazy. Had he done his job, for which he was well paid, he would never have needed to arrest Piers. But he was lazy, and that was the long and the short of it. He had his conviction, and now he had no reason to want Piers freed.

No reason.

The flame of hope flickered into existence. Slowly it rose. *A reason to want Piers freed.* Suzanne found a line of thought that did not come to a dead end. What if Pepper did have one? What if he did have a reason to want Piers exonerated? She sat up on the sofa, her thoughts rushing about like a cat after a mouse. What if? What if? What could Pepper want that might make him change his mind about Piers?

Then a real idea came to her. It burst in her brain like the flare of Greek fire, lighting all in a clear, luminous vision. Brilliant, undeniable. Joyous laughter rose in her, for it had been before her all along and she'd not seen it until now.

She rose from the sofa and hurried to her desk, where she opened the ink bottle, dipped a quill, and began to write. In her hurry the ink spattered and ran, and she would have to copy the letter, but just then she couldn't write fast enough to keep up with her idea and she hurried to put it down on paper.

Once the sun was up, still without sleep, Suzanne dressed in her most conservative outfit, mahogany brown and showing very little bosom. In such a hurry, she didn't bother with cloak or vizard, and pattens would only slow her down. She took Horatio with her, carrying the crossbow in a sack, and hurried to the office of the constable. She walked through the streets so quickly, tall Horatio found himself skipping a step every so often to keep up with her. His wig slipped on his bald head, and he had to shove it back into place several times. By the time they reached Pepper's office he was puffing hard. Suzanne was also breathing hard, but it was impossible to say it was because of the walk and not for the urgency of her mission.

They burst into Pepper's office at full speed. The clerk looked up and opened his mouth as if he might say something. But they both walked straight past him, so he said nothing and only went wide-eyed at Horatio's size and stared as he passed.

Inside the inner office, Suzanne and Horatio found Pepper was not in. Suzanne groaned in frustration and returned to the outer office, where the clerk was still gawping at the intrusion. "Where might I find the constable? It's terribly important. I can't tell you just how important it is I see him immediately. Where is he?"

The clerk blinked, thinking. "Ah . . . at home, perhaps. He sometimes is late coming to the office of a morning, mistress."

She straightened and looked down her nose at the clerk. "How remarkable he should show such temperance with his brandy."

Horatio swallowed a snort of laughter.

"Where does he live? I must talk to him now."

"I couldn't tell you, mistress."

"Your loyalty is commendable." She reached through the slit in her skirt for her pocket. "I'm certain I can ease your conscience—"

"I can't tell you because I don't know, mistress. The constable is very close with information regarding himself. I know not where he lives, nor where he is now."

Suzanne retrieved her hand from the pocket. Suddenly the situation appeared impossible again. The sun was peeking over the tops of buildings now, and they were running out of time. In a matter of short hours the hangman will have executed Piers and it would be too late. She said, "We'll just wait . . ." She looked about the room and saw two wooden armchairs standing against the wall opposite the clerk's writing desk. "We'll wait over here." Before the clerk could reply, she and Horatio claimed both chairs.

The clerk gawped some more, then apparently decided he didn't care much what they did, and returned to his work, nose to the paper.

Suzanne and Horatio waited in silence. Each second that passed was an eternity and an agony. Nevertheless they flew as time never had before. The light through the window by the door brightened, and she willed it to stop, but it did not.

Eventually the street door opened and in came Constable Pepper. Suzanne leapt to her feet and blurted his name. Horatio rose beside her. On sight of his visitors, Pepper's mouth went agape much as the clerk's had. Then he recovered himself and proceeded toward his office, saying as he went, "What brings you here, Mistress Thornton?" His face was pinched with annoyance. His jacket hung open. His wig had slipped forward. He had to shove it back to get the hair out of his eyes, and without a mirror he shoved it too far. It revealed his high forehead and a few strands of his own gray hair.

"Good day to you, too, constable. I have something for you."

He stopped and considered her presence for a moment, glanced at Horatio and the sack he held, then sighed and said, "Let us do this inside." He went into his office and the two followed. Pepper plopped himself heavily into his chair without offering seats to Suzanne and Horatio. Suzanne preferred to stand during this in any case, and pulled from the pocket beneath her skirts the papers she'd spent the night writing.

"Constable Pepper," she began, "I've come to share a letter with you. One I intend to have delivered to the king, via a friend of mine, Daniel Stockton, Earl of Throckmorton." She hadn't spoken to Daniel of this, but was certain he would do this much for her. Besides, just then it only mattered what Pepper thought Daniel would do.

"I see," said the constable, not the least moved. "I daresay you'll have no luck with a complaint to the king. I've done my job correctly where your son is concerned, and the case is, quite literally, closed. He will hang shortly." He leaned back in his chair with his fingers laced over his belly, his habitual posture. A glance at the window to his left told her he was checking the time to see whether it was noon yet.

A chill skittered down her spine at his words, and she pressed on, more urgent than ever. "Hear this, Pepper." She opened the pages she'd folded into a letter packet. On the outside of the packet she'd printed "Charles, King of England, Scotland, Ireland, and Wales" in large, plain letters, the better for Pepper to read them and know she was serious.

She began to read, in a clear, strong voice. "Your majesty, my dearest Charles." Her gaze flicked to Pepper's face to read it, for she hoped he would take note of the too-familiar salutation.

Pepper was yet unmoved. Suzanne wondered what it would take to budge him, and hoped the approach she'd chosen would do the trick.

She continued, "I hope this finds you well, and that the Lord has graced you with fine health since our last meeting. I hope your children are well, and your business with Parliament goes your way."

A puzzled frown came over Pepper's face. That last had been a mite silly, but that was what she was after, to disarm Pepper. And if necessary the king himself, should he ever actually read this letter.

Suzanne continued, "You may be aware of a certain case of murder here in Southwark. A man, one William Wainwright, was shot with a crossbow in the Globe Theatre, and fell to the stage during a performance. It was a terrible thing, and a shock to all who witnessed it. None of us quite knew what to do, but there was one man who stepped to the fore and calmly brought the situation under control. I wish to tell you of the heroic and industrious constable who solved the crime, one Samuel Pepper. Without him, the mystery of the death of Wainwright might never have been found out."

Pepper's puzzlement deepened, but he was too fascinated to stop her. He sat up in his chair, possibly for the first time in his tenure as constable, crossed his arms over his chest, and listened closely, his head tilted slightly, like a dog hearing a strange sound.

"Oh, your majesty, it was a thing to behold! Constable Pepper was on the case immediately, and his diligence in pursuing the truth was unmatched. He doggedly tracked down and interviewed witnesses. He examined the scene and the surrounding areas. Through his brilliant reconstruction of the incident, he was able to piece together what had happened as if he'd witnessed it himself."

Now Pepper tried to say something, but Suzanne quickly spoke over him, louder now.

"*When he found the weapon* that killed Wainwright and determined what had happened, your majesty, everyone in our little theatre troupe was quite surprised, and impressed with his powers of deduction." She nodded to Horatio, and he reached into the sack to pull out the crossbow and set it on Pepper's desk. "We all had assumed Wainwright had been shot while standing in the gallery, but we were all most egregiously wrong. It was Constable Pepper who thought to search the roof over the stage. His was the brilliant mind that sought the facts and deduced the truth."

Here Pepper sat back in his chair, with raised eyebrows, a look of consideration on his face. Plainly he liked the direction this narrative had taken.

Suzanne continued quickly, "Constable Pepper was the one who found the broken rain gutter where Wainwright had been standing on the roof. It was *Constable Pepper* who found the murder weapon, where it had lodged behind a downspout after Wainwright dropped it in his fall. It was *Constable Pepper* who located a witness who had seen Wainwright in the 'tiring room from whence the lethal crossbow had been stolen. It was *Constable Pepper* who found the broken rain gutter and drops of blood on the roof over our stage. Brilliantly, Constable Pepper deduced that Wainwright had stolen the crossbow, taken it to the roof, and then fallen when the gutter gave way. The death had not been a murder at all, but rather a nasty accident. An accident that befell a would-be assassin, for Constable Pepper concluded that the reason for Wainwright's climb to the roof with a crossbow was to shoot someone in the audience. His vantage point suggests he meant to loose his bolt at someone sitting in the third floor gallery just over the entrance doors. Thank God for the accident, or someone far more important than William Wainwright might have been shot."

Pepper was smiling now, and when she looked up to see his reaction, he gestured that she should finish.

"So, your majesty, I expect you would wish to show favor to Constable Pepper for his fine job in solving this mystery. It is through his untiring efforts that my son, the innocent man who was convicted of Wainwright's killing in error, was set free, mere"—here her glance flickered toward Pepper in askance—"mere hours before he was to be executed." She glanced over at him again, but he showed no reaction, so she continued. "Constable Pepper is a fine and true enforcer of the law, a seeker of justice, and a credit to the crown in all he does. He goes in God's grace, a treasure to us all. Most sincerely, Suzanne Thornton."

Suzanne folded the letter into its packet once more and looked at Pepper.

"I see," he said. "It was an accident, as I said in the beginning."

"It was." Embarrassment made her look down, for it was true he'd been the one to say that at the first. To be sure, it was almost the only true thing about his involvement as stated in the letter. And she didn't care to mention that he'd thought it for all the wrong reasons.

"And Wainwright's intended victim? You've neglected to mention a name in your letter."

"The king."

That made Pepper's eyebrows go up. "Indeed? The king himself was in the theatre that night?"

"He was. He sat in one of those seats that night, and so would understand who the intended victim was. I saw no need to set it down in writing."

Pepper gave a slow, sage nod. "I expect if it came out that Wainwright intended to assassinate Charles, even had Wainwright been murdered, it would be unpopular to have hung the murderer. It would at least make us all appear silly. Wouldn't want that bandied about, for a certainty. One wouldn't wish for the commons to ever be confused about the king's position on the subject of regicide."

"I'm certain of that. And the fact remains that William wasn't murdered at all. Further, the king has you to thank for your skilled—and timely—work, as it says so lavishly in this letter."

Pepper thought about that for a moment. She could see wheels and gears clanking behind his eyes.

"I pray you," she continued, "my son is set to be hung very shortly." She looked toward the window, and the angle of light through it made her heart skip and flop in her chest. "We must hurry to stop the hangman, or Piers will die. And you will look most foolish when the king reads this letter if my son does die."

Finally Pepper took out a piece of paper from a desk drawer and laid it on his blotter. He chose a quill from a stack in that same drawer, then uncorked the bottle of ink that sat atop his desk and began to write. Suzanne and Horatio waited in silence. Pepper signed the page with a flourish and blotted the ink. He blew on it a couple of times, made one last press of the blotter, and folded the page into a small packet. He held out his hand for Suzanne's letter as he offered her his.

"Here is the order to release your son; take it to Newgate and he will be remanded to your care until his pardon can be obtained. I'll make certain your message is delivered to the king with proper haste."

Eagerly Suzanne took the order and handed over her missive. Pepper said, "It's been a pleasure doing business with you, madam."

"And you, constable." She said it over her shoulder as she

ran from the room. Horatio stuffed the crossbow back into the sack and followed.

Suzanne and Horatio waved down a carriage and offered the driver an excessive tip for all speed. The coach bounced over cobbles and careened around corners nearly on two wheels in its race to the prison. Suzanne kept her head out the window the entire way, as if she could speed the horses by looking where they should go.

On arrival at the prison, she was out of the carrige before it had quite stopped. She reached the door of the keeper's house at a dead run, leaving Horatio to pay the driver. There she waved Pepper's letter at the guards and informed them she was there to stop an execution.

The short one commented that the crowd gathered around the gibbet would be disappointed. Conversationally, the tall one said he thought the execution had already taken place.

Suzanne's heart nearly stopped. "That's not possible."

"I'm telling you," said the tall one. "There's nothing and nobody to save. The thing is done. The transport cart must be well gone by now."

"Take me to his cell. He must still be there. For the love of Jesus Christ, take me there now!"

"Very well, then." The short one picked up his pike and showed her the way. She remembered it quite well. The guard moved so slowly, more than once she passed him up and he had to trot to keep up with her. At the corridor containing Piers's cell, she found the door to it wide open and the cell empty. An uneaten breakfast sat on the table next to a guttering candle. She wavered, turned a circle, looking for the way he must have gone. The guard proceeded past her, through the doors, and out to a yard. She followed. Bright noon sunlight blinded her, and for a moment she saw nothing but white.

When her vision had cleared, she found the guard responsible for the condemned prisoners loitering as if reluctant to return to his post.

"Where is the cart?" Suzanne asked, breathless.

He turned around and looked to the street behind him. Suzanne followed his glance and found clusters of spectators watching a rickety wooden cart move off down Hart Row Street toward Snow Hill. The crowd had let the cart move past them, and now they were gathering behind to follow it along its route toward the Tyburn Gallows several miles to the west. Five men and one woman stood in the cart with the hangman, staring out across the crowd. One of them was Piers, wearing exactly the look of terror Suzanne had imagined in her worst moments.

She screamed and burst into tears. At a run, she waved the paper from Constable Pepper and shouted for the cart to halt. But the cheering and jeering from the onlookers drowned her out. She pressed her way between them, shoving and carrying her skirts in one fist.

Struggling through the crowd, she continued to shout, "Stop! Stop the cart!" Those around her shoved back, but she insisted and pressed her way through them, the letter raised above them in her other fist.

Finally she reached the cart and clutched the side of it as she thrust the paper into the face of the startled hangman. Guards on horseback came to remove her, but she clung with the desperation that Piers should live. Amidst hoots and boos from the crowd expecting to see the condemned die, the hangman halted his cart to have a look at the paper.

"You must remand my son to me. 'Tis an order from the constable."

It seemed to take forever for the hangman to read the

letter—longer than it had taken Pepper to write it. But finally he folded it to slip it into his pocket, and he borrowed a knife to cut the rope tying Piers's wrists. Suzanne's son then leapt over the side of the cart to hug his mother, and he burst into tears.

PIERS had been home for several days when Daniel appeared at the theatre on business. Suzanne and her son were at breakfast, anticipating an ordinary day, both of them grateful for the ordinariness of it, when there was a knock at the outer door of the quarters. It was early yet, and nobody else was awake, so the two of them fell silent, alert to whom it might be at this hour. Sheila went to answer the knock. They heard her let someone in.

Daniel's voice came. "Is the mistress in?" Suzanne and Piers each looked to the other, neither sure why Daniel would have come unbidden.

Sheila replied, "She is, my lord. Please come in and have a seat whilst I tell her you're here." She hurried into the kitchen. "Mistress, Himself is here."

"You let him in?"

Sheila gave a half-curtsey of apology. "With all due respect, mistress, I could hardly have done aught but that. He's an earl, after all. Send him on his way if you've a mind, but I'm ill-equipped for rudeness toward the peerage."

"Very well, Sheila. Perhaps you're well enough equipped to clear the breakfast dishes, then?"

"Aye, mistress. Immediately." Sheila began cleaning up while Suzanne rose and straightened her clothing to be presentable to the earl before she would find a convenient reason to leave. Then she said to Piers, "Are you coming?"

He made a sour face. "I think Sheila needs me to supervise the clearing of the table."

"Well, that shouldn't take terribly long, then you'll have enough time to speak to your father before I send him away."

"Unlikely, I'd say."

Suzanne considered that, then allowed as he might be right in not wanting to talk to Daniel, but he should consider it. So she went to the other room by herself. "Good morning," she greeted Daniel.

"Good day, Suzanne."

"Mistress Thornton, if you please."

Daniel's face fell, then he recovered his dignity, smiled, and nodded. "Mistress Thornton, as you wish."

"What can I do for you this morning, your lordship?"

He seemed at a loss and uncertain, for the first time ever since she'd known him. Suzanne thought it possible he had come to make an apology he now saw would not be well received. He said, "I came to have a look at the theatre. I'm told there's been damage to it, and I wish to know the extent of it so I can assess the cost."

"The damage was minimal, my lord. Only a section of rain gutter and some boards on the stage will need to be replaced. The cost can be borne by our receipts, so there will be no need for more capital from you. My son is capable of handling that business himself. It's really not anything at all." Her voice took on an edge to suggest she knew that was not the real reason he'd come all the way across London to see her.

He removed his hat, but she did not summon Sheila to take it. He held it by the rim in both hands. "I hope you and Piers are well today."

"As well as can be expected."

"Is his arm recovering?"

She wondered how he'd heard about Piers's injury, and gathered that Daniel might have been asking after him among the players or at the prison when he'd paid for Piers's accommodations. Some of her anger abated, and she gave him a long, gentle, assessing look. Daniel had once been the love of her life. He was no longer, but there was no denying he'd been a very important part of her life at one time. He still was, in other ways. She sighed and offered him a seat on the sofa.

He sat, and she sat in a chair opposite. "Piers is recovering as only a young man can. Physically, he'll be quite well in a few weeks."

"That's good to hear."

"Emotionally, however, he may never again be himself."

"I had no choice, Suzanne."

"You had a choice. You chose your wife and your political power."

"Without that, I am nothing."

"Daniel, without Piers I am nothing. I am and have nothing without my son. You have told me you couldn't know me because I had no room for you. That Piers took up too much of my life for you to be part of my life. Now I'm telling you that to know me at all is to know my son. I cannot be one person to you and another to everyone else. And I'm appalled you would think any mother could do that.

"You think you are separable from your responsibility as a father, and in that you are wrong. You think that your duty to Piers only starts once your own place in the world is secure, and in that you are also wrong."

Daniel opened his mouth to speak, but she continued. "*Furthermore*, I would point out to you that when you went to York with Charles's father, you left not only us, but also you left your wife behind. You chose king and country over everyone who was ever family to you. It was your choice."

"It's a man's duty to fight for what he thinks is right."

"Only a fool would accept that excuse. It was your choice to go where you thought you might gain political power. Power and glory, all for yourself. It was never about duty, it was about self-aggrandizement."

Color rose to his cheeks and he fidgeted in his seat. "You speak carelessly for someone whose livelihood depends on a theatre I own. I could very well evict you and sell the property away."

"If you evict me and my troupe, then where would you and your wife go to see plays and have the best seats in the house?" The sudden sharpness of his gaze told her Anne had mentioned her visit, and that he realized she had not gone to his house to invite him to see a play. "Besides, you won't, for that would only demonstrate my point. If you wish to prove me wrong, you'll keep our arrangement."

Daniel's gaze moved from her face to focus on something behind her, and she turned to see Piers standing in the kitchen doorway. Nobody spoke for a moment, then Piers said, "Good morning, your lordship."

Daniel stood, and gave a nodding bow. "Pleasant good morning to you, Piers. How fare you today?"

"Well enough, and good of you to ask."

"I came to enquire whether you and your mother needed anything."

"Only to be left alone, if you please."

Daniel pressed his lips together at the harsh words.

Suzanne said, "Piers, if I may be blunt for a moment . . ." Piers attended to her, with a slight nod of permission. "I believe the earl is sincere in his regret, and in his wish for all to be well between us."

"That would be convenient for him."

Daniel spoke up for himself. "You say that as if it's not possible I could be sincere."

"You've never shown us anything but self-interest. I have no reason to think you've changed. Easy enough at this point to say you have."

"What do you want from me?"

"Nothing. Nothing whatsoever. I've gotten on well enough without you; I think I can continue to do so."

Daniel stood silent for a long moment, thinking, gazing at his son. The son gazed back. Finally he said, "Very well, Master Thornton. Continue to manage this theatre as well as you have so far, and all will be well between us as far as I'm concerned. Is that fair enough?"

"Eminently fair. Though I would wish that you might treat my mother with equal respect."

"Of course." Daniel gave Suzanne a graceful, nodding bow.

"Then there's nothing more to discuss." Piers glanced at the door as if his words weren't sufficient hint that Daniel should leave.

Daniel chose to accept that hint, set his hat back on his head, and said, "I'll take my leave now. I bid you both a good day, until we meet again." Then he took Suzanne's hand before she could reasonably keep it from him, and he kissed the back of it in the Continental manner. Another slight bow to Piers, and he made his graceful exit.

Suzanne and Piers watched him go. She hoped that in time things between her son and his father would eventually right themselves.

Through the tiny window in the kitchen that looked on the cellarage came the sound of Horatio and some other players vocalizing, warming up for the day's rehearsals and performance. Suzanne's life and the theatre beckoned.

Declaration of Dramatic License

In my associations with my fellow authors, often I'm drawn into debate about the moral obligation of historical fiction writers to be true to historical fact. I think most people agree that accuracy is desired, at least so far as the commonly known facts are concerned. I don't know any writers of historical fiction who don't claim at least due diligence in their research. But some feel that reading one general history is plenty, while some are trained historians who bring to bear years of studying primary sources. Several authors I know claim their stories never deviate from history by so much as a single word or thought. Anything less, they say, is Untruth and perpetuates Confusion among the uneducated and ill-read masses.

They all lie.

I agree that unless one is deliberately and openly writing what is called "alternate history" one should stick as close to the known facts as humanly possible. Hollywood often makes us groan and fidget to see, for instance, William Wallace in a kilt or Jane Grey dewy-eyed and in love with the puppet-king husband foisted on her by her father. Or Mary I fat and ugly, and therefore evil and wrong. Or a svelte Henry VIII with a buzz cut and bedroom eyes. I could go on, but I'm sure Gentle Reader knows what I mean. Hollywood often gets it wrong, and we've learned to accept that. But we expect better from literature. We desire accuracy in print.

However, in any work of historical fiction there is a level of detail at which known fact fails us and the drama must be served. It is impossible to know exactly what was said or done in private chambers long ago, and even more difficult to know the inner thoughts of the people whose stories the author is trying to tell. At some point in the narrative one must start making things up.

Storytelling is the glue that makes sense out of random facts. One does one's best to keep the conjecture to a minimum and to stay within reasonable limits of plausibility, but there is no getting away from the fact that one's job is to fill in blanks left by historical documents that tell only a fraction of what went on.

The Opening Night Murder is a work of fiction, set in a historical period. To avoid being chained to the well-known history of either the King's Company or the Duke's Men, ordinarily I would have invented a fictional theatre to house my fictional troupe and fictional characters for my story. But then I still would have had to place it on an actual London street where no theatre existed. I might even have placed it on the spot where the Globe had stood, and called it something else. No matter how hard one tries, there's always the line where fact butts up against fiction.

So why not use Shakespeare's Globe Theatre, located near what is now Porter Street in the Southwark district of London?

Unfortunately, that theatre was torn down in 1644, sixteen years before our story opens.

However, this is fiction. If I can invent a theatre and place it on a spot where no theatre actually stood in 1660, then why not simply resurrect the Old Globe and put it where it was originally?

Further, with only a little hand waving, why not let this fictional troupe of actors perform Shakespeare's plays even though the two royal theatres were granted a monopoly on "serious" dramas? It's true that the King's Company and the Duke's Men were given patents and Shakespeare's works divided between them, and lesser companies were limited to older forms of comedy, mummeries, and mime. But it is also true that one reason for the patents given to the King's and the Duke's companies was to control new playwrights who might satirize the king. So my fictional troupe has been given fictional permission to perform the works of Shakespeare, which could not ever be about the current regime.

Although it is my sincere wish not to annoy my Gentle Reader, who might cry, "But no! That didn't happen!" I reply, "Of course it didn't happen. In the words of another great playwright, Oscar Wilde: *That's what fiction means.*"

Anne Rutherford
January 2012

About the Author

Anne Rutherford can be reached at anne@julianneardianlee
.com, or visit www.julianneardianlee.com/anne/anneruther
ford.html.